Postern of Fate

Agatha Christie

This low-priced Bantam Book
has been completely reset in a type face
designed for easy reading, and was printed
from new plates. It contains the complete
text of the original hard-cover edition.
NOT ONE WORD HAS BEEN OMITTED.

POSTERN OF FATE
A Bantam Book / published by arrangement with
Dodd, Mead & Company

PRINTING HISTORY
Dodd, Mead edition published November 1973

2nd printing	January 1974	3rd printing	February 1974

Bantam edition / October 1974

2nd printing	October 1974	8th printing	August 1976
3rd printing ..	November 1974	9th printing	October 1976
4th printing ..	December 1974	10th printing	August 1977
5th printing	March 1975	11th printing	May 1978
6th printing	May 1975	12th printing	July 1978
7th printing ..	December 1975	13th printing ..	February 1980

ISBN 0-553-13775-1

Bantam Books are published by Bantam Books, Inc. Its trademark, consisting of the words "Bantam Books" and the por-
trayal of a bantam, is Registered in U.S. Patent and Trademark
Office and in other countries. Marca Registrada. Bantam
Books, Inc., 666 Fifth Avenue, New York, New York 10019.

PRINTED IN THE UNITED STATES OF AMERICA

"MARY JORDAN DID NOT DIE NATURALLY."

"What did she die of?"

"Somebody brought a few foxglove leaves in with some spinach from the garden, by accident, and then they ate it. Mind you, that probably wouldn't kill you."

"No," said Mr. Robinson. "But if you then put a strong dose of digitalin alkaloid in the coffee and just made sure that Mary Jordan got it in her coffee, or in a cocktail earlier, then the foxglove leaves would be blamed and it would all be taken to be an accident. But Alexander Parker, or whatever the schoolboy's name was, was too sharp for that. He had other ideas, did he? Anything else, Beresford? When was this? First World War, Second World War, or before that?"

"Before. Rumors say she was a German spy."

POSTERN OF FATE
by Agatha Christie

Bantam Books by Agatha Christie
Ask your bookseller for the books you have missed

DEATH ON THE NILE
HOLIDAY FOR MURDER
THE MYSTERIOUS AFFAIR AT STYLES
POIROT INVESTIGATES
POSTERN OF FATE
THE SECRET ADVERSARY
THE SEVEN DIALS MYSTERY

Four great gates has the city of Damascus . . .
Postern of Fate, the Desert Gate, Disaster's Cavern,
    Fort of Fear . . .
Pass not beneath, O Caravan, or pass not singing.
    Have you heard
That silence where the birds are dead yet something
    pipeth like a bird?

JAMES ELROY FLECKER
From "Gates of Damascus"

For Hannibal and his master

Contents

BOOK ONE

1	Mainly Concerning Books	3
2	*The Black Arrow*	10
3	Visit to the Cemetery	19
4	Lots of Parkinsons	25
5	The White Elephant Sale	32
6	Problems	41
7	More Problems	49
8	Mrs. Griffin	54

BOOK TWO

9	A Long Time Ago	59
10	Introduction to Mathilde, Truelove and KK	64
11	Six Impossible Things Before Breakfast	74
12	Expedition on Truelove; Oxford and Cambridge	82
13	Methods of Research	99
14	Mr. Robinson	106

BOOK THREE

15	Mary Jordan	127
16	Research by Tuppence	139
17	Tommy and Tuppence Compare Notes	144
18	Possibility of Surgery on Mathilde	150
19	Interview with Colonel Pikeaway	164
20	Postern of Fate	177
21	The Inquest	182

22 Reminiscences About an Uncle   189
23 Junior Brigade   202
24 Attack on Tuppence   214
25 Hannibal Takes Action   231
26 Oxford, Cambridge and Lohengrin   237
27 Visit from Miss Mullins   241
28 Garden Campaign   246
29 Hannibal Sees Active Service with
       Mr. Crispin   251
30 The Birds Fly South   262
31 Last Words: Dinner with Mr. Robinson   267

Book One

1

Mainly Concerning Books

"Books!" said Tuppence.

She produced the word rather with the effect of a bad-tempered explosion.

"What did you say?" said Tommy.

Tuppence looked across the room at him.

"I said 'books,'" she said.

"I see what you mean," said Thomas Beresford.

In front of Tuppence were three large packing cases. From each of them various books had been extracted. The larger part of them were still filled with books.

"It's incredible," said Tuppence.

"You mean the room they take up?"

"Yes."

"Are you trying to put them all on the shelves?"

"I don't know what I'm trying to do," said Tuppence. "That's the awkward part of it. One doesn't know ever, exactly, what one wants to do. Oh dear," she sighed.

"Really," said her husband, "I should have thought that that was not at all characteristic of you. The trouble with you has always been that you knew much too well what you *do* want to do."

"What I mean is," said Tuppence, "that here we are, getting older, getting a bit—well, let's face it—definitely rheumatic, especially when one is stretching; you know, stretching putting in books or lifting down things from shelves for something, then finding it a bit difficult to get up again."

"Yes, yes," said Tommy, "that's an account of our

3

general disabilities. Is that what you started to say?"

"No, it isn't what I started to say. What I started to say was, it was lovely to be able to buy a new home and find just the place we wanted to go and live in, and just the house there we'd always dreamt of having—with a little alteration, of course."

"Knocking one or two rooms into each other," said Tommy, "and adding to it what you call a veranda and your builder calls a lodger, though I prefer to call it a loggia."

"And it's going to be very nice," said Tuppence firmly.

"When you've done with it, I shan't know it! Is that the answer?" said Tommy.

"Not at all. All I said was that when you see it finished, you're going to be delighted and say what an ingenious and clever and artistic wife you have."

"All right," said Tommy. "I'll remember the right thing to say."

"You won't need to remember," said Tuppence. "It will burst upon you."

"What's that got to do with books?" said Tommy.

"Well, we brought two or three cases of books with us. I mean, we sold off the books we didn't much care about. We brought the ones we really couldn't bear to part with, and then, of course, the what-you-call-'ems—I can't remember their name now, but the people who were selling us this house—they didn't want to take a lot of their own things with them, and they said if we'd like to make an offer, they would leave things including books, and we came and looked at things—"

"And we made some offers," said Tommy.

"Yes. Not as many as they hoped we would make, I expect. Some of their furniture and ornaments were too horrible. Well, fortunately we didn't have to take those, but when I came and saw the various books—there were some nursery ones, you know, some down in the sitting room—and there were one or two old favorites. I mean, there still are. There are one or two of my own special favorites. And so I thought it'd be such fun to have them. You know, the story of Androcles and the Lion." she said. "I remember reading that when I was eight years old. Andrew Lang."

"Tell me, Tuppence, were you clever enough to read at eight years old?"

"Yes," said Tuppence, "I read at five years old. Everybody could, when I was young. I didn't know one even had to sort of learn. I mean, somebody would read stories aloud, and you liked them very much and you remembered where the book went back on the shelf and you were always allowed to take it out and have a look at it yourself, and so you found you were reading it, too, without bothering to learn to spell or anything like that. It wasn't so good later," she said, "because I've never been able to spell very well. And if somebody had taught me to spell when I was about four years old, I can see it would have been very good indeed. My father did teach me to do addition and subtraction and multiplication, of course, because he said the multiplication table was the most useful thing you could learn in life, and I learnt long division, too."

"What a clever man he must have been!"

"I don't think he was specially clever," said Tuppence, "but he was just very, very nice."

"Aren't we getting away from the point?"

"Yes, we are," said Tuppence. "Well, as I said, when I thought of reading 'Androcles and the Lion' again—it came in a book of stories about animals, I think, by Andrew Lang. Oh, I loved that. And there was a story about 'a day in my life at Eton' by an Eton schoolboy. I can't think why I wanted to read that, but I did. It was one of my favorite books. And there were some stories from the classics, and there was Mrs. Molesworth, *The Cuckoo Clock, Four Winds Farm*—"

"Well, that's all right," said Tommy. "No need to

give me a whole account of your literary triumphs in
early youth."

"What I mean is," said Tuppence, "that you can't
get them nowadays. I mean, sometimes you get
reprints of them, but they've usually been altered and
have different pictures in them. Really, the other day
I couldn't recognize *Alice in Wonderland* when I saw
it. Everything looks so peculiar in it. There are the
books I really could get still. Mrs. Molesworth, one or
two of the old fairy books—Pink, Blue and Yellow—
and then, of course, lots of later ones which I'd enjoyed. Lots of Stanley Weymans and things like that.
There are quite a lot here, left behind."

"All right," said Tommy. "You were tempted. You
felt it was a good buy."

"Yes. At least— What d'you mean 'a goodbye'?"

"I mean b-u-y," said Tommy.

"Oh. I thought you were going to leave the room
and were saying goodbye to me."

"Not at all," said Tommy. "I was deeply interested.
Anyway, it *was* a good b-u-y."

"And I got them very cheap, as I tell you. And—
and here they all are among our own books and others. Only, we've got such a terrible lot of books now,
and the shelves we had made I don't think are going
to be nearly enough. What about your special sanc-
tum? Is there room there for more books?"

"No, there isn't," said Tommy. "There's not going to
be enough for my own."

"Oh dear, oh dear," said Tuppence, "that's so like
us. Do you think we might have to build on an extra
room?"

"No," said Tommy, "we're going to economize. We
said so the day before yesterday. Do you remember?"

"That was the day before yesterday," said Tuppence. "Time alters. What I am going to do now is
to put on these shelves all the books I really can't
bear to part with. And then—and then we can look at
the others and—well, there might be a children's hos-

pital somewhere and there might, anyway, be places which would like books."

"Or we could sell them," said Tommy.

"I don't suppose they're the sort of books people would want to buy very much. I don't think there are any books of rare value or anything like that."

"You never know your luck," said Tommy. "Let's hope something out of print will fulfil some bookseller's long-felt want."

"In the meantime," said Tuppence, "we have to put them into the shelves, and look inside them, of course, each time, to see whether it's a book I do really want and I can really remember. I'm trying to get them roughly—well, you know what I mean, sort of sorted. I mean, adventure stories, fairy stories, children's stories and those stories about schools where the children were always very rich—L. T. Meade, I think. And some of the books we used to read to Deborah when she was small, too. How we all used to love *Winnie the Pooh*. And there was *The Little Grey Hen*, too, but I didn't care very much for that."

"I think you're tiring yourself," said Tommy. "I think I should leave off what you're doing now."

"Well, perhaps I will," said Tuppence, "but I think if I could just finish this side of the room, just get the books in here . . ."

"Well, I'll help you," said Tommy.

He came over, tilted the case more so that the books fell out, gathered up armfuls of them and went to the shelves and shoved them in.

"I'm putting the same-sized ones together; it looks neater," he said.

"Oh, I don't call that sorting," said Tuppence.

"Sorting enough to get on with. We can do more of that later. You know, make everything really nice. We'll sort it on some wet day when we can't think of anything else to do."

"The trouble is we always can think of something else to do."

"Well now, there's another seven in there. Now then, there's only this top corner. Just bring me that wooden chair over there, will you? Are its legs strong enough for me to stand on it? Then I can put some on the top shelf."

With some care he climbed on the chair. Tuppence lifted up to him an armful of books. He insinuated them with some care onto the top shelf. Disaster only happened with the last three, which cascaded to the floor, narrowly missing Tuppence.

"Oh," said Tuppence, "that was painful."

"Well, I can't help it. You handed me up too many at once."

"Oh well, that does look wonderful," said Tuppence, standing back a little. "Now then, if you'll just put these on the second shelf from the bottom, there's a gap there, that will finish up this particular caseful anyway. It's a good thing. too. These ones I'm doing this morning aren't really ours; they're the ones we bought. We may find treasures."

"We may," said Tommy.

"I think we shall find treasures. I think I really shall find something. Something that's worth a lot of money, perhaps."

"What do we do then? Sell it?"

"I expect we'll have to sell it, yes," said Tuppence. "Of course we might just keep it and show it to people. You know, not exactly boasting, but just say, you know: 'Oh yes, we've got really one or two interesting finds.' I think we shall make an interesting find, too."

"What—one old favorite you've forgotten about?"

"Not exactly that. I meant something startling, surprising. Something that'll make all the difference to our lives."

"Oh, Tuppence," said Tommy, "what a wonderful mind you've got. Much more likely to find something that's an absolute disaster."

"Nonsense," said Tuppence. "One must have hope.

It's the great thing you have to have in life. Hope. Remember? I'm always full of hope."

"I know you are," said Tommy. He sighed. "I've often regretted it."

2

The Black Arrow

Mrs. Thomas Beresford replaced *The Cuckoo Clock*, by Mrs. Molesworth, choosing a vacant place on the third shelf from the bottom. The Mrs. Molesworths were congregated here together. Tuppence drew out *The Tapestry Room* and held it thoughtfully in her fingers. Or she might read *Four Winds Farm*. She couldn't remember *Four Winds Farm* as well as she could remember *The Cuckoo Clock* and *The Tapestry Room*. Her fingers wandered . . . Tommy would be back soon.

She was getting on. Yes, surely she was getting on. If only she didn't stop and pull out old favorites and read them. Very agreeable, but it took a lot of time. And when Tommy asked her in the evening when he came home how things were going and she said, "Oh, very well now," she had to employ a great deal of tact and finesse to prevent him from going upstairs and having a real look at how the bookshelves were progressing. It all took a long time. Getting into a house always took a long time—much longer than one thought. And so many irritating people. Electricians, for instance, who came and appeared to be displeased with what they had done the last time they came and took up more large areas in the floor and, with cheerful faces, produced more pitfalls for the unwary housewife to walk along and put a foot wrong and be rescued just in time by the unseen electrician who was groping beneath the floor.

"Sometimes," said Tuppence, "I really wish we hadn't left Bartons Acre."

"Remember the dining-room roof," Tommy had said, "and remember those attics, and remember what happened to the garage. Nearly wrecked the car, you know it did."

"I suppose we could have had it patched up," said Tuppence.

"No," said Tommy, "we'd have had to practically replace the damaged building, or else we had to move. This is going to be a very nice house someday. I'm quite sure of that. Anyway, there's going to be room in it for all the things we want to do."

"When you say the things we want to do," Tuppence had said, "you mean the things we want to find places for and to keep."

"I know," said Tommy. "One keeps far too much. I couldn't agree with you more."

At that moment Tuppence considered something— whether they ever were going to do anything with this house, that is to say, beyond getting into it. It had sounded simple but had turned out complex. Partly, of course, all these books.

"If I'd been a nice ordinary child of nowadays," said Tuppence, "I wouldn't have learned to read so easily when I was young. Children nowadays who are four, or five, or six, don't seem to be able to read, and quite a lot of them don't seem to be able to read when they get to ten or eleven. I can't think why it was so easy for all of us. We could all read. Me and Martin next door and Jennifer down the road and Cyril and Winifred. All of us. I don't mean we could all spell very well, but we could read anything we wanted to. I don't know how we learnt. Asking people, I suppose. Things about posters and Carter's Little Liver Pills. We used to read all about them in the fields when trains got near London. It was very exciting. I always wondered what they were. Oh dear, I must think of what I'm doing."

She removed some more books. Three-quarters of an hour passed with her absorbed first in *Alice*

Through the Looking-Glass, then with Charlotte
Yonge's *Unknown to History.* Her hands lingered
over the fat shabbiness of *The Daisy Chain.*

"Oh, I must read that again," said Tuppence. "To
think of the years and years and years it is since I did
read it. Oh dear, how exciting it was, wondering, you
know, whether Norman was going to be allowed to
be confirmed or not. And Ethel and—what was the
name of the place? Coxwell or something like that—
and Flora, who was worldly. I wonder why everyone
was 'worldly' in those days, and how poorly it was
thought of, being worldly. I wonder what we are
now. Do you think we're all worldly or not?"

"I beg your pardon, ma'am?"

"Oh, nothing," said Tuppence, looking round at her
devoted henchman, Albert, who had just appeared in
the doorway.

"I thought you called for something, madam. And
you rang the bell, didn't you?"

"Not really," said Tuppence. "I just leant on it getting up on a chair to take a book out."

"Is there anything I can take down for you?"

"Well, I wish you would," said Tuppence. "I'm falling off those chairs. Some of their legs are very wob-
bly, some of them rather slippery."

"Any book in particular?"

"Well, I haven't got on very far with the third shelf
up. Two shelves down from the top, you know. I
don't know what books are there."

Albert mounted on a chair and banging each book
in turn to dislodge such dust as it had managed to
gather on it, handed things down. Tuppence received
them with a good deal of rapture.

"Oh, fancy! All these. I really have forgotten a lot
of these. Oh, here's *The Amulet* and here's *The Psa-
mayad.* Here's *The New Treasure Seekers.* Oh, I love
all those. No, don't put them on shelves yet, Albert. I
think I'll have to read them first. Well, I mean, one or
two of them first, perhaps. Now, what's this one? Let

me see. *The Red Cockade*. Oh yes, that was one of
the historical ones. That was very exciting. And
there's *Under the Red Robe*, too. Lots of Stanley
Weyman. Lots and lots. Of course I used to read
those when I was about ten or eleven. I shouldn't be
surprised if I don't come across *The Prisoner of
Zenda*." She sighed with enormous pleasure at the
remembrance. "*The Prisoner of Zenda*. One's first in-
troduction, really, to the romantic novel. The ro-
mance of Princess Flavia. The King of Ruritania. Ru-
dolph Rassendyll, some name like that, whom one
dreamt of at night."

Albert handed down another selection.

"Oh yes," said Tuppence, "that's better, really.
That's earlier again. I must put the early ones all together. Now, let me see. What have we got here?
Treasure Island. Well, that's nice, but of course I
have read *Treasure Island* again, and I've seen, I
think, two films of it. I don't like seeing it on films, it
never seems right. Oh—and here's *Kidnapped*. Yes, I
always liked that."

Albert stretched up, overdid his armful, and *Catriona* fell more or less on Tuppence's head.

"Oh, sorry, madam. Very sorry."

"It's quite all right," said Tuppence, "it doesn't matter. *Catriona*. Yes. Any more Stevensons up there?"

Albert handed the books down now more gingerly.
Tuppence uttered a cry of excessive delight.

"*The Black Arrow*. I declare! *The Black Arrow!*
Now that's one of the first books really I ever got
hold of and read. Yes. I don't suppose you ever did,
Albert. I mean, you wouldn't have been born, would
you? Now let me think. Let me think. *The Black Arrow*. Yes, of course, it was that picture on the wall
with eyes—real eyes—looking through the eyes of the
picture. It was splendid. So frightening, just that. Oh
yes. *The Black Arrow*. What was it? It was all
about—oh yes, the cat, the dog? No. *The cat, the rat
and Lovell, the dog. Rule all England under the hog.*

That's it. The hog was Richard the Third, of course. Though nowadays they all write books saying he was really wonderful. Not a villain at all. But I don't believe that. Shakespeare didn't either. After all, he started his play by making Richard say, 'I am determined to prove a villain.' Ah yes. *The Black Arrow*."

"Some more, madam?"

"No, thank you, Albert. I think I'm rather too tired to go on now."

"That's all right. By the way, the master rang up and said he'd be half an hour late."

"Never mind," said Tuppence.

She sat down in the chair, took *The Black Arrow*, opened the pages and engrossed herself.

"Oh dear," she said, "how wonderful this is. I've really forgotten it quite enough to enjoy reading it all over again. It was so exciting."

Silence fell. Albert returned to the kitchen. Tuppence leaned back in the chair. Time passed. Curled up in the rather shabby armchair, Mrs. Thomas Beresford sought the joys of the past by applying herself to the perusal of Robert Louis Stevenson's *The Black Arrow*.

In the kitchen time also passed. Albert applied himself to various maneuvers with the stove. A car drove up. Albert went to the side door.

"Shall I put it in the garage, sir?"

"No," said Tommy, "I'll do that. I expect you're busy with dinner. Am I very late?"

"Not really, sir, just about when you said. A little early, in fact."

"Oh." Tommy disposed of the car and then came into the kitchen, rubbing his hands. "Cold out. Where's Tuppence?"

"Oh, missis, she's upstairs with the books."

"What, still those miserable books?"

"Yes. She's done a good many more today and she's spent most of the time reading."

"Oh dear," said Tommy. "All right, Albert. What are we having?"

"Fillets of lemon sole, sir. It won't take long to do."

"All right. Well, make it about quarter of an hour or so anyway. I want to wash first."

Upstairs, on the top floor, Tuppence was still sitting in the somewhat shabby armchair engrossed in *The Black Arrow*. Her forehead was slightly wrinkled. She had come across what seemed to her a somewhat curious phenomenon. There seemed to be what she could only call a kind of interference. The particular page she had got to—she gave it a brief glance, 64 or was it 65?—she couldn't see—anyway, apparently somebody had underlined some of the words in the page. Tuppence had spent the last quarter of an hour studying this phenomenon. She didn't see why the words had been underlined. They were not in sequence, they were not a quotation, therefore, in the book. They seemed to be words that had been apparently singled out and had then been underlined in red ink. She read under her breath: "Matcham could not restrain a little cry. Dick started with surprise and dropped the windack from his fingers. They were all afoot, loosing sword and dagger in the sheath. Ellis held up his hand. The white of his eyes shone Let, large—" Tuppence shook her head. It didn't make sense. None of it did.

She went over to the table where she kept her writing things, picked out a few sheets recently sent by a firm of notepaper printers for the Beresfords to make a choice of the paper to be stamped with their new address: The Laurels.

"Silly name," said Tuppence, "but if you go changing names all the time, then all your letters go astray."

She copied things down. Now she realized something she hadn't realized before.

"That makes all the difference," said Tuppence.

She traced letters on the page.

"So there you are," said Tommy's voice suddenly. "Dinner's practically in. How are the books going?"

"This lot's terribly puzzling," said Tuppence. "Dreadfully puzzling."

"What's puzzling?"

"Well, this is *The Black Arrow* of Stevenson's and I wanted to read it again and I began. It was all right, and then suddenly—all the pages were rather queer because I mean a lot of the words had been underlined in red ink."

"Oh well, one does that," said Tommy. "I don't mean solely in red ink, but I mean one does underline things. You know, something you want to remember, or a quotation or something. Well, you know what I mean."

"I know what you mean," said Tuppence, "but it doesn't go like that. And it's—it's letters, you see."

"What do you mean by letters?" said Tommy.

"Come here," said Tuppence.

Tommy came and sat on the arm of the chair. He read: " 'Matcham could not restrain a little cry and even died starter started with surprise and dropped the window from his fingers the two big fellows on the—something I can't read—shell was an expected signal. They were all afoot together tightening loosing sword and dagger.' It's mad," he said.

"Yes," said Tuppence, "that's what I thought at first. It was mad. But it isn't mad, Tommy."

Some cowbells rang from downstairs.

"That's supper in."

"Never mind," said Tuppence, "I've got to tell you this first. We can get down to things about it later, but it's really so extraordinary. I've got to tell you this straightaway."

"Oh, all right. Have you got one of your mare's nests?"

"No, I haven't. It's just that I took out the letters, you see. Well—on this page, you see, well—the M of Matcham which is the first word, the M is underlined

and the A and after that there are three more, three
or four more words. They don't come in sequence in
the book. They've just been picked out, I think, and
they've been underlined—the letters in them—because
they wanted the right letters and the next one, you
see, is the R from 'restrained' underlined and the Y of
'cry,' and then there's J from 'Jack,' O from 'shot,' R
from 'ruin,' D from 'death' and A from 'death' again,
N from 'murrain'—"

"For goodness' sake," said Tommy, "do stop."

"Wait," said Tuppence. "I've got to find out. Now
you see because I've written out these, do you see
what this is? I mean, if you take those letters out and
write them in order on this piece of paper, do you see
what you get with the ones I've done first? M-a-r-y.
Those four were underlined."

"What does that make?"

"It makes Mary."

"All right," said Tommy, "it makes Mary. Somebody called Mary. A child with an inventive nature, I
expect, who is trying to point out that this was her
book. People are always writing their names in books
and things like that."

"All right. Mary," said Tuppence. "And the next
thing that comes underlined makes the word J-o-r-
d-a-n."

"You see? Mary Jordan," said Tommy. "It's quite
natural. Now you know her whole name. Her name
was Mary Jordan."

"Well, this book didn't belong to her. In the beginning it says in a rather silly, childish-looking writing,
it says 'Alexander.' Alexander Parkinson, I think."

"Oh well. Does it really matter?"

"Of course it matters," said Tuppence.

"Come on, I'm hungry," said Tommy.

"Restrain yourself," said Tuppence. "I'm only going
to read you the next bit until the writing stops—or at
any rate stops in the next four pages. The letters are
picked from odd places on various pages. They don't

run in sequence—there can't be anything in the words that matters—it's just the letters. Now then. We've got M-a-r-y J-o-r-d-a-n. That's right. Now do you know what the next four words are? D-i-d n-o-t, not, d-i-e n-a-t-u-r-a-l-y. That's meant to be 'naturally,' but they didn't know it had two 'ls.' Now then, what's that? *Mary Jordan did not die naturally.* There you are," said Tuppence. "Now the next sentence made is *It was one of us. I think I know which one.* That's all. Can't find anything else. But it is rather exciting, isn't it?"

"Look here, Tuppence," said Tommy, "you're not going to get a thing about this, are you?"

"What do you mean, a thing, about this?"

"Well, I mean working up a sort of mystery."

"Well, it's a mystery to me," said Tuppence. "*Mary Jordan did not die naturally. It was one of us. I think I know which one.* Oh, Tommy, you must say that it is very intriguing."

3

Visit to the Cemetery

"Tuppence!" Tommy called as he came into the
house.

There was no answer. With some annoyance, he
ran up the stairs and along the passage on the first
floor. As he hastened along it, he nearly put his foot
through a gaping hole, and swore promptly.

"Some other bloody careless electrician," he said.

Some days before he had had the same kind of
trouble. Electricians arriving in a kindly tangle of op-
timism and efficiency had started work. "Coming
along fine now, not much more to do," they said.
"We'll be back this afternoon." But they hadn't been
back that afternoon; Tommy was not precisely surprised. He was used, now, to the general pattern of
labor in the building trade, electrical trade, gas em-
ployees and others. They came, they showed efficiency, they made optimistic remarks, they went
away to fetch something. They didn't come back. One
rang up numbers on the telephone, but they always
seemed to be the wrong numbers. If they were the
right numbers, the right man was not working at this
particular branch of the trade, whatever it was. All
one had to do was be careful not to sprain an ankle,
fall through a hole, damage yourself in some way or
another. He was far more afraid of Tuppence damag-
ing herself than he was of doing the damage to himself. He had had more experience than Tuppence.
Tuppence, he thought, was more at risk from scalding
herself from kettles or disasters with the heat of the

19

stove. But where was Tuppence now? He called again.

"Tuppence! Tuppence!"

He worried about Tuppence. Tuppence was one of those people you had to worry about. If you left the house, you gave her last words of wisdom and she gave you last promises of doing exactly what you counseled her to do: No, she would not be going out except just to buy half a pound of butter, and after all you couldn't call that dangerous, could you?

"It could be dangerous if *you* went out to buy half a pound of butter," said Tommy.

"Oh," said Tuppence, "don't be an idiot."

"I'm not being an idiot," Tommy had said. "I am just being a wise and careful husband, looking after something which is one of my favorite possessions. I don't know why it is—"

"Because," said Tuppence, "I am so charming, so good-looking, such a good companion and because I take so much care of you."

"That also, maybe," said Tommy, "but I could give you another list."

"I don't feel I should like that," said Tuppence. "No, I don't think so. I think you have several saved-up grievances. But don't worry. Everything will be quite all right. You've only got to come back and call me when you get in."

But now where was Tuppence?

"The little devil," said Tommy. "She's gone out somewhere."

He went on into the room upstairs where he had found her before. Looking at another child's book, he supposed. Getting excited again about some silly words that a silly child had underlined in red ink. On the trail of Mary Jordan, whoever she was. Mary Jordan, who hadn't died a natural death. He couldn't help wondering. A long time ago, presumably, the people who'd had the house and sold it to them had been named Jones. They hadn't been there very long, only three or four years. No, this child of the Robert Louis Stevenson book dated from further back than that. Anyway, Tuppence wasn't here in this room. There seemed to be no loose books lying about with signs of having had interest shown in them.

"Ah, where the hell can she be?" said Thomas.

He went downstairs again, shouting once or twice. There was no answer. He examined one of the pegs in the hall. No signs of Tuppence's mackintosh. Then she'd gone out. Where had she gone? And where was Hannibal? Tommy varied the use of his vocal cords and called for Hannibal.

"Hannibal—Hannibal—Hanny-boy. Come on, Hannibal."

No Hannibal.

Well, at any rate, she's got Hannibal with her, thought Tommy.

He didn't know if it was worse or better that Tuppence should have Hannibal. Hannibal would certainly allow no harm to come to Tuppence. The question was, might Hannibal do some damage to other people? He was friendly when taken visiting people, but people who wished to visit Hannibal, to enter any house in which he lived, were always definitely suspect in Hannibal's mind. He was ready at all risks to both bark and bite if he considered it necessary. Anyway, where was everybody?

He walked a little way along the street, could see no signs of any small black dog with a medium-size woman in a bright red mackintosh walking in the distance. Finally, rather angrily, he came back to the house.

Rather an appetizing smell met him. He went quickly to the kitchen, where Tuppence turned from the stove and gave him a smile of welcome.

"You're ever so late," she said. "This is a casserole. Smells rather good, don't you think? I put some rather unusual things in it this time. There were some herbs in the garden, at least I hope they were herbs."

"If they weren't herbs," said Tommy, "I suppose they were deadly nightshade, or digitalin leaves pretending to be something else, but really foxglove. Where on earth have you been?"

"I took Hannibal for a walk."

Hannibal, at this moment, made his own presence felt. He rushed at Tommy and gave him such a rapturous welcome as nearly to fell him to the ground. Hannibal was a small black dog, very glossy, with interesting tan patches on his behind and each side of his cheeks. He was a Manchester terrier of very pure pedigree and he considered himself to be on a much higher level of sophistication and aristocracy than any other dog he met.

"Oh, good gracious. I took a look round. Where've you been? It wasn't very nice weather."

"No, it wasn't. It was very sort of foggy and misty. Ah—I'm quite tired, too."

"Where did you go? Just down the street for the shops?"

"No, it's early closing day for the shops. No. Oh no, I went to the cemetery."

"Sounds gloomy," said Tommy. "What did you want to go to the cemetery for?"

"I went to look at some of the graves."

"It still sounds rather gloomy," said Tommy. "Did Hannibal enjoy himself?"

"Well, I had to put Hannibal on the lead. There was something that looked like a verger who kept coming out of the church and I thought he wouldn't like Hannibal because—well, you never know, Hannibal mightn't like him and I didn't want to prejudice people against us the moment we'd arrived."

"What did you want to look in the cemetery for?"

"Oh, to see what sort of people were buried there. Lots of people, I mean it's very, very full up. It goes back a long way. It goes back well in the eighteen-hundreds and I think one or two older than that, only the stone's so rubbed away you can't really see."

"I still don't see why you wanted to go to the cemetery."

"I was making my investigation," said Tuppence.

"Investigation about what?"

"I wanted to see if there were any Jordans buried there."

"Good gracious," said Tommy. "Are you still on that? Were you looking for—"

"Well, Mary Jordan died. We know she died. We know because we had a book that said she didn't die a natural death, but she'd still have to be buried somewhere, wouldn't she?"

"Undeniably," said Tommy, "unless she was buried in this garden."

"I don't think that's very likely," said Tuppence, "because I think that it was only this boy or girl—it must have been a boy, I think—of course it was a boy, his name was Alexander—and he obviously thought he'd been rather clever in knowing that she'd not died a natural death. But if he was the only person who'd made up his mind about that or who'd discovered it—well, I mean, nobody else had, I suppose. I mean, she just died and was buried and nobody said . . ."

"Nobody said there had been foul play," suggested Tommy.

"That sort of thing, yes. Poisoned or knocked on the head or pushed off a cliff or run over by a car or—oh, lots of ways I can think of."

"I'm sure you can," said Tommy. "Only good thing about you, Tuppence, is that at least you have a kindly heart. You wouldn't put them into execution just for fun."

"But there wasn't any Mary Jordan in the cemetery. There weren't any Jordans."

"Disappointing for you," said Tommy. "Is that

thing you're cooking ready yet, because I'm pretty hungry. It smells rather good."

"It's absolutely done *à point*," said Tuppence. "So, as soon as you've washed, we eat."

4

Lots of Parkinsons

"Lots of Parkinsons," said Tuppence as they ate. "A long way back, but an amazing lot of them. Old ones, young ones and married ones. Bursting with Parkinsons. And Capes, and Griffins and Underwoods and Overwoods. Curious to have both of them, isn't it?"

"I had a friend called George Underwood," said Tommy.

"Yes, I've known Underwoods, too. But not Overwoods."

"Male or female?" said Thomas, with slight interest.

"A girl, I think it was. Rose Overwood."

"Rose Overwood," said Tommy, listening to the sound of it. "I don't think somehow it goes awfully well together." He added, "I must ring up those electricians after lunch. Be very careful, Tuppence, or you'll put your foot through the landing upstairs."

"Then I shall be a natural death, or an unnatural death, one of the two."

"A curiosity death," said Tommy. "Curiosity killed the cat."

"Aren't you at all curious?" asked Tuppence.

"I can't see any earthly reason for being curious. What have we got for pudding?"

"Treacle tart."

"Well, I must say, Tuppence, it was a delicious meal."

"I'm very glad you liked it," said Tuppence.

"What is that parcel outside the back door? Is it that wine we ordered?"

"No," said Tuppence, "it's bulbs."

"Oh," said Tommy, "bulbs."

"Tulips," said Tuppence. "I'll go and talk to old Isaac about them."

"Where are you going to put them?"

"I think along the center path in the garden."

"Poor old fellow, he looks as if he might drop dead any minute," said Tommy.

"Not at all," said Tuppence. "He's enormously tough, is Isaac. I've discovered, you know, that gardeners are like that. If they're very good gardeners, they seem to come to their prime when they're over eighty, but if you get a strong, hefty-looking young man about thirty-five who says, 'I've always wanted to work in a garden,' you may be quite sure that he's probably no good at all. They're just prepared to brush up a few leaves now and again and anything you want them to do they always say it's the wrong time of year, and as one never knows oneself when the right time of year is, at least I don't, well then, you see, they always get the better of you. But Isaac's wonderful. He knows about everything." Tuppence added, "There ought to be some crocuses as well. I wonder if they're in the parcel, too. Well, I'll go out and see. It's his day for coming and he'll tell me all about it."

"All right," said Tommy, "I'll come out and join you presently."

Tuppence and Isaac had a pleasant reunion. The bulbs were unpacked, discussions were held as to where things would show to best advantage. First the early tulips, which were expected to rejoice the heart at the end of February, then a consideration of the handsome fringed parrot tulips, and some tulips called, as far as Tuppence could make out, *viridiflora,* which would be exceptionally beautiful with long stems in the month of May and early June. As these were of an interesting green pastel color, they agreed to plant them as a collection in a quiet part of the garden where they could be picked and arranged in interesting floral arrangements in the drawing room, or by the short approach to the house through the front gate where they would arouse envy and jealousy among callers. They must even rejoice the artistic feelings of tradesmen delivering joints of meat and crates of grocery.

At four o'clock Tuppence produced a brown teapot full of good strong tea in the kitchen, placed a sugar basin full of lumps of sugar and a milk jug by it, and called Isaac in to refresh himself before departing. She went in search of Tommy.

I suppose he's asleep somewhere, thought Tuppence to herself as she looked from one room into another. She was glad to see a head sticking up on the landing out of the sinister pit in the floor.

"It's all right now, ma'am," said an electrician. "No need to be careful any more. It's all fixed." He added that he was starting work on a different portion of the house on the following morning.

"I do hope," said Tuppence, "that you will really come." She added, "Have you seen Mr. Beresford anywhere?"

"Aye, your husband, you mean? Yes, he's up on an upper floor, I think. Dropping things, he was. Yes, rather heavy things, too. Must have been some books, I think."

"Books!" said Tuppence. "Well, I never!"

The electrician retreated down into his own personal underworld in the passage and Tuppence went up to the attic converted to the extra book library at present devoted to children's books.

Tommy was sitting on the top of a pair of steps. Several books were around him on the floor and there were noticeable gaps in the shelves.

"So there you are," said Tuppence, "after pretending you weren't interested or anything. You've been looking at lots of books, haven't you? You've disarranged a lot of the things that I put away so neatly."

"Well, I'm sorry about that," said Tommy, "but, well, I thought I'd perhaps just have a look round."

"Did you find any other books that have got any underlined things in them in red ink?"

"No. Nothing else."

"How annoying," said Tuppence.

"I think it must have been Alexander's work, Master Alexander Parkinson," said Tommy.

"That's right," said Tuppence. "One of the Parkinsons, the numerous Parkinsons."

"Well, I think he must have been rather a lazy boy, although of course it must have been rather a bother doing that underlining and all. But there's no more information re Jordan," said Tommy.

"I asked old Isaac. He knows a lot of people round here. He says he doesn't remember any Jordans."

"What are you doing with that brass lamp you've put by the front door?" asked Tommy, as he came downstairs.

"I'm taking it to the white elephant sale," said Tuppence.

"Why?"

"Oh, because it's always been a thorough nuisance. We bought it somewhere abroad, didn't we?"

"Yes, I think we must have been mad. You never liked it. You said you hated it. Well, I agree. And it's awfully heavy, too—very heavy."

"But Miss Sanderson was terribly pleased when I said that they could have it. She offered to fetch it, but I said I'd run it down to them in the car. It's today we take the things."

"I'll run down with it if you like."

"No, I'd rather like to go."

"All right," said Tommy. "Perhaps I'd better come with you and just carry it in for you."

"Oh, I think I'll find someone who'll carry it in for me," said Tuppence.

"Well, you might or you might not. Don't go and strain yourself."

"All right," said Tuppence.

"You've got some other reason for wanting to go, haven't you?"

"Well, I just thought I'd like to chat a bit with people," said Tuppence.

"I never know what you're up to, Tuppence, but I know the look in your eye when you *are* up to something."

"You take Hannibal for a walk," said Tuppence. "I can't take him to the white elephant sale. I don't want to get into a dog-fight."

"All right. Want to go for a walk, Hannibal?"

Hannibal, as was his habit, immediately replied in the affirmative. His affirmatives and his negatives were always quite impossible to miss. He wriggled his body, wagged his tail, raised one paw, put it down again and came and rubbed his head hard against Tommy's leg.

"That's right," he obviously said, "that's what you exist for, my dear slave. We're going out for a lovely walk down the street. Lots of smells, I hope."

"Come on," said Tommy. "I'll take the lead with me, and don't run into the road like you did last time. One of those awful great 'long vehicles' was nearly the end of you."

Hannibal looked at him with the expression of "I'm always a very good dog who'll do exactly what I am told." False as the statement was, it often succeeded in deceiving even those people who were in closest contact with Hannibal.

Tommy put the brass lamp into the car, murmuring it was rather heavy. Tuppence drove off in the car. Having seen her turn the corner, Tommy attached the lead to Hannibal's collar and took him down the street. Then he turned up the lane towards the church, and removed Hannibal's lead, since very little traffic came up this particular road. Hannibal acknowledged the privilege by grunting and sniffing in various tufts of grass with which the pavement next to the wall was adorned. If he could have used human language, it was clear that what he would have said was—"Delicious! Very rich. Big dog here. Believe it's that beastly Alsatian." Low growl. "I don't like Alsatians. If I see the one again that bit me once, I'll bite him. Ah! Delicious, delicious. Very nice little bitch here. Yes—yes—I'd like to meet her. I wonder if she lives far away. Expect she comes out of this house. I wonder now."

"Come out of that gate, now," said Tommy. "Don't go into a house that isn't yours."

Hannibal pretended not to hear.

"Hannibal!"

Hannibal redoubled his speed and turned a corner which led toward the kitchen.

"Hannibal!" shouted Tommy. "Do you hear me?"

"Hear you, Master?" said Hannibal. "Were you calling me? Oh yes, of course."

A sharp bark from inside the kitchen caught his ear. He scampered out to join Tommy. Hannibal walked a few inches behind Tommy's heel.

"Good boy," said Tommy.

"I am a good boy, aren't I?" said Hannibal. "Any moment you need me to defend you, here I am less than a foot away."

They had arrived at a side gate which led into the churchyard. Hannibal, who in some way had an extraordinary knack of altering his size when he wanted to, instead of appearing somewhat broad-shouldered, possibly a somewhat too plump dog, he could at any moment make himself like a thin black thread. He now squeezed himself through the bars of the gate with no difficulty at all.

"Come back, Hannibal," called Tommy. "You can't go into the churchyard."

Hannibal's answer to that, if there had been any, would have been, "I am in the churchyard already, Master." He was scampering gaily round the churchyard with the air of a dog who has been let out in a singularly pleasant garden.

"You awful dog!" said Tommy.

He unlatched the gate, walked in and chased Hannibal, lead in hand. Hannibal was now at a far corner of the churchyard, and seemed to have every intention of trying to gain access through the door of the church, which was slightly ajar. Tommy, however, reached him in time and attached the lead. Hannibal looked up with the air of one who had intended this to happen all along. "Putting me on the lead, are you?" he said. "Yes, of course, I know it's a kind of prestige. It shows that I am a very valuable dog." He wagged his tail. Since there seemed nobody to oppose Hannibal walking in the churchyard with his master, suitably secured as he was by a stalwart lead, Tommy wandered round, checking perhaps Tuppence's researches of a former day.

He looked first at a worn stone monument more or less behind a little side door into the church. It was, he thought, probably one of the oldest. There were several of them there, most of them bearing dates in the eighteen-hundreds. There was one, however, that Tommy looked at longest.

"Odd," he said, "damned odd."

Hannibal looked up at him. He did not understand this piece of his master's conversation. He saw nothing about the gravestone to interest a dog. He sat down, looked up at his master inquiringly.

5

The White Elephant Sale

Tuppence was pleasurably surprised to find the brass lamp which she and Tommy now regarded with such repulsion welcomed with the utmost warmth.

"How very good of you, Mrs. Beresford, to bring us something as nice as that. Most interesting, most interesting. I suppose it must have come from abroad on your travels once."

"Yes. We bought it in Egypt," said Tuppence.

She was quite doubtful by this time, a period of eight to ten years having passed, as to where she had bought it. It might have been Damascus, she thought, and it might equally well have been Baghdad or possibly Tehran. But Egypt, she thought, since Egypt was doubtless in the news at this moment, would be far more interesting. Besides, it looked rather Egyptian. Clearly, if she had got it from any other country, it dated from some period when they had been copying Egyptian work.

"Really," she said, "it's rather big for our house, so I thought—"

"Oh, I think really we ought to raffle it," said Miss Little.

Miss Little was more or less in charge of things. Her local nickname was "The Parish Pump," mainly because she was so well informed about all things that happened in the parish. Her surname was misleading. She was a large woman of ample proportions. Her Christian name was Dorothy, but she was always called Dodo.

"I hope you're coming to the sale, Mrs. Beresford?"

Tuppence assured her that she was coming.

"I can hardly wait to buy," she said chattily.

"Oh, I'm so glad you feel like that."

"I think it's a very good thing," said Tuppence. "I mean, the white elephant idea, because it's—well, it is so true, isn't it? I mean, what's one person's white elephant is somebody else's pearl beyond price."

"Ah, really, we *must* tell that to the vicar," said Miss Price-Ridley, an angular lady with a lot of teeth. "Oh yes, I'm sure he would be very much amused."

"That papier-mâché basin, for instance," said Tuppence, raising this particular trophy up.

"Oh really, do you think anyone will buy that?"

"I shall buy it myself if it's for sale when I come here tomorrow," said Tuppence.

"But surely, nowadays, they have such pretty plastic washing-up bowls."

"I'm not very fond of plastic," said Tuppence. "That's a really good papier-mâché bowl that you've got there. I mean, if you put things down in that, lots of china together, they wouldn't break. And there's an old-fashioned tin-opener, too. The kind with a bull's head that one never sees nowadays."

"Oh, but it's such hard work, that. Don't you think the ones that you put on an electric thing are much better?"

Conversation on these lines went on for a short time and then Tuppence asked if there were any services that she could render.

"Ah, dear Mrs. Beresford, perhaps you would arrange the curio stall. I'm sure you're very artistic."

"Not really artistic at all," said Tuppence, "but I would love to arrange the stall for you. You must tell me if I'm doing it wrong," she added.

"Oh, it's so nice to have some extra help. We are so pleased to meet you, too. I suppose you've nearly settled into your house by now?"

"I thought we should be settled by now," said Tuppence, "but it seems as though there's a long time to go still. It's so very hard with electricians and then carpenters and people. They're always coming back."

A slight dispute arose with people near her supporting the claims of electricians and the Gas Board.

"Gas people are the worst," said Miss Little with firmness, "because, you see, they come all the way over from Lower Stamford. The electricity people only have to come from Wellbank."

The arrival of the vicar to say a few words of encouragement and good cheer to the helpers changed the subject. He also expressed himself very pleased to meet his new parishioner, Mrs. Beresford.

"We know all about you," he said. "Oh yes indeed. And your husband. A most interesting talk I had the other day about you both. What an interesting life you must have had. I dare say it's not supposed to be spoken of, so I won't. I mean, in the last war. A wonderful performance on your and your husband's part."

"Oh, do tell us, Vicar," said one of the ladies, detaching herself from the stall where she was setting up jars of jam.

"I was told in strict confidence," said the vicar. "I think I saw you walking round the churchyard yesterday, Mrs. Beresford."

"Yes," said Tuppence. "I looked into the church first. I see you have one or two very attractive windows."

"Yes, yes, they date back to the fourteenth century. That is, the one in the north aisle does. But of course most of them are Victorian."

"Walking round the churchyard," said Tuppence, "it seemed to me there were a great many Parkinsons buried there."

"Yes, yes indeed. There've always been big contingents of Parkinsons in this part of the world, though of course I don't remember any of them myself, but you do, I think, Mrs. Lupton."

Mrs. Lupton, an elderly lady who was supporting herself on two sticks, looked pleased.

"Yes, yes," she said. "I remember when Mrs. Parkinson was alive—you know, old Mrs. Parkinson, *the* Mrs. Parkinson who lived in the Manor House, wonderful old lady she was. Quite wonderful."

"And there were some Somers I saw, and the Chattertons."

"Ah, I see you're getting up well with our local geography of the past."

"I think I heard something about a Jordan—Annie or Mary Jordan, was it?"

Tuppence looked round her in an inquiring fashion. The name of Jordan seemed to cause no particular interest.

"Somebody had a cook called Jordan, I think. Mrs. Blackwell. Susan Jordan, I think it was. She only stayed six months, I think. Quite unsatisfactory in many ways."

"Was that a long time ago?"

"Oh no. Just about eight or ten years ago, I think. Not more than that."

"Are there any Parkinsons living here now?"

"Oh no. They're all gone long ago. One of them married a first cousin and went to live in Kenya, I believe."

"I wonder," said Tuppence, managing to attach herself to Mrs. Lupton, whom she knew had something to do with the local children's hospital, "I wonder if you want any extra children's books. They're all old ones, I mean. I got them in an odd lot when we were bidding for some of the furniture that was for sale in our house."

"Well, that's very kind of you, I'm sure, Mrs. Beresford. Of course we do have some very good ones given to us, you know. Special editions for children nowadays. One does feel it's a pity they should have to read all those old-fashioned books."

"Oh, do you think so," said Tuppence. "I loved the

books that I had as a child. Some of them," she said, "had been my grandmother's when she was a child. I believe I liked those best of all. I shall never forget reading *Treasure Island*, and Mrs. Molesworth's *Four Winds Farm* and some of Stanley Weyman's."

She looked round her inquiringly—then, resigning herself, she looked at her wrist watch, exclaimed at finding how late it was and took her leave.

Tuppence, having got home, put the car away in the garage and walked round the house to the front door. The door was open, so she walked in. Albert then came from the back premises and bowed to greet her.

"Like some tea, madam? You must be very tired."

"I don't think so," said Tuppence. "I've had tea. They gave me tea down at the Institute. Quite good cake, but very nasty buns."

"Buns is difficult. Buns is nearly as difficult as doughnuts. Ah," he sighed. "Lovely doughnuts Amy used to make."

"I know. Nobody's were like them," said Tuppence.

Amy had been Albert's wife, now some years deceased. In Tuppence's opinion, Amy had made wonderful treacle tart, but had never been very good with doughnuts.

"I think doughnuts are dreadfully difficult," said Tuppence. "I've never been able to do them myself."

"Well, it's a knack."

"Where's Mr. Beresford? Is he out?"

"Oh no, he's upstairs. In that room. You know. The book-room or whatever you like to call it. I can't get out of the way of calling it the attic still, myself."

"What's he doing up there?" asked Tuppence, slightly surprised.

"Well, he's still looking at the books, I think. I suppose he's still arranging them, getting them finished, as you might say."

"Still seems to me very surprising," said Tuppence. "He's really been very rude to us about those books."

"Ah well," said Albert, "gentlemen are like that, aren't they? They likes big books mostly, you know, don't they? Something scientific that they can get their teeth into."

"I shall go up and rout him out," said Tuppence. "Where's Hannibal?"

"I think he's up there with the master."

But at that moment Hannibal made his appearance. Having barked with the ferocious fury he considered necessary for a good guard dog, he had correctly assumed that it was his beloved mistress who had returned and not someone who had come to steal the teaspoons or to assault his master and mistress. He came wriggling down the stairs, his pink tongue hanging out, his tail wagging.

"Ah," said Tuppence, "pleased to see your mother?"

Hannibal said he was very pleased to see his mother. He leapt upon her with such force that he nearly knocked her to the ground.

"Gently," said Tuppence, "gently. You don't want to kill me, do you?"

Hannibal made it clear that the only thing he wanted to do was to eat her because he loved her so much.

"Where's Master? Where's Father? Is he upstairs?"

Hannibal understood. He ran up a flight, turned his head over his shoulder and waited for Tuppence to join him.

"Well, I never," said Tuppence as, slightly out of breath, she entered the book-room, to see Tommy astride a pair of steps, taking books in and out. "Whatever are you doing? I thought you were going to take Hannibal for a walk."

"We have been for a walk," said Tommy. "We went to the churchyard."

"Why on earth did you take Hannibal into the churchyard? I'm sure they wouldn't like dogs there."

"He was on the lead," said Tommy, "and anyway I

didn't take him. He took me. He seemed to like the churchyard."

"I hope he hasn't got a thing about it," said Tuppence. "You know what Hannibal is like. He likes arranging a routine always. If he's going to have a routine of going to the churchyard every day, it will really be very difficult for us."

"He's really been very intelligent about the whole thing," said Tommy.

"When you say he's intelligent, you just mean he's self-willed," said Tuppence.

Hannibal turned his head and came and rubbed his nose against the calf of her leg.

"He's telling you," said Tommy, "that he is a very clever dog. Cleverer than you or I have been so far."

"And what do you mean by that?" asked Tuppence.

"Have you been enjoying yourself?" asked Tommy, changing the subject.

"Well, I wouldn't go as far as that," said Tuppence. "People were very kind to me and nice to me and I think soon I shan't get them mixed up so much as I do at present. It's awfully difficult at first, you know, because people look rather alike and wear the same sort of clothes and you don't know at first which is which. I mean, unless somebody is very beautiful or very ugly. And that doesn't seem to happen so noticeably in the country, does it?"

"I'm telling you," said Tommy, "that Hannibal and I have been extremely clever."

"I thought you said it was Hannibal."

Tommy reached out his hand and took a book from the shelf in front of him.

"*Kidnapped*," he remarked. "Oh yes, another Robert Louis Stevenson. Somebody must have been very fond of Robert Louis Stevenson. *The Black Arrow, Kidnapped, Catriona* and two others, I think. All given to Alexander Parkinson by a fond grandmother and one from a generous aunt."

"Well," said Tuppence, "what about it?"

"And I've found his grave," said Tommy.

"Found what?"

"Well, Hannibal did. It's right in the corner against one of the small doors into the church. I suppose it's the door to the vestry, something like that. It's very rubbed and not well kept up, but that's it. He was fourteen when he died. Alexander Richard Parkinson. Hannibal was nosing about there. I got him away from it and managed to make out the inscription, in spite of its being so rubbed."

"Fourteen," said Tuppence. "Poor little boy."

"Yes," said Tommy, "it's sad and—"

"You've got something in your head," said Tuppence. "I don't understand."

"Well, I wondered. I suppose, Tuppence, you've infected me. That's the worst of you. When you get keen on something, you don't go on with it by yourself, you get somebody else to take an interest in it, too."

"I don't quite know what you mean," said Tuppence.

"I wondered if it was a case of cause and effect."

"What do you mean, Tommy?"

"I was wondering about Alexander Parkinson who took a lot of trouble, though no doubt he enjoyed himself doing it, making a kind of code, a secret message in a book. *Mary Jordan did not die naturally.* Supposing that was true? Supposing Mary Jordan, whoever she was, didn't die naturally? Well then, don't you see, perhaps the next thing that happened was that Alexander Parkinson died."

"You don't mean—you don't think—"

"Well, one wonders," said Tommy. "It started me wondering—fourteen years old. There was no mention of what he died of. I suppose there wouldn't be on a gravestone. There was just a text: *In thy presence is the fullness of joy.* Something like that. But—it might have been because he knew something that was dangerous to somebody else. And so—and so he died."

"You mean he was killed? You're just imagining things," said Tuppence.

"Well, you started it. Imagining things, or wondering. It's much the same thing, isn't it?"

"We shall go on wondering, I suppose," said Tuppence, "and we shan't be able to find out anything because it was all such years and years and years ago."

They looked at each other.

"Round about the time we were trying to investigate the Jane Finn business," said Tommy.

They looked at each other again, their minds going back to the past.

6

Problems

Moving house is often thought of beforehand as an agreeable exercise which the movers are going to enjoy, but it does not always turn out as expected. Relations have to be reopened or adjusted with electricians, with builders, with carpenters, with painters, with wallpapers, with providers of refrigerators, gas stoves, electric appliances, with upholsterers, makers of curtains, hangers-up of curtains, those who lay linoleum, those who supply carpets. Every day has not only its appointed task but usually something between four and twelve extra callers, either long expected or those whose coming was quite forgotten.

But there were moments when Tuppence with sighs of relief announced various finalities in different fields.

"I really think our kitchen is almost perfect by now," she said. "Only I can't find the proper kind of flour bin yet."

"Oh," said Tommy, "does it matter very much?"

"Well, it does rather. I mean, you buy flour very often in three-pound bags and it won't go into these kind of containers. They're all so dainty. You know, one has a pretty rose on it and the other's got a sunflower and they'll not take more than a pound. It's all so silly."

At intervals, Tuppence made other suggestions.

"The Laurels," she said. "Silly name for a house, I think. I don't see why it's called The Laurels. It hasn't got any laurels. They could have called it The

41

Plane Trees much better. Plane trees are very nice," said Tuppence.

"Before The Laurels it was called Long Scofield, so they told me," said Tommy.

"That name doesn't seem to mean anything either," said Tuppence. "What is a Scofield, and who lived in it then?"

"That was the Waddingtons."

"One gets so mixed," said Tuppence. "Waddingtons and then the Joneses, the people who sold it to us. And before that the Blackmores? And once, I suppose, the Parkinsons. Lots of Parkinsons. I'm always running into more Parkinsons."

"What way do you mean?"

"Well, I suppose it's that I'm always asking," said Tuppence. "I mean, if I could find out something about the Parkinsons, we could get on with our—well, with our problem."

"That's what one always seems to call everything nowadays. The problem of Mary Jordan, is that it?"

"Well, it's not just that. There's the problem of the Parkinsons and the problem of Mary Jordan and there must be a lot of other problems, too. Mary Jordan didn't die naturally, then the next thing the message said was, 'It was one of us.' Now did that mean one of the Parkinson family or did it mean just someone who lived in the house? Say there were two or three Parkinsons, and some older Parkinsons, and people with different names who were aunts to the Parkinsons or nephews and nieces of the Parkinsons, and I suppose something like a housemaid and a parlormaid and a cook and perhaps a governess and perhaps—well, not an *au pair* girl, it would be too long ago for an *au pair* girl—but 'one of us' must mean a householdful. Households were fuller then than they are now. Well, Mary Jordan could have been a housemaid or a parlormaid or even the cook. And why should someone want her to die, and not die naturally? I mean, somebody must have wanted her to die or else her death would have been natural, wouldn't it?—I'm going to another coffee morning the day after tomorrow," said Tuppence.

"You seem to be always going to coffee mornings."

"Well, it's a very good way of getting to know one's neighbors and the people who live in the same village. After all, it's not very big, this village. And people are always talking about their old aunts or people they knew. I shall try and start on Mrs. Griffin, who was evidently a great character in the neighborhood. I should say she ruled everyone with a rod of iron. You know. She bullied the vicar and she bullied the doctor and I think she bullied the district nurse and all the rest of it."

"Wouldn't the district nurse be helpful?"

"I don't think so. She's dead. I mean, the one who would have been there in the Parkinsons' time is dead, and the one who is here now hasn't been here very long. No sort of interest in the place. I don't think she even knew a Parkinson."

"I wish," said Tommy desperately, "oh, how I wish that we could forget *all* the Parkinsons."

"You mean, then we shouldn't have a problem?"

"Oh dear," said Tommy. "Problems again."

"It's Beatrice," said Tuppence.

"What's Beatrice?"

"Who introduced problems. Really, it's Elizabeth. The cleaning help we had before Beatrice. She was always coming to me and saying, 'Oh, madam, could I speak to you a minute? You see, I've got a problem,' and then Beatrice began coming on Thursdays and she must have caught it, I suppose. So she has problems, too. It's just a way of saying something—but you always call it a problem."

"All right," said Tommy. "We'll admit that's so. You've got a problem—I've got a problem. We've both got problems."

He sighed and departed.

Tuppence came down the stairs slowly, shaking her

head. Hannibal came up to her hopefully, wagging
his tail and wriggling in hopes of favors to come.

"No, Hannibal," said Tuppence. "You've had a
walk. You've had your morning walk."

Hannibal intimated that she was quite mistaken, he
hadn't had a walk.

"You are one of the worst liars among dogs I have
ever known," said Tuppence. "You've been for a walk
with Father."

Hannibal made his second attempt, which was to
endeavor to show by various dog attitudes that any
dog could have a second walk if only he had an
owner who could see things in that light. Disappointed in this effort, he went down the stairs and
proceeded to bark loudly and make every pretense of
being about to make a sharp snap bite at a tousle-
haired girl who was wielding a Hoover. He did not
like the Hoover, and he objected to Tuppence having
a lengthy conversation with Beatrice.

"Oh, don't let him bite me," said Beatrice.

"He won't bite you," said Tuppence. "He only pre-
tends he's going to."

"Well, I think he'll really do it one day," said
Beatrice. "By the way, madam, I wonder if I could
speak to you for a moment."

"Oh," said Tuppence. "You mean—"

"Well, you see, madam, I've got a problem."

"I thought that was it," said Tuppence. "What sort
of problem is it? And, by the way, do you know any
family here or anyone who lived here at one time
called Jordan?"

"Jordan now. Well, I can't really say. There was
the Johnsons, of course, and there was—ah yes, one of
the constables was a Johnson. And so was one of the
postmen. George Johnson. He was a friend of mine."
She giggled.

"You never heard of a Mary Jordan who died?"

Beatrice merely looked bewildered—and she shook
her head and went back to the assault.

"About this problem, madam?"

"Oh yes, your problem."

"I hope you don't mind my asking you, madam, but it's put me in a very queer position, you see, and I don't like—"

"Well, if you can tell me quickly," said Tuppence. "I've got to go out to a coffee morning."

"Oh yes. At Mrs. Barber's, isn't it?"

"That's right," said Tuppence. "Now what's the problem?"

"Well, it's a coat. Ever such a nice coat it was. At Simmonds it was, and I went in and I tried it on and it seemed to me very nice, it did. Well, there was one little spot on the skirt, you know, just round near the hem, but that didn't seem to me would matter much. Anyway, well, it—er—"

"Yes," said Tuppence, "it what?"

"It made me see why it was so inexpensive, you see. So I got it. And so that was all right. But when I got home I found there was a label on it and instead of saying £3.70 it was labeled £6. Well, ma'am, I didn't like to do that, so I didn't know what to do. I went back to the shop and I took the coat with me—I thought I'd better take it back and explain, you see, that I hadn't meant to take it away like that and then you see the girl who sold it to me—very nice girl she is, her name is Gladys, yes, I don't know what her other name is—but anyway she was ever so upset, she was, and I said, 'Well that's quite all right, I'll pay extra,' and she said, 'No, you can't do that because it's all entered up.' You see—you do see what I mean?"

"Yes, I think I see what you mean," said Tuppence.

"And so, she said, 'Oh, you can't do that. It will get *me* into trouble.'"

"Why should it get her into trouble?"

"Well, that's what I felt. I mean to say, well, I mean it'd been sold to me for less and I'd brought it back and I didn't see why it could put *her* in trouble. She said if there was any carelessness like that and they hadn't noticed the right ticket and they'd charged me the wrong price, as likely as not she'd get the sack for it."

"Oh, I shouldn't think that would happen," said Tuppence. "I think you were quite right. I don't see what else you could do."

"Well, but there it is, you see. She made such a fuss and she was beginning to cry and everything, so I took the coat away again and now I don't know whether I've cheated the shop or whether—I don't really know what to do."

"Well," said Tuppence, "I really think I'm too old to know what one ought to do nowadays because everything is so odd in shops. The prices are odd and everything is difficult. But if I were you and you want to pay something extra, well, perhaps you'd better give the money to what's-her-name—Gladys something. She can put the money in the till or somewhere."

"Oh well, I don't know as I'd like to do that because she might keep it, you see. I mean, if she kept the money, oh well, I mean it wouldn't be difficult would it, because I suppose I've stolen the money and I wouldn't have stolen it really. I mean, then it would have been Gladys who stole it, wouldn't it, and I don't know that I trust her all that much. Oh dear."

"Yes," said Tuppence, "life is very difficult, isn't it? I'm terribly sorry, Beatrice, but I really think you've got to make up your own mind about this. If you can't trust your friend—"

"Oh, she's not exactly a friend. I only buy things there. And she's ever so nice to talk to. But I mean, well, she's not exactly a friend, you know. I think she had a little trouble once before the last place she was in. You know, they said she kept back money on something she'd sold."

"Well, in that case," said Tuppence in slight desperation, "I shouldn't do anything."

The firmness of her tone was such that Hannibal

came into the consultation. He barked loudly at Beatrice and took a running leap at the Hoover which he considered one of his principal enemies. "I don't trust that Hoover," said Hannibal. "I'd like to bite it up."

"Oh, be quiet, Hannibal. Stop barking. Don't bite anything or anyone," said Tuppence. "I'm going to be awfully late."

She rushed out of the house.

"Problems," said Tuppence, as she went down the hill and along Orchard Road. Going along there, she wondered as she'd done before if there'd ever been an orchard attached to any of the houses. It seemed unlikely nowadays.

Mrs. Barber received her with great pleasure. She brought forward some very delicious-looking éclairs.

"What lovely things," said Tuppence. "Did you get them at Betterby's?"

Betterby's was the local confectionery shop.

"Oh no, my aunt made them. She's wonderful, you know. She does wonderful things."

"Éclairs are very difficult things to make," said Tuppence. "I could never succeed with them."

"Well, you have to get a particular kind of flour. I believe that's the secret of it."

The ladies drank coffee and talked about the difficulties of certain kinds of home cookery.

"Miss Bolland was talking about you the other day, Mrs. Beresford."

"Oh?" said Tuppence. "Really? Bolland?"

"She lives next to the vicarage. Her family has lived here a long time. She was telling us the other day how she'd come and stayed here when she was a child. She used to look forward to it. She said, because there were such wonderful gooseberries in the garden. And greengage trees, too. Now that's a thing you practically never see nowadays, not real greengages.

Something else called gage plums or something, but they're not a bit the same to taste."

The ladies talked about things in the fruit line which did not taste like the things used to which they remembered from their childhood.

"My great-uncle had greengage trees," said Tuppence.

"Oh yes. Is that the one who was a canon at Anchester? Canon Henderson used to live here, with his sister, I believe. Very sad it was. She was eating seed cake one day, you know, and one of the seeds got the wrong way. Something like that and she choked and she choked and she choked and she died of it. Oh dear, that's very sad, isn't it?" said Mrs. Barber. "Very sad indeed. One of my cousins died choking," she said. "A piece of mutton. It's very easy to do, I believe, and there are people who die of hiccups because they can't stop, you know. They don't know the old rhyme," she explained. " 'Hic-up, hic-down, hic to the next town, three hics and one cup sure to cure the hiccups.' You have to hold your breath while you say it."

7

More Problems

"Can I speak to you a moment, ma'am?"

"Oh dear," said Tuppence. "Not more problems?"

She was descending the stairs from the book-room, brushing dust off herself because she was dressed in her best coat and skirt, to which she was thinking of adding a feather hat and then proceeding out to a tea she had been asked to attend by a new friend she had met at the white elephant sale. It was no moment, she felt, to listen to the further difficulties of Beatrice.

"Well, no, no, it's not exactly a problem. It's just something I thought you might like to know about."

"Oh," said Tuppence, still feeling that this might be another problem in disguise. She came down carefully. "I'm in rather a hurry because I have to go out to tea."

"Well, it was just about someone as you asked about, it seems. Name of Mary Jordan, that was right? Only they thought perhaps it was Mary Johnson. You know, there was a Belinda Johnson as worked at the post office, but a good long time ago."

"Yes," said Tuppence, "and there was a policeman called Johnson, too, so someone told me."

"Yes, well, anyway, this friend of mine—Gwenda, her name is—you know the shop, the post office is one side and envelopes and dirty cards and things the other side, and some china things too, before Christmas, you see, and—"

"I know," said Tuppence, "it's called Mrs. Garrison's or something like that."

"Yes, but it isn't really Garrisons nowadays as keep it. Quite a different name. But anyway, this friend of mine, Gwenda, she thought you might be interested to know because she says as she had heard of a Mary Jordan what lived here a long time ago. A very long time ago. Lived here, in this house, I mean."

"Oh, lived in The Laurels?"

"Well, it wasn't called that then. And she'd heard something about her, she said. And so she thought you might be interested. There was some rather sad story about her, she had an accident or something. Anyway, she died."

"You mean that she was living in this house when she died? Was she one of the family?"

"No. I think the family was called Parker, a name of that kind. A lot of Parkers there were. Parkers or Parkistons—something like that. I think she was just staying here. I believe Mrs. Griffin knows about it. Do you know Mrs. Griffin?"

"Oh, very slightly," said Tuppence. "Matter of fact, that's where I'm going to tea this afternoon. I talked to her the other day at the sale. I hadn't met her before."

"She's a very old lady. She's older than she looks, but I think she's got a very good memory. I believe one of the Parkinson boys was her godson."

"What was his Christian name?"

"Oh, it was Alec, I think. Some name like that. Alec or Alix."

"What happened to him? Did he grow up—go away—become a soldier or sailor or something like that?"

"Oh no. He died. Oh yes, I think he's buried right here. It's one of those things, I think, as people usedn't to know much about. It's one of those things with a name like a Christian name."

"You mean somebody's disease?"

"Hodgkin's disease, or something. No, it was a

Christian name of some kind. I don't know, but they say as your blood grows the wrong color or something. Nowadays I believe they take blood away from you and give you some good blood again, or something like that. But even then you usually die, they say. Mrs. Billings—the cakeshop, you know—she had a little girl died of that and she was only seven. They say it takes them very young."

"Leukemia?" suggested Tuppence.

"Oh, now, fancy you knowing. Yes, it was that name, I'm sure. But they say now as one day there'll maybe be a cure for it, you know. Just like nowadays they give you inoculations and things to cure you from typhoid, or whatever it is."

"Well," said Tuppence, "that's very interesting. Poor little boy."

"Oh, he wasn't very young. He was at school somewhere, I think. Must have been about thirteen or fourteen."

"Well," said Tuppence, "it's all very sad." She paused, then said, "Oh dear, I'm very late now. I must hurry off."

"I dare say Mrs. Griffin could tell you a few things. I don't mean things as she'd remember herself, but she was brought up here as a child and she heard a lot of things, and she tells people a lot sometimes about the families that were here before. Some of the things are real scandalous, too. You know, goings-on and all that. That was, of course, in what they called Edwardian times or Victorian times. I don't know which. You know. I should think it was Victorian, really. They talk about it as Edwardian and something called 'the Marlborough House set.' Sort of high society, wasn't it?"

"Yes," said Tuppence, "yes. High society."

"And goings-on," said Beatrice with some fervor.

"A good many goings-on," said Tuppence.

"Young girls doing what they shouldn't do," said Beatrice, loath to part with her mistress just when something interesting might be said.

"No," said Tuppence, "I believe the girls led very—well, pure and austere lives and they married young, though often into the peerage."

"Oh dear," said Beatrice, "how nice for them. Lots of fine clothes, I suppose, race meetings and going to dances and ballrooms."

"Yes," said Tuppence, "lots of ballrooms."

"Well, I knew someone once, and her grandmother had been a housemaid in one of those smart houses, you know, as they all came to, and the Prince of Wales—the Prince of Wales as was then, you know, he was Edward VII afterwards, that one, the early one—well, he was there and he was ever so nice. Ever so nice to all the servants and everything else. And when she left, she took away the cake of soap that he'd used for his hands, and she kept it always. She used to show it to some of us children once."

"Very thrilling for you," said Tuppence. "It must have been very exciting times. Perhaps he stayed here in The Laurels."

"No, I don't think as I ever heard that, and I would have heard it. No, it was only Parkinsons here. No countesses and marchionesses and lords and ladies. The Parkinsons, I think, were mostly in trade. Very rich, you know, and all that, but still there's nothing exciting in trade, is there?"

"It depends," said Tuppence. She added, "I think I ought—"

"Yes, you'd best be going along, ma'am."

"Yes. Well, thank you very much. I don't think I'd better put on a hat. I've got my hair awfully mussed now."

"Well, you put your head in that corner where the cobwebs is. I'll dust it off in case you do it again."

Tuppence ran down the stairs.

"Alexander ran down here," she said. "Many times, I expect. And he knew it was 'one of them.' I wonder. I wonder more than ever now."

8

Mrs. Griffin

"I am so very pleased that you and your husband have come here to live, Mrs. Beresford," said Mrs. Griffin, as she poured out tea. "Sugar? Milk?"

She pressed forward a dish of sandwiches, and Tuppence helped herself.

"It makes so much difference, you know, in the country where one has nice neighbors with whom one has something in common. Did you know this part of the world before?"

"No," said Tuppence, "not at all. We had, you know, a good many different houses to go and view—particulars of them were sent us by the estate agents. Of course, most of them were very often quite frightful. One was called Full of Old World Charm."

"I know," said Mrs. Griffin, "I know exactly. Old world charm usually means that you have to put a new roof on and that the damp is very bad. And 'thoroughly modernized'—well, one knows what that means. Lots of gadgets one doesn't want and usually a very bad view from the windows of really hideous houses. But The Laurels is a charming house. I expect, though, you have had a good deal to do to it. Everyone has in turn."

"I suppose a lot of different people have lived there," said Tuppence.

"Oh yes. Nobody seems to stay very long anywhere nowadays, do they? The Cuthbertsons were here and the Redlands, and before that the Seymours. And after them the Joneses."

54

"We wondered a little why it was called The Laurels," said Tuppence.

"Oh well, that was the kind of name people liked to give a house. Of course, if you go back far enough, probably to the time of the Parkinsons, I think there *were* laurels. Probably a drive, you know, curling round and a lot of laurels, including those speckled ones. I never liked speckled laurels."

"No," said Tuppence, "I do agree with you. I don't like them either. There seem to have been a lot of Parkinsons here," she added.

"Oh yes. I think they occupied it longer than anyone else."

"Nobody seems able to tell one much about them."

"Well, it was a long time ago, you see, dear. And after the—well, I think after the—the trouble you know, and there was some feeling about it and of course one doesn't wonder they sold the place."

"It had a bad reputation, did it?" said Tuppence, taking a chance. "Do you mean the house was supposed to be insanitary, or something?"

"Oh no, not the house. No, really, the people you see. Well, of course, there was the—the disgrace, in a way—it was during the First War. Nobody could believe it. My grandmother used to talk about it and say that it was something to do with naval secrets—about a new submarine. There was a girl living with the Parkinsons who was said to have been mixed up with it all."

"Was that Mary Jordan?" said Tuppence.

"Yes. Yes, you're quite right. Afterwards they suspected that it wasn't her real name. I think somebody had suspected her for some time. The boy had, Alexander. Nice boy. Quite sharp, too."

Book Two

9

A Long Time Ago

Tuppence was selecting birthday cards. It was a
wet afternoon and the post office was almost empty.
People dropped letters into the post box outside or
occasionally made a hurried purchase of stamps.
Then they usually departed to get home as soon as
possible. It was not one of those crowded shopping
afternoons. In fact, Tuppence thought, she had chosen this particular day very well.

Gwenda, whom she had managed to recognize easily from Beatrice's description, had been only too
pleased to come to her assistance. Gwenda represented the household shopping side of the post office. An
elderly woman with gray hair presided over the government business of Her Majesty's mails. Gwenda, a
chatty girl, interested always in new arrivals to the
village, was happy among the Christmas cards, valentines, birthday cards, comic post cards, notepaper and
stationery, various types of chocolates and sundry
china articles of domestic use. She and Tuppence
were already on friendly terms.

"I'm so glad that house has been opened up again.
Princes Lodge, I mean."

"I thought it had always been The Laurels."

"Oh no. I don't think it was ever called that.
Houses change names a lot around here. People do
like giving new names to houses, you know."

"Yes, they certainly seem to," said Tuppence
thoughtfully. "Even we have thought of a name or
two. By the way, Beatrice told me that you knew
someone once living here called Mary Jordan."

59

"I didn't know her, but I have heard her mentioned. In the war it was, not the last war. The one long before that when there used to be zeppelins."

"I remember hearing about zeppelins," said Tuppence.

"In nineteen fifteen or nineteen sixteen—they came over London."

"I remember I'd gone to the Army and Navy Stores one day with an old great-aunt and there was an alarm."

"They used to come over at night sometimes, didn't they? Must have been rather frightening, I should think."

"Well, I don't think it was really," said Tuppence. "People used to get quite excited. It wasn't nearly as frightening as the flying bombs—in this last war. One always felt rather as though *they* were following you to places. Following you down a street, or something like that."

"Spend all your nights in the tube, did you? I had a friend in London. She used to spend all the nights in the tubes. Warren Street, I think it was. Everyone used to have their own particular tube station."

"I wasn't in London in the last war," said Tuppence. "I don't think I'd have liked to spend all night in the tube."

"Well, this friend of mine, Jenny her name was, oh, she used to love the tubes. She said it was ever so much fun. You know, you had your own particular stair in the tube. It was kept for you always, you slept there, and you took sandwiches in and things, and you had fun together and talked. Things went on all night and never stopped. Wonderful, you know. Trains going on right up to the morning. She told me she couldn't bear it when the war was over and she had to go home again, felt it was so dull, you know."

"Anyway," said Tuppence, "there weren't any flying bombs in nineteen fourteen. Just the zeppelins."

Zeppelins had clearly lost interest for Gwenda.

"It was someone called Mary Jordan I was asking about," said Tuppence. "Beatrice said you knew about her."

"Not really—I just heard her name mentioned once or twice, but it was ages ago. Lovely golden hair she had, my grandmother said. German she was—one of those Frowlines, as they were called. Looked after children—a kind of nurse. Had been with a naval family somewhere. That was up in Scotland, I think. And afterwards she came down here. Went to a family called Parks or Perkins. She used to have one day off a week, you know, and go to London, and that's where she used to take the things, whatever they were."

"What sort of things?" said Tuppence.

"I don't know—nobody ever said much. Things she'd stolen, I expect."

"Was she discovered stealing?"

"Oh no, I don't think so. They were beginning to suspect, but she got ill and died before that."

"What did she die of? Did she die down here? I suppose she went to hospital?"

"No—I don't think there were any hospitals to go to then. Wasn't any Welfare in those days. Somebody told me it was some silly mistake the cook made. Brought foxglove leaves into the house by mistake for spinach—or for lettuce, perhaps. No, I think that was someone else. Someone told me it was deadly nightshade but I don't believe *that* for a moment because, I mean, everyone knows about deadly nightshade, don't they, and anyway that's berries. Well, I think this was foxglove leaves brought in from the garden by mistake. Foxglove is Digoxo or some name like Digit—something that sounds like fingers. It's got something very deadly in it—the doctor came and he did what he could, but I think it was too late."

"Were there many people in the house when it happened?"

"Oh, there was quite a lot I should think—yes, because there were always people staying, so I've heard, and children, you know, and weekenders and a nursery maid and a governess, I think, and parties. Mind you, I'm not knowing all about this myself. It's only what Granny used to tell me. And old Mr. Bodlicott talks now and then. You know, the old gardener chap as works here now and then. He was gardener there, and they blamed him at first for sending in the wrong leaves, but it wasn't *him* as did it. It was someone who came out of the house, and wanted to help and picked the vegetables in the garden, and took them in to the cook. You know, spinach and lettuce and things like that and—er—I suppose they just made a mistake not knowing much about growing vegetables. I think they said at the inquest or whatever they had afterwards that it was a mistake that *anyone* could make because the spinach or the sorrel leaves were growing near the digi—digit-what-not, you see, so I suppose they just took a great handful of both leaves, possibly in a bunch together. Anyway, it was very sad because Granny said she was a very good-looking girl with golden hair and all that, you know."

"And she used to go up to London every week? Naturally she'd have to have a day off."

"Yes. Said she had friends there. Foreigner, she was—Granny says there was some as said she was actually a German spy."

"And was she?"

"I shouldn't think so. The gentlemen liked her all right, apparently. You know, the naval officers and the ones up at Shelton Military Camp, too. She had one or two friends there, you know. The military camp it was."

"Was she really a spy?"

"Shouldn't think so. I mean, my grandmother said that was what people *said*. It wasn't in the last war. It was ages before that."

"Funny," said Tuppence, "how easy it is to get

mixed up over the wars. I knew an old man who had a friend in the battle of Waterloo."

"Oh, fancy that. Years before nineteen fourteen. People did have foreign nurses—what were called Mamoselles as well as Frowlines, whatever a Frowline is. Very nice with children she was, Granny said. Everyone was very pleased with her and always liked her."

"That was when she was living here, living at The Laurels?"

"Wasn't called that then—at least I don't think so. She was living with the Parkinsons or the Perkins, some name like that," said Gwenda. "What we call nowadays an *au pair* girl. She came from that place where the patty comes from, you know, Fortnum and Mason keep it—expensive patty for parties. Half German, half French, so someone told me."

"Strasbourg?" suggested Tuppence.

"Yes, that was the name. She used to paint pictures. Did one of an old great-aunt of mine. It made her look too old, Aunt Fanny always said. Did one of one of the Parkinson boys. Old Mrs. Griffin's got it still. The Parkinson boy found out something about her, I believe—the one she painted the picture of, I mean. Godson of Mrs. Griffin, I believe he was."

"Would that have been Alexander Parkinson?"

"Yes, that's the one. The one who's buried near the church."

10

Introduction to Mathilde, Truelove and KK

Tuppence, on the following morning, went in search of that well-known public character in the village known usually as old Isaac, or, on formal occasions if one could remember, Mr. Bodlicott. Isaac Bodlicott was one of the local "characters." He was a character because of his age—he claimed to be ninety (not generally believed)—and he was able to do repairs of many curious kinds. If your efforts to ring up the plumber met with no response, you went to old Isaac Bodlicott. Mr. Bodlicott, whether or not he was in any way qualified for the repairs he did, had been well acquainted for many of the years of his long life with every type of sanitation problem, bath water problems, difficulties with geysers, and sundry electrical problems on the side. His charges compared favorably with a real live qualified plumber, and his repairs were often surprisingly successful. He could do carpentering, he could attend to locks, he could hang pictures—rather crookedly sometimes—he understood about the springs of derelict armchairs. The main disadvantage of Mr. Bodlicott's attentions was his garrulous habit of incessant conversation slightly hampered by a difficulty in adjusting his false teeth in such a way as to make what he said intelligible in his pronunciation. His memories of past inhabitants of the neighborhood seemed to be unlimited. It was difficult, on the whole, to know how reliable they might be. Mr. Bodlicott was not one to shirk giving himself the pleasure of retailing some really good story of past days. These flights of fancy, claimed usually as flights of memory, were ushered in with the same type of statement.

"You'd be surprised, you would, if I could tell you what I knew about that one. Yes indeed. Well, you know, everybody thought they knew all about it, but they were wrong. Absolutely wrong. It was the elder sister, you know. Yes, it was. Such a nice girl, she seemed. It was the butcher's dog that gave them all the clue. Followed her home, he did. Yes. Only it wasn't her own home, as you might say. Ah well, I could tell you a lot more about *that*. Then there was old Mrs. Atkins. Nobody knew as she kept a revolver in the house, but I knew. I knew when I was sent for to mend her tallboy—that's what they call those high chests, isn't it? Yes. Tallboys. Well, that's right. Well, there she was, seventy-five, and in that drawer, the drawer of the tallboy as I went, you know, to mend—the hinges had gone, the lock too—that's where the revolver was. Wrapped up, it was, with a pair of women's shoes. Number three size. Or, I'm not sure as it wasn't number two. White satin. Tiny little foot. Her great-grandmother's wedding shoes, she said. Maybe. But somebody said she bought them at a curiosity shop once, but I don't know about that. And there was the revolver wrapped up, too. Yes. Well, they said as her son had brought it back. Brought it back from East Africa, he did. He'd been out there shooting elephants or something of that kind. And when he come home, he brought this revolver. And do you know what that old lady used to do? Her son had taught her how to shoot. She'd sit by her drawing-room window looking out and when people came up the drive, she'd have her revolver with her and she'd shoot either side of them. Yes. Got them frightened to death and they ran away. She said she wouldn't have anyone coming in and disturbing the birds. Very keen on the birds, she was. Mind you, she never shot a bird. No, she didn't want to do that. Then there was all the stories about Mrs. Letherby.

Nearly had up, *she* was. Yes, shoplifting. Very clever
at it, so they say. And yet as rich as they make them."

Having persuaded Mr. Bodlicott to replace the skylight in the bathroom, Tuppence wondered if she
could direct his conversation to any memory of the
past which would be useful to Tommy and herself in
solving the mystery of the concealment in their house
of some treasure or interesting secret of whose real
nature they had no knowledge whatever.

Old Isaac Bodlicott made no difficulties about coming to do repairs for the new tenants to the place. It
was one of his pleasures in life to meet as many new-
comers as possible. It was in his life one of the main
events to be able to come across people who had not
so far heard any of his splendid memories and reminiscences. Those who were well acquainted with them
did not often encourage him to repeat these tales. But
a new audience! That was always a pleasant happening. That and displaying the wonderful amount of
trades that he managed to combine among his various
services to the community in which he lived. It was
his pleasure to indulge in a running commentary.

"Luck it was, as old Joe didn't get cut. Might have
ripped his face open."

"Yes, it might indeed."

"There's a bit more glass wants sweeping up on the
floor still, missus."

"I know," said Tuppence. "We haven't had time
yet."

"Ah, but you can't take risks with glass. You know
what glass is. A little splinter can do you all the harm
in the world. Die of it, you can, if it gets into a blood
vessel. I remember Miss Lavinia Shotacomb. You
wouldn't believe ..."

Tuppence was not somehow tempted by Miss Lavinia Shotacomb. She had heard her mentioned by
other local characters. She had apparently been between seventy and eighty, quite deaf and almost
blind.

"I suppose," said Tuppence, breaking in before Isaac's reminiscences of Lavinia Shotacomb could begin, "that you must know a lot about all the various people and the extraordinary things that have happened in this place in the past."

"Aw well, I'm not as young as I was, you know. Over eighty-five, I am. Going on for ninety. I've always had a good memory. There are things, you know, you don't forget. No. However long it is, something reminds you of it, you know, and brings it all back to you. The things I could tell you, you wouldn't believe."

"Well, it's really wonderful, isn't it," said Tuppence, "to think how much you must know about what a lot of extraordinary people."

"Ah no, there's no accounting for people, is there? Ones that aren't what you think they are, sometimes things as you wouldn't have believed in about them."

"Spies, I suppose, sometimes," said Tuppence, "or criminals."

She looked at him hopefully. . . . Old Isaac bent and picked up a splinter of glass.

"Here you are," he said. "How'd you feel if *that* got in the sole of your foot?"

Tuppence began to feel that the replenishing of a glass skylight was not going to yield much in the way of Isaac's more exciting memories of the past. She mentioned that the small so-called greenhouse attached to a wall of the house near the dining-room window was also in need of repair and replacement by an outlay of money upon glass. Would it be worth repairing or would it be better to have it pulled down? Isaac was quite pleased to transfer himself to this fresh problem. They went downstairs, and outside the house walked round its walls until they came to the erection in question.

"Ah, you mean that there, do you?"

Tuppence said yes, she did mean that there.

"Kay-kay," said Isaac.

Tuppence looked at him. Two letters of the alphabet such as KK really meant nothing to her.

"What did you say?"

"I said KK. That's what it used to be called in old Mrs. Lottie Jones's time."

"Oh. Why did she call it KK?"

"I dunno. It was a sort of—sort of name I suppose they used to have for places like this. You know, it wasn't grand. Bigger houses have a real conservatory. You know, where they'd have maidenhair ferns in pots."

"Yes," said Tuppence, her own memories going back easily to such things.

"And a greenhouse you can call it, too. But this here, KK old Mrs. Lottie Jones used to call it. I dunno why."

"Did they have maidenhair ferns in it?"

"No, it wasn't used for that. No. The children had it for toys mostly. Well, when you say toys I expect they're here still if nobody has turned them out. You see, it's half falling down, isn't it? They just stuck up a bit, then they put a bit of roofing over and I don't suppose that anyone will use it again. They used to bring the broken toys or chairs out here and things like that. But then, you see, they already had the rocking-horse there and Truelove in the far corner."

"Can we get inside it?" asked Tuppence, trying to apply her eye to a slightly clearer portion of a pane of window. "There must be a lot of queer things inside."

"Ah well, there's the key," said Isaac, "I expect it's hanging up in the same place."

"Where's the same place?"

"Ah, there's a shed round here."

They went round an adjacent path. The shed was hardly worthy of being called a shed. Isaac kicked its door open, removed various bits of branches of trees, kicked away some rotting apples and, removing an old doormat hanging on the wall, showed three or four rusty keys hanging up on a nail.

"Lindop's keys, those," he said. "Last but one as was living here as gardener. Retired basketmaker, he was. Didn't do no good at anything. If you'd like to see inside KK—?"

"Oh yes," said Tuppence hopefully. "I'd like to see inside KK. How do you spell it?" she asked.

"How do I spell what?"

"I mean KK. Is it just two letters?"

"No. I think it was something different. I think it was two foreign words. I seem to remember now K-A-I and then another K-A-I. Kay-Kay, or Kye-Kye almost, they used to say it. I think it was a Japanese word."

"Oh," said Tuppence. "Did any Japanese people ever live here?"

"Oh no, nothing like that. No. Not that kind of foreigner."

The application of a little oil, which Isaac seemed to produce and apply quite quickly, had a wonderful effect on the rustiest of the keys which, inserted in the door and turned with a grinding noise, could be pushed open. Tuppence and her guide went in.

"There you are," said Isaac, not displaying any particular pride in the objects within. "Nothing but old rubbish, is it?"

"That's a rather wonderful-looking horse," said Tuppence.

"That's Mackild, that is," said Isaac.

"Mack-ild?" said Tuppence, rather doubtfully.

"Yes. It's a woman's name of some kind. Queen somebody, it was. Somebody said as it was William the Conqueror's wife, but I think they were just boasting about that. Come from America, it did. American godfather brought it to one of the children."

"To one of the—?"

"One of the Bassington children, that was. Before

the other lot. I dunno. I suppose it's all rusted up now."

Mathilde was a rather splendid-looking horse even in decay. Its length was quite the length of any horse or mare to be found nowadays. Only a few hairs were left of what must once have been a prolific mane. One ear was broken off. It had once been painted gray. Its front legs splayed out in front and its back legs at the back; it had a wispy tail.

"It doesn't work like any rocking-horse I've ever seen before," said Tuppence, interested.

"No, it don't, do it?" said Isaac. "You know, they go up and down, up and down, front to back. But this one here, you see—it sort of springs forwards. Once first, the front legs do it—whooop—and then the back legs do it. It's a very good action. Now if I was to get on it and show you—"

"Do be careful," said Tuppence. "It might—there might be nails or something which would stick into you, or you might fall off."

"Ah. I've ridden on Mathilde, fifty or sixty years ago it must have been, but I remember. And it's still pretty solid, you know. It's not really falling to bits yet."

With a sudden, unexpected, acrobatic action he sprang upon Mathilde. The horse raced forwards, then raced backwards.

"Got action, hasn't it?"

"Yes, it's got action," said Tuppence.

"Ah, they loved that, you know. Miss Jenny, she used to ride it day after day."

"Who was Miss Jenny?"

"Why, she was the eldest one, you know. She was the one that had the godfather as sent her this. Sent her Truelove, too," he added.

Tuppence looked at him inquiringly. The remark did not seem to apply to any of the other contents of Kay-Kay.

"That's what they call it, you know. That little horse and cart what's there in the corner. Used to ride it down the hill, Miss Pamela did. Very serious, she was, Miss Pamela. She'd get in at the top of the hill and she'd put her feet on there—you see, it's meant to have pedals but they don't work, so she'd take it to the top of the hill and then she'd let it begin to go down the hill, and she'd put the brakes on, as it were, with her feet. Often she'd end up landing in the monkey puzzle, as a matter of fact."

"That sounds very uncomfortable," said Tuppence, "I mean, to land in the monkey puzzle."

"Ah well, she could stop herself a bit before that. Very serious, she was. She used to do that by the hour—three or four hours I've watched her. I was doing the Christmas rose bed very often, you know, and the pampas grass, and I'd see her going down. I didn't speak to her because she didn't like being spoken to. She wanted to go on with what she was doing or what she thought she was doing."

"What did she think she was doing?" said Tuppence, beginning suddenly to get more interested in Miss Pamela than she had been in Miss Jenny.

"Well, I don't know. She used to say sometimes she was a princess, you know, escaping, or Mary, Queen of What-is-it—do I mean Ireland or Scotland?"

"Mary Queen of Scots," suggested Tuppence.

"Yes, that's right. She went away or something, or escaped. Went into a castle. Lock something it was called. Not a real lock, you know, a piece of water, it was."

"Ah yes, I see. And Pamela thought she was Mary Queen of Scots escaping from her enemies?"

"That's right. Going to throw herself into England on Queen Elizabeth's mercy, she said, but I don't think as Queen Elizabeth was very merciful."

"Well," said Tuppence, masking any disappointment she felt, "it's all very interesting, I'm sure. Who were these people, did you say?"

"Oh, they were the Listers, they were."

"Did you ever know a Mary Jordan?"

"Ah, I know who you mean. No, she was before my time a bit, I think. You mean the German spy girl, don't you?"

"Everyone seems to know that about her here," said Tuppence.

"Yes. They called her the Frow Line, or something. Sounds like a railway."

"It does rather," said Tuppence.

Isaac suddenly laughed. "Ha, ha, ha," he said. "If it was a railway, a line a railway line, oh, it didn't run straight, did it? No, indeed." He laughed again.

"What a splendid joke," said Tuppence kindly.

Isaac laughed again.

"It's about time," he said, "you thought of putting some vegetables in, isn't it? You know, if you want to get your broad beans on in good time you ought to put 'em in and prepare for the peas. And what about some early lettuce? Tom Thumbs now? Beautiful lettuce, those, small but crisp as anything."

"I suppose you've done a lot of gardening work round here. I don't mean just this house, but a lot of places."

"Ah yes, I've done odd jobbing, you know. I used to come along to most of the houses. Some of the gardeners they had weren't any good at all and I'd usually come in and help at certain times or other. Had a bit of an accident here once, you know. Mistake about vegetables. Before my time— But I heard about it."

"Something about foxglove leaves, wasn't it?" said Tuppence.

"Ah, fancy you having heard of that already. That was a long time ago, too. Yes, several was taken ill with it. One of them died. At least so I heard. That was only hearsay. Old pal of mine told me that."

"I think it was the Frow Line," said Tuppence.

"What, the Frow Line as died? Well, I never heard that."

"Well, perhaps I'm wrong," said Tuppence. "Supposing you take Truelove," she said, "or whatever this thing's called, and put it on the hill in the place where that child, Pamela, used to take it down the hill—if the hill is still there."

"Well, of course the hill is still there. What do you think? It's all grass still, but be careful now. I don't know how much of Truelove is rusted away. I'll have a bit of a clean-up on it first, shall I?"

"That's right," said Tuppence, "and then you can think of a list of vegetables that we ought to be getting on with."

"Ah well, I'll be careful you don't get foxglove and spinach planted together. Shouldn't like to hear that something happened to you when you've just got into a new house. Nice place here if you can just have a little money to spend on it."

"Thank you very much," said Tuppence.

"And I'll just see to that there Truelove so as it won't break down under you. It's very old, but you'd be surprised the way some old things work. Why, I knew a cousin of mine the other day and he got out an old bicycle. You wouldn't think it would go—nobody had ridden it for about forty years. But it went all right with a bit of oil. Ah, it's wonderful what a bit of oil can do."

11

Six Impossible Things
Before Breakfast

"What on earth—" said Tommy.

He was used to finding Tuppence in unlikely spots when he returned to the house, but on this occasion he was more startled than usual.

Inside the house there was no trace of her, although outside there was a very slight patter of rain. It occurred to him that she might be engrossed in some portion of the garden, and he went out to see if this might be the case. And it was then that he remarked, "What on earth—"

"Hullo, Tommy," said Tuppence; "you're back a bit earlier than I thought you would be."

"What is that thing?"

"You mean Truelove?"

"What did you say?"

"I said Truelove," said Tuppence; "that's the name of it."

"Are you trying to go for a ride on it—it's much too small for you."

"Well, of course it is. It's a child's sort of thing—what you had, I suppose, before you had fairy-cycles, or whatever one had in my youth."

"It doesn't really *go*, does it?" asked Tommy.

"Well, not exactly," said Tuppence, "but, you see, you take it up to the top of the hill and then it—well, its wheels turn of their own accord, you see, and because of the hill you go down."

"And crash at the bottom, I suppose. Is that what you've been doing?"

"Not at all," said Tuppence. "You brake it with

your feet. Would you like me to give you a demonstration?"

"I don't think so," said Tommy. "It's beginning to rain rather harder. I just wanted to know why you—well, why you're doing it. I mean, it can't be very enjoyable, can it?"

"Actually," said Tuppence, "it's rather frightening. But you see I just wanted to find out and—"

"And are you asking this tree? What is this tree, anyway? A monkey puzzle, isn't it?"

"That's right," said Tuppence. "How clever of you to know."

"Of course I know," said Tommy. "I know its other name, too."

"So do I," said Tuppence.

They looked at each other.

"Only at the moment I've forgotten it," said Tommy. "Is it an arti—"

"Well, it's something very like that," said Tuppence. "I think that's good enough, don't you?"

"What are you doing inside a prickly thing like that?"

"Well, because when you get to the end of the hill, I mean, if you didn't put your feet down to stop completely you could be in the arti—or whatever it is."

"Do I mean arti—? What about urticaria? No, that's nettles, isn't it? Oh well," said Tommy, "everyone to their own kind of amusement."

"I was just doing a little investigation, you know, of our latest problem."

"Your problem? My problem? Whose problem?"

"I don't know," said Tuppence. "Both our problems, I hope."

"But not one of Beatrice's problems, or anything like that?"

"Oh no. It's just that I wondered what other things there might be hidden in this house, so I went and looked at a lot of toys that seem to have been shoved away in a sort of queer old greenhouse probably years and years ago and there was this creature and there was Mathilde, which is a rocking-horse with a hole in its stomach."

"A hole in its stomach?"

"Well, yes. People, I suppose, used to shove things in there. Children—for fun—and lots of old leaves and dirty papers and bits of sort of queer dusters and flannel, oily stuff that had been used to clean things with."

"Come on, let's go into the house," said Tommy.

"Well, Tommy," said Tuppence, as she stretched out her feet to a pleasant wood fire which she had lit ready for his return in the drawing room, "let's have your news. Did you go to the Ritz Hotel Gallery to see the show?"

"No. As a matter of fact, I didn't. I hadn't time, really."

"What do you mean, you hadn't time? I thought that's what you went for."

"Well, one doesn't always do the things that one went for."

"You must have gone somewhere and done *something*," said Tuppence.

"I found a new possible place to park a car."

"That's always useful," said Tuppence. "Where was that?"

"Near Hounslow."

"What on earth did you want to go to Hounslow for?"

"Well, I didn't actually go to Hounslow. There's a sort of car park there, then I took a tube, you know."

"What, a tube to London?"

"Yes. Yes, it seemed the easiest way."

"You have rather a guilty look about you," said Tuppence. "Don't tell me I have a rival who lives in Hounslow?"

"No," said Tommy. "You ought to be pleased with what I've been doing."

"Oh. Have you been buying me a present?"

"No. No," said Tommy, "I'm afraid not. I never know what to give you, as a matter of fact."

"Well, your guesses are very good sometimes," said Tuppence hopefully. "What have you been really doing, Tommy, and why should I be pleased?"

"Because I, too," said Tommy, "have been doing research."

"Everyone's doing research nowadays," said Tuppence. "You know, all the teen-agers and all one's nephews or cousins or other people's sons and daughters, they're all doing research. I don't know actually what they do research into nowadays, but they never seem to do it, whatever it is, afterwards. They just have the research and a good time doing the research and they're very pleased with themselves and—well, I don't quite know what does come next."

"Betty, our adopted daughter, went to East Africa," said Tommy. "Have you heard from her?"

"Yes, she loves it there—loves poking into African families and writing articles about them."

"Do you think the families appreciate her interest?" asked Tommy.

"I shouldn't think so," said Tuppence. "In my father's parish, I remember, everyone disliked the District Visitors—Nosey Parkers they called them."

"You may have something there," said Tommy. "You are certainly pointing out to me the difficulties of what I am undertaking, or trying to undertake."

"Research into what? Not lawn mowers, I hope."

"I don't know why you mention lawn mowers."

"Because you're eternally looking at catalogues of them," said Tuppence. "You're mad about getting a lawn mower."

"In this house of ours it is historic research we are doing into things—crimes and others that seem to have happened at least sixty or seventy years ago."

"Anyway, come on, tell me a little more about your research projects, Tommy."

"I went to London," said Tommy, "and put certain things in motion."

"Ah," said Tuppence. "Research? Research in motion. In a way I've been doing the same thing that you are, only our methods are different. And my period is very far back."

"Do you mean that you're really beginning to take an interest in the problem of Mary Jordan? So that's how you put it on the agenda nowadays," said Tommy. "It's definitely taken shape, has it? The mystery, or the problem of Mary Jordan."

"Such a very ordinary name, too. Couldn't have been her right name if she was German," said Tuppence, "and she was said to be a German spy or something like that, but she could have been English, I suppose."

"I think the German story is just a kind of legend."

"Do go on, Tommy. You're not telling me anything."

"Well, I put certain—certain—certain—"

"Don't go on saying certain," said Tuppence. "I really can't understand."

"Well, it's very difficult to explain things sometimes," said Tommy, "but I mean, there are certain ways of making inquiries."

"You mean, things in the past?"

"Yes. In a sense. I mean, there are things that you can find out. Things that you could obtain information from. Not just by riding old toys and asking old ladies to remember things and cross-questioning an old gardener who probably will tell you everything quite wrong or going round to the post office and upsetting the staff by asking the girls there to tell their memories of what their great-great-aunts once said."

"All of them have produced a little something," said Tuppence.

"So will mine," said Tommy.

"You've been making inquiries? Who do you go to to ask your questions?"

"Well, it's not quite like that, but you must remember, Tuppence, that occasionally in my life I have been in connection with people who do know how to go about these sort of things. You know, there are people you pay a certain sum to and they do the research for you from the proper quarters so that what you get is quite authentic."

"What sort of things? What sort of places?"

"Well, there are lots of things. To begin with you can get someone to study deaths, births and marriages, that sort of thing."

"Oh, I suppose you send them to Somerset House. Do you go there for deaths as well as marriages?"

"And births—one needn't go oneself, you get someone to go for you. And find out when someone dies or read somebody's will, look up marriages in churches or study birth certificates. All those things can be inquired into."

"Have you been spending a lot of money?" asked Tuppence. "I thought we were going to try and economize once we'd paid the expense of moving in here."

"Well, considering the interest you're taking in problems, I consider that this can be regarded in the way of money well spent."

"Well, did you find out anything?"

"Not as quickly as this. You have to wait until the research has been made. Then if they can get answers for you—"

"You mean somebody comes up and tells you that someone called Mary Jordan was born at Little Sheffield-on-the-Wold or something like that and then you go and make inquiries there later. Is that the sort of thing?"

"Not exactly. And then there are census returns and death certificates and causes of death and, oh, quite a lot of things that you can find out about."

"Well," said Tuppence, "it sounds rather interesting anyway, which is always something."

"And there are files in newspaper offices that you can read and study."

"You mean accounts of something—like murders or court cases?"

"Not necessarily, but one has had contact with certain people from time to time. People who know things—one can look them up—ask a few questions—renew old friendships. Like the time we were being a private detective firm in London. There are a few people, I expect, who could give us information or tell us where to go. Things do depend a bit on who you know."

"Yes," said Tuppence, "that's quite true. I know that myself from experience."

"Our methods aren't the same," said Tommy. "I think yours are just as good as mine. I'll never forget the day I came suddenly into that boarding-house, or whatever it was, Sans Souci. The first thing I saw was you sitting there knitting and calling yourself Mrs. Blenkinsop."

"All because I *hadn't* applied research, or got anyone to do research for me," said Tuppence.

"No," said Tommy, "you got inside a wardrobe next door to the room where I was being interviewed in a very interesting manner, so you knew exactly where I was being sent and what I was meant to do, and you managed to get there first. Eavesdropping. Neither more nor less. Most dishonorable."

"With very satisfactory results," said Tuppence.

"Yes," said Tommy. "You have a kind of feeling for success. It seems to happen to you."

"Well, someday we shall know all about everything here, only it's all such years and years ago. I can't help thinking that the idea of something really important being hidden round here or owned by someone here, or something to do with this house or people who once lived in it being important—I can't just believe it somehow. Oh well, I see what we shall have to do next."

"What?" said Tommy.

"Believe six impossible things before breakfast, of course," said Tuppence. "It's quarter to eleven now, and I want to go to bed. I'm tired. I'm sleepy and extremely dirty because of playing around with all those dusty, ancient toys and things. I expect there are even more things in that place that's called—by the way, why is it called Kay-Kay?"

"I don't know. Do you spell it at all?"

"I don't know—I think it's spelt k-a-i. Not just KK."

"Because it sounds more mysterious?"

"It sounds Japanese," said Tuppence doubtfully.

"I can't see why it should sound to you like Japanese. It doesn't to me. It sounds more like something you eat. A kind of rice, perhaps."

"I'm going to bed and to wash thoroughly and to get all the cobwebs off me somehow," said Tuppence.

"Remember," said Tommy, "six impossible things before breakfast."

"I expect I shall be better at that than you would be," said Tuppence.

"You're very unexpected sometimes," said Tommy.

"*You're* more often right than *I* am," said Tuppence. "*That's* very annoying sometimes. Well, these things are sent to try us. Who used to say that to us? Quite often, too."

"Never mind," said Tommy. "Go and clean the dust of bygone years off you. Is Isaac any good at gardening?"

"He considers he is," said Tuppence. "We might experiment with him—"

"Unfortunately we don't know much about gardening ourselves. Yet another problem."

12

Expedition on Truelove; Oxford and Cambridge

"Six impossible things before breakfast indeed," said Tuppence as she drained a cup of coffee and considered a fried egg remaining in the dish on the sideboard, flanked by two appetizing-looking kidneys. "Breakfast is more worthwhile than thinking of impossible things. Tommy is the one who has gone after impossible things. Research, indeed. I wonder if he'll get anything out of it all."

She applied herself to a fried egg and kidneys.

"How nice," said Tuppence, "to have a different kind of breakfast."

For a long time she had managed to regale herself in the morning with a cup of coffee and either orange juice or grapefruit. Although satisfactory so long as any weight problems were thereby solved, the pleasures of this kind of breakfast were not much appreciated. From the force of contrasts, hot dishes on the sideboard animated the digestive juices.

"I expect," said Tuppence, "it's what the Parkinsons used to have for breakfast here. Fried eggs or poached eggs and bacon and perhaps—" she threw her mind a good long way back to remembrances of old novels—"perhaps, yes, perhaps cold grouse on the sideboard, delicious! Oh yes, I remember, delicious it sounded. Of course, I suppose children were so unimportant that they only let them have the legs. Legs of game are very good because you can nibble at them." She paused with the last piece of kidney in her mouth.

Very strange noises seemed to be coming through the doorway.

"I wonder," said Tuppence. "It sounds like a concert gone wrong somewhere."

She paused again, a piece of toast in her hand, and looked up as Albert entered the room.

"What is going on, Albert?" demanded Tuppence. "Don't tell me that's our workmen playing something? A harmonium or something like that?"

"It's the gentleman what's come to do the piano," said Albert.

"Come to do what to the piano?"

"To tune it. You said I'd have to get a piano tuner."

"Good gracious," said Tuppence, "you've done it already? How wonderful you are, Albert."

Albert looked pleased, though at the same time conscious of the fact that he *was* very wonderful in the speed with which he could usually supply the extraordinary demands made upon him sometimes by Tuppence and sometimes by Tommy.

"He says it needs it very bad," he said.

"I expect it does," said Tuppence.

She drank half a cup of coffee, went out of the room and into the drawing room. A young man was at work at the grand piano, which was revealing to the world large quantities of its inside.

"Good morning, madam," said the young man.

"Good morning," said Tuppence. "I'm so glad you've managed to come."

"Ah, it needs tuning, it does."

"Yes," said Tuppence, "I know. You see, we've only just moved in and it's not very good for pianos, being moved into houses and things. And it hasn't been tuned for a long time."

"No, I can soon tell that," said the young man.

He pressed three different chords in turn, two cheerful ones in a major key, two very melancholy ones in A minor.

"A beautiful instrument, madam, if I may say so."

"Yes," said Tuppence. "It's an Erard."

"And a piano you wouldn't get so easily nowadays."

"It's been through a few troubles," said Tuppence. "It's been through bombing in London. Our house there was hit. Luckily we were away, but it was mostly outside that was damaged."

"Yes. Yes, the works are good. They don't need so very much doing to them."

Conversation continued pleasantly. The young man played the opening bars of a Chopin Prelude and passed from that to a rendering of "The Blue Danube." Presently he announced that his ministrations had finished.

"I shouldn't leave it too long," he warned her. "I'd like the chance to come and try it again before too much time has gone by because you don't know quite when it might not—well, I don't know how I should put it—relapse a bit. You know, some little thing that you haven't noticed or haven't been able to get at."

They parted with mutually appreciative remarks on music in general and on piano music in particular, and with the polite salutations of two people who agreed very largely in their ideas as to the joys that music generally played in life.

"Needs a lot doing to it, I expect, this house," he said, looking round him.

"Well, I think it had been empty some time when we came into it."

"Oh yes. It's changed hands a lot, you know."

"Got quite a history, hasn't it?" said Tuppence. "I mean, the people who lived in it in the past and the sort of queer things that happened."

"Ah well, I expect you're talking of that time long ago. I don't know if it was the last war or the one before."

"Something to do with naval secrets or something," said Tuppence hopefully.

"Could be, I expect. There was a lot of talk, so they

tell me, but of course I don't know anything about it myself."

"Well before your time," said Tuppence, looking appreciatively at his youthful countenance.

When he had gone, she sat down at the piano.

"I'll play 'The Rain on the Roof,'" said Tuppence, who had had this Chopin memory revived in her by the piano tuner's execution of one of the other preludes. Then she dropped into some chords and began playing the accompaniment to a song, humming it first and then murmuring the words as well.

> "Where has my true love gone a-roaming?
> Where has my true love gone from me?
> High in the woods the birds are calling.
> When will my true love come back to me?

I'm playing it in the wrong key, I believe," said Tuppence, "but at any rate, the piano's all right again now. Oh, it is great fun to be able to play the piano again. 'Where has my true love gone a-roaming?'" she murmured. "'When will my true love'—Truelove," said Tuppence thoughtfully. "True love? Yes, I'm thinking of that perhaps as a sign. Perhaps I'd better go out and do something with Truelove."

She put on her thick shoes and a pullover, and went out into the garden. Truelove had been pushed, not back into his former home in KK, but into the empty stable. Tuppence took him out, pulled him to the top of the grass slope, gave him a sharp flick with the duster she had brought out with her to remove the worst of the cobwebs which still adhered in many places, got into Truelove, placed her feet on the pedals and induced Truelove to display his paces as well as he could in his condition of general age and wear.

"Now, my true love," she said, "down the hill with you and not too fast."

She removed her feet from the pedals and placed

them in a position where she could brake with them when necessary.

Truelove was not inclined to go very fast in spite of the advantage to him of having only to go by weight down the hill. However, the slope increased in steepness suddenly. Truelove increased his pace, Tuppence applied her feet as brakes rather more sharply and she and Truelove arrived together at a rather more uncomfortable portion than usual of the monkey puzzle at the bottom of the hill.

"Most painful," said Tuppence, excavating herself.

Having extricated herself from the pricking of various portions of the monkey puzzle, Tuppence brushed herself down and looked around her. She had come to a thick bit of shrubbery leading up the hill in the opposite direction. There were rhododendron bushes here and hydrangeas. It would look, Tuppence thought, very lovely later in the year. At the moment, there was no particular beauty about it, it was a mere thicket. However, she did seem to notice that there had once been a pathway leading up between the various flower bushes and shrubs. Everything was much grown together now, but you could trace the direction of the path. Tuppence broke off a branch or two, pressed her way through the first bushes and managed to follow the hill. The path went winding up. It was clear that nobody had ever cleared it or walked down it for years.

"I wonder where it takes one," said Tuppence. "There must be a reason for it."

Perhaps, she thought, as the path took a couple of sharp turns in opposite directions, making a zigzag and making Tuppence feel that she knew exactly what Alice in Wonderland had meant by saying that a path would suddenly shake itself and change direction. There were fewer bushes, there were laurels now, possibly fitting in with the name given to the property, and then a rather stony, difficult, narrow path wound up between them. It came very suddenly to four moss-covered steps leading up to a kind of niche made of what had once been metal and later seemed to have been replaced by bottles. A kind of shrine, and in it a pedestal and on this pedestal a stone figure, very much decayed. It was the figure of a boy with a basket on his head. A feeling of recognition came to Tuppence.

"This is the sort of thing you could date a place with," she said. "It's very like the one Aunt Sarah had in her garden. She had a lot of laurels, too."

Her mind went back to Aunt Sarah, whom she had occasionally visited as a child. She had played herself, she remembered, a game called River Horses. For River Horses you took your hoop out. Tuppence, it may be said, had been six years old at the time. Her hoop represented the horses. White horses with manes and flowing tails. In Tuppence's imagination, with that you had gone across a green, rather thick patch of grass and you had then gone round a bed planted with pampas grass waving feathery heads into the air, up the same kind of path, and leaning there among some beech trees in the same sort of summerhouse niche was a figure and a basket. Tuppence, when riding her winning horses here, had taken a gift always, a gift you put in the basket on top of the boy's head; at the same time you said it was an offering and you made a wish. The wish, Tuppence remembered, was nearly always to come true.

"But that," said Tuppence, sitting down suddenly on the top step of the flight she had been climbing, "that, of course, was because I cheated really. I mean, I wished for something that I knew was almost sure to happen, and then I could feel that my wish had come true and it really *was* a magic. It was a proper offering to a real god from the past. Though it wasn't a god really, it was just a podgy-looking little boy. Ah well—what fun it is, all the things one used to invent and believe in and play at."

She sighed, went down the path again and found her way to the mysteriously named KK.

KK looked in just the same mess as ever. Mathilde was still looking forlorn and forsaken, but two more things attracted Tuppence's attention. They were in porcelain—porcelain stools with the figures of white swans curled round them. One stool was dark blue and the other stool was pale blue.

"Of course," said Tuppence, "I've seen things like that before when I was young. Yes, they used to be on verandas. One of my other aunts had them, I think. We used to call them Oxford and Cambridge. Very much the same. I think it was ducks—no, it *was* swans they had round them. And then there was the same sort of queer thing in the seat, a sort of hole that was like a letter S. The sort of thing you could put things into. Yes, I think I'll get Isaac to take these stools out of here and give them a good wash, and then we'll have them on the loggia, or lodger as he will insist on calling it, though the veranda comes more natural to me. We'll put them on that and enjoy them when the good weather comes."

She turned and started to run towards the door. Her foot caught in Mathilde's obtrusive rocker.

"Oh dear!" said Tuppence. "Now what have I done?"

What she had done was to catch her foot in the dark blue porcelain stool and it had rolled down onto the floor and smashed in two pieces.

"Oh dear," said Tuppence, "now I've really killed Oxford, I suppose. We shall have to make do with Cambridge. I don't think you could stick Oxford together again. The pieces are too difficult."

She sighed and wondered what Tommy was doing.

Tommy was sitting exchanging memories with some old friends.

"World's in a funny way nowadays," said Colonel Atkinson. "I hear you and your what's-her-name, Prudence—no, you had a nickname for her, Tuppence, that's right—yes, I hear you've gone to live in the country. Somewhere down near Hollowquay. I wonder what took you there. Anything particular?"

"Well, we found this house fairly cheap," said Tommy.

"Ah. Well, that's lucky always, isn't it? What's the name? You must give me your address."

"Well, we think we may call it Cedar Lodge because there's a very nice cedar there. Its original name was The Laurels, but that's rather a Victorian hangover, isn't it?"

"The Laurels. The Laurels, Hollowquay. My word, what are *you* up to, eh? What are *you* up to?"

Tommy looked at the elderly face with the sprouting white mustache.

"On to something, are you?" said Colonel Atkinson. "Are you employed in the service of your country again?"

"Oh, I'm too old for that," said Tommy. "I'm retired from all that sort of stuff."

"Ah, I wonder now. Perhaps that's just the thing you say. Perhaps you've been told to say that. After all, you know, there's a good deal was never found out about all that business."

"What business?" said Tommy.

"Well, I expect you've read about it or heard about it. The Cardington scandal. You know, came after that other thing—the what-you-call-'em letters—and the Emlyn Johnson submarine business."

"Oh," said Tommy, "I seem to remember something vaguely."

"Well, it wasn't actually the submarine business, but that's what called attention to the whole thing. And there were those letters, you see. Gave the whole show away politically. Yes. Letters. If they'd been able to get hold of *them*, it would have made a big difference. It would have drawn attention to several people who at the time were the most highly trusted people in the government. Astonishing how these things happen, isn't it? You know! The traitors in one's midst, always highly trusted, always splendid fellows, always the last people to be suspected—and all the time—well, a lot of all that never came to light." He winked one eye. "Perhaps you've been sent down there to have a look round, eh, my boy?"

"A look round at what?" said Tommy.

"Well, this house of yours, The Laurels, did you say? There used to be some silly jokes about The Laurels sometimes. Mind you, they'd had a good look round, the Security people and the rest of them. They thought that somewhere in that house was valuable evidence of some kind. There was an idea it had been sent overseas—Italy was mentioned—just before people got alerted. But other people thought it might be still hidden there in that part of the world somewhere. You know, it's the sort of place that has cellars and flagstones and various things. Come now, Tommy, my boy, I feel you're on the hunt again."

"I assure you I don't do anything of that kind nowadays."

"Well, that's what one thought before about you when you were at that other place. Beginning of the last war. You know, where you ran down that German chap. That and the woman with the nursery rhyme books. Yes. Sharp bit of work, all that. And now, perhaps, they've set you on another trail."

"Nonsense," said Tommy. "You mustn't get all these ideas in your head. I'm an old gaffer now."

"You're a cunning old dog. I bet you're better than some of these young ones. Yes. You sit there looking innocent, and really I expect, well, one mustn't ask you questions. Mustn't ask you to betray state secrets, must I? Anyway, be careful of your missus. You know she's always one to stick herself forward too much. She had a narrow escape last time in the N or M days."

"Ah well," said Tommy, I think Tuppence is just interested in the general antiquity of this place, you

know. Who lived there and where. And pictures of
the old people who used to live in the houses and all
the rest of it. That and planning the garden. That's all
we're really interested in nowadays. Gardens. Gardens and bulb catalogues and all the rest of it."

"Well, maybe I'll believe that if a year passes and
nothing exciting has happened. But I know you,
Beresford, and I know our Mrs. Beresford, too. The
two of you together, you're a wonderful couple and I
bet you'll come up with something. I tell you, if those
papers ever come to light, it'll have a very, very great
effect on the political front and there are several people who won't be pleased. No indeed. And those people who won't be pleased are looked on as—pillars of
rectitude at the moment! But by some they are
thought to be dangerous. Remember that. They're
dangerous, and the ones that aren't dangerous are in
contact with those who *are* dangerous. So you be
careful and make your missus be careful, too."

"Really," said Tommy, "your ideas, you make me
feel quite excited."

"Well, go on feeling excited but look after Mrs.
Tuppence. I'm very fond of Tuppence. She's a nice
girl, always was and still is."

"Hardly a girl," said Tommy.

"Now don't say that of your wife. Don't get in that
habit. One in a thousand, she is. But I'm sorry for
someone who has her in the picture sleuthing him
down. She's probably out on the hunt today."

"I don't think she is. More likely gone to tea with
an elderly lady."

"Ah well. Elderly ladies can sometimes give you
useful information. Elderly ladies and children five
years old. All the unlikely people come out sometimes
with a truth nobody had ever dreamed of. I could tell
you things—"

"I'm sure you could, Colonel."

"Ah well, one mustn't give away secrets."

Colonel Atkinson shook his head.

On his way home Tommy stared out of the railway
carriage window and watched the rapidly retreating
countryside. "I wonder," he said to himself, "I really
wonder. That old boy, he's usually in the know.
Knows things. But what can there be that could matter *now?* It's all in the past—I mean there's nothing,
can't be anything left from that war. Not nowadays."
Then he wondered. New ideas had taken over—Common Market ideas. Somewhere, as it were *behind* his
mind rather than *in* it, because there were grandsons
and nephews, new generations—younger members of
families that had always meant something, that had
pull, had got positions of influence, of power because
they were born who they were, and if by any chance
they were not loyal, they *could* be approached, could
believe in new creeds or in old creeds revived,
whichever way you liked to think of it. England was
in a funny state, a different state from what it had
been. Or was it really always in the same state? Always underneath the smooth surface there was some
black mud. There wasn't clear water down to the
pebbles, down to the shells, lying on the bottom of
the sea. There was something moving, something
sluggish somewhere, something that had to be found,
suppressed. But surely not—surely not in a place like
Hollowquay. Hollowquay was a has-been if there
ever was. Developed first as a fishing village and then
further developed as an English Riviera—and now a
mere summer resort, crowded in August. Most people
now preferred package trips abroad.

"Well," said Tuppence, as she left the dinner table
that night and went into the other room to drink coffee, "was it fun or not fun? How were all the old
boys?"

"Oh, very much the old boys," said Tommy. "How
was your old lady?"

"Oh, the piano tuner came," said Tuppence, "and it
rained in the afternoon, so I didn't see her. Rather a

pity, the old lady might have said some things that were interesting."

"My old boy did," said Tommy. "I was quite surprised. What do you think of this place really, Tuppence?"

"Do you mean the house?"

"No, I don't mean the house. I think I mean Hollowquay."

"Well, I think it's a nice place."

"What do you mean by nice?"

"Well, it's a good word really. It's a word one usually despises, but I don't know why one should. I suppose a place that's nice is a place where things don't happen and you don't want them to happen. You're glad they don't."

"Ah. That's because of our age, I suppose."

"No, I don't think it's because of that. It's because it's nice to know there *are* places where things don't happen. Though I must say something nearly happened today."

"What do you mean by nearly happened? Have you been doing anything silly, Tuppence?"

"No, of course I haven't."

"Then what do you mean?"

"I mean that pane of glass at the top of the greenhouse, you know, it was trembling the other day a bit, had the twitches. Well, it practically came down on my head. Might have cut me to bits."

"It doesn't seem to have cut you to bits," said Tommy, looking at her.

"No. I was lucky. But still, it made me jump rather."

"Oh, we'll have to get our old boy who comes and does things, what's-his-name? Isaac, isn't it? Have to get him to look at some of the other panes—I mean, we don't want you being done in, Tuppence."

"Well, I suppose when you buy an old house there's always something wrong with it."

"Do you think there's something wrong with this house, Tuppence?"

"What on earth do you mean by wrong with this house?"

"Well, because I heard something rather queer about it today."

"What—queer about this house?"

"Yes."

"Really, Tommy, that seems impossible," said Tuppence.

"Why does it seem impossible? Because it looks so nice and innocent? Well painted and done up?"

"No. Well painted and done up and looking innocent, that's all due to us. It looked rather shabby and decayed when we bought it."

"Well, of course, that's why it was cheap."

"You look peculiar, Tommy," said Tuppence. "What is it?"

"Well, it was old Moustachio-Monty, you know."

"Oh, dear old boy, yes. Did he send his love to me?"

"Yes, he certainly did. He told me to make you take care of yourself, and me to take care of you."

"He always says that. Though why I should take care of myself here, I don't know."

"Well, it seems it's the sort of place you might have to take care of yourself."

"Now what on earth do you mean by that, Tommy?"

"Tuppence, what would you think if I said that he suggested or hinted, whatever way you like, that we were here not as old retired has-beens but as people on active service. That we were once more, as in the N or M days, on duty here. Sent here by the forces of security and order to discover something. To find out what was wrong with this place."

"Well, I don't know if you're dreaming, Tommy, or if it was old Moustachio-Monty who was, if it was he who suggested it."

"Well, he did. He seemed to think that we were definitely here on some kind of mission, to find something."

"To find something? What sort of thing?"

"Something that might be hidden in this house."

"Something that might be hidden in this house! Tommy, are you mad, or was he mad?"

"Well, I rather thought he might be mad, but I'm not so sure."

"What could there be to find in this house?"

"Something that I suppose was once hidden here."

"Buried treasure, are you talking about? Russian crown jewels hidden in the basement, that sort of thing?"

"No. Not treasure. Something that would be dangerous to someone."

"Well, that's very odd," said Tuppence.

"Why, have you found something?"

"No, of course I haven't found anything. But it seems there was a scandal about this place donkey's years ago. I don't mean anyone actually remembers, but it's the sort of thing that your grandmother told you, or the servants gossiped about. Actually, Beatrice has a friend who seemed to know something about it. And Mary Jordan was mixed up in it. It was all very hush-hush."

"Are you imagining things, Tuppence? Have you gone back to the glorious days of our youth, to the time when someone gave a girl on the *Lusitania* something secret, the days when we had adventure, when we tracked down the enigmatic Mr. Brown?"

"Goodness, that was a long time ago, Tommy. The Young Adventurers, we called ourselves. Doesn't seem real now, does it?"

"No, it doesn't. Not a bit. But it was real, yes, it was real all right. Such a lot of things are real though you can't really bring yourself to believe it. Must be at least sixty or seventy years ago. More than that, even."

"What did Monty actually say?"

"Letters or papers of some kind," said Tommy. "Something that would have created or did create some great political upheaval of some kind. Someone in a position of power and who oughtn't to have been in a position of power, and there were letters, or papers, or something that would definitely cook his goose if they ever came to light. All sorts of intrigues and all happening years ago."

"In the time of Mary Jordan? It sounds very unlikely," said Tuppence. "Tommy, you must have gone to sleep in the train coming back and dreamt all this."

"Well, perhaps I did," said Tommy. "It certainly doesn't seem likely."

"Well, I suppose we might as well have a look around," said Tuppence, "as we are living here."

Her eyes passed round the room.

"I shouldn't think there would be anything hidden here, do you, Tommy?"

"It doesn't seem the sort of house where anything would have been likely to be hidden. Lots of other people have lived in the house since those days."

"Yes. Family after family, as far as I can make out. Well, I suppose it might be hidden up in an attic or down in the cellar. Or perhaps buried under the summerhouse floor. Anywhere.

"Anyway, it'll be quite fun," said Tuppence. "Perhaps, you know, when we haven't got anything else to do and our backs are aching because of planting tulip bulbs, we might have a little sort of look round. You know, just to think. Starting from the point: 'If I wanted to hide something, where would I choose to put it, and where would it be likely to remain undiscovered?' "

"I don't think anything could remain undiscovered here," said Tommy. "Not with gardeners and people, you know, tearing up the place, and different families living here, and house agents and everything else."

"Well, you never know. It might be in a teapot somewhere."

Tuppence rose to her feet, went towards the mantelpiece, stood up on a stool and took down a Chinese teapot. She took off the lid and peered inside.

"Nothing there," she said.

"A most unlikely place," said Tommy.

"Do you think," said Tuppence with a voice that was more hopeful than despondent, "that somebody was trying to put an end to me and loosened that glass skylight in the conservatory so that it would fall on me?"

"Most unlikely," said Tommy. "It was probably meant to fall on old Isaac."

"That's a disappointing thought," said Tuppence. "I would like to feel that I had had a great escape."

"Well, you'd better be careful of yourself. I shall be careful of you, too."

"You always fuss over me," said Tuppence.

"It's very nice of me to do so," said Tommy. "You should be very pleased to have a husband who fusses about you."

"Nobody tried to shoot *you* in the train or disrail it or anything, did they?" said Tuppence.

"No," said Tommy. "But we'd better look at the car brakes before we go out driving in it next time. Of course this is all completely ridiculous," he added.

"Of course it is," said Tuppence. "Absolutely ridiculous. All the same—"

"All the same what?"

"Well, it's sort of fun just to *think* of things like that."

"You mean Alexander was killed because he knew something?" asked Tommy.

"He knew something about who killed Mary Jordan. *It was one of us* . . ." Tuppence's face lit up. "US," she said with emphasis. "We'll have to know just all about US. An 'US' here in this house in the past. It's a crime we've got to solve. Go back to the past to solve it—to where it happened and why it happened. That's a thing we've never tried to do before."

13

Methods of Research

"Where on earth have you been, Tuppence?" demanded her husband when he returned to the family mansion the following day.

"Well, last of all I've been in the cellar," said Tuppence.

"I can see that," said Tommy. "Yes, I do see. Do you know that your hair is absolutely full of cobwebs?"

"Well, it would be, of course. The cellar is full of cobwebs. There wasn't anything there, anyway," said Tuppence. "At least there were some bottles of bay rum."

"Bay rum?" said Tommy. "That's interesting."

"Is it?" said Tuppence. "Does one drink it? It seems to me most unlikely."

"No," said Tommy, "I think people used to put it on their hair. I mean men, not women."

"I believe you're right," said Tuppence. "I remember my uncle—yes, I had an uncle who used bay rum. A friend of his used to bring it to him from America."

"Oh, really? That seems very interesting," said Tommy.

"I don't think it is particularly interesting," said Tuppence. "It's no help to us, anyway. I mean, you couldn't hide anything in a bottle of bay rum."

"Oh, so that's what you've been doing."

"Well, one has to start somewhere," said Tuppence. "It's just possible if what your pals said to you was true, something *could* be hidden in this house, though it's rather difficult to imagine where it could be or what

it could be, because, you see, when you sell a house
or die and go out of it, the house is then of course
emptied, isn't it? I mean, anyone who inherits it takes
the furniture out and sells it, or if it's left, the next
person comes in and *they* sell it, and so anything
that's left in it now would have belonged to the last
tenant but one and certainly not much further back
than that."

"Then why should somebody want to injure you or
injure me or try to get us to leave this house—unless,
I mean, there was something here that they didn't
want us to find?"

"Well, that's all *your* idea," said Tuppence. "It
mightn't be true at all. Anyway, it's not been an entirely wasted day. I have found *some* things."

"Anything to do with Mary Jordan?"

"Not particularly. The cellar, as I say, is not much
good. It had a few old things to do with photography,
I think. You know, a developing lamp or something
like they used to use in the old days, with red glass in
it and the bay rum. But there were no sort of flagstones that looked as though you could pull them up
and find anything underneath. There were a few decayed trunks, some tin trunks and a couple of old
suitcases, but things that just couldn't be used to put
anything in any more. They'd fall to bits if you
kicked them. No. It was a wash-out."

"Well, I'm sorry," said Tommy. "So no satisfaction."

"Well, there *were* some things that were interesting. I said to myself, one has to say something to
oneself—'I think I'd better go upstairs now and take
the cobwebs off before I go on talking.'"

"Well, I think perhaps you had," said Tommy. "I
shall like looking at you better when you've done
that."

"If you want to get the proper Darby and Joan
feeling," said Tuppence, "you must always look at me
and consider that your wife, no matter what her age,
still looks lovely to you."

"Tuppence dearest," said Tommy, "you look excessively lovely to me. And there is a kind of roly-poly of a cobweb hanging down over your left ear which is most attractive. Rather like the curl that the Empress Eugénie is sometimes represented as having in pictures. You know, running along the corner of her neck. Yours seems to have got a spider in it, too."

"Oh," said Tuppence, "I don't like that."

She brushed the web away with her hand. She duly went upstairs and returned to join Tommy later. A glass was awaiting her. She looked at it doubtfully.

"You aren't trying to make *me* drink bay rum, are you?"

"No. I don't think I particularly want to drink bay rum myself."

"Well," said Tuppence, "if I may get on with what I was saying—"

"I should like you to," said Tommy. "You'll do it anyway, but I would like to feel it was because I'd urged you to do so."

"Well, I said to myself, 'Now if I was going to hide anything in this house that I didn't want anyone else to find, what sort of place would I choose?' "

"Yes," said Tommy, "very logical."

"And so I thought, what places are there where one can hide things? Well, one of them of course is Mathilde's stomach."

"I beg your pardon," said Tommy.

"Mathilde's stomach. The rocking-horse. I told you about the rocking-horse. It's an American rocking-horse."

"A lot of things seem to have come from America," said Tommy. "The bay rum too, you said."

"Well, anyway, the rocking-horse did have a hole in its stomach because old Isaac told me about it; it had a hole in its stomach and a lot of sort of queer old paper stuff came out of it. Nothing interesting. But anyway, that's the sort of place where anyone might have hidden anything, isn't it?"

"Quite possibly."

"And Truelove, of course. I examined Truelove again. You know it's got a sort of rather old decayed mackintosh seat, but there was nothing there. And of course there were no personal things belonging to anyone. So I thought again, Well, after all, there's still the bookcase and books. People hide things in books. And we haven't quite finished doing the bookroom upstairs, have we?"

"I thought we had," said Tommy hopefully.

"Not really. There was the bottom shelf still."

"That doesn't really need doing. I mean, one hasn't got to get up a ladder and take things down."

"No. So I went up there and sat down on the floor and looked through the bottom shelf. Most of it was sermons. Sermons of somebody in old times written by a Methodist minister, I think. Anyway, they weren't interesting, there was nothing in them. So I pulled all those books out on the floor. And then I did make a discovery. Underneath, sometime or other, somebody had made a sort of gaping hole, and pushed all sorts of things into it, books all torn to pieces more or less. There was one rather big one. It had a brown paper cover on it and I just pulled it out to see. After all, one never knows, does one? And what do you think it was?"

"I've no idea. First edition of *Robinson Crusoe* or something valuable like that?"

"No. It was a birthday book."

"A birthday book. What's that?"

"Well, they used to have them. Goes back a long time. Back to the Parkinsons, I think. Probably before that. Anyway, it was rather battered and torn. Not worth keeping, and I don't suppose anyone would have bothered about it. But it *does* date back and one *might* find something in it, I thought."

"I see. You mean the sort of thing people might have slipped something into."

"Yes. But nobody had done that, of course. Nothing

so simple. But I'm still going through it quite carefully. I haven't gone through it properly yet. You see, it might have interesting names in it and one might find out something."

"I suppose so," said Tommy, sounding skeptical.

"Well, that's one thing. That's the only thing in the book line that I came across. There was nothing else on the bottom shelf. The other thing to look through, of course, is cupboards."

"What about furniture?" said Tommy. "Lots of things like secret drawers in furniture, and all that."

"No, Tommy, you're not looking at things straight. I mean, all the furniture in the house now is *ours*. We moved into an empty house and brought our furniture with us. The only thing we found here from really old times is all that mess out in the place called KK, old decayed toys and garden seats. I mean, there's no proper antique furniture left in the house. Whoever it was lived here last took it away or else sent it to be sold. There's been lots of people, I expect, since the Parkinsons, so there wouldn't be anything of theirs here. But, I *did* find something. I don't know, it may mean something helpful."

"What was that?"

"China menu cards."

"China menu cards?"

"Yes. In that old cupboard we haven't been able to get into. The one off the larder. You know, they'd lost the key. Well, I found the key in an old box. Out in KK, as a matter of fact. I put some oil on it and I managed to get the cupboard door open. And, well, there was nothing in it. It was just a dirty cupboard with a few broken bits of china left in it. I should think from the last people who were here. But shoved up on the top shelf there was a little heap of the Victorian china menus people used to have at parties. Fascinating, the things they ate—really the most delicious meals. I'll read you some after we've had dinner. It was fascinating. You know, two soups, clear

and thick, and on top of that there were two kinds of
fish and then there were two entrées, I think, and
then you had a salad or something like that. And then
after that you had the joint and after that—I'm not
quite sure what came next. I think a sorbet—that's ice
cream, isn't it? And actually after that—lobster salad!
Can you believe it?"

"Hush, Tuppence," said Tommy, "I don't really
think I can stand any more."

"Well, anyway, I thought it might be interesting. It
dates back, you know. It dates back, I should think,
quite a long time."

"And what do you hope to get from all these discoveries?"

"Well, the only thing with possibilities is the birthday book. In it I see there is a mention of somebody
called Winifred Morrison."

"Well?"

"Well, Winifred Morrison, I gather, was the maiden
name of old Mrs. Griffin. That's the one I went to tea
with the other day. She's one of the oldest inhabitants, you know, and she remembers or knows about
a lot of things that happened before her time. Well, I
think she might remember or have heard of some of
the other names in the birthday book. We might get
something from that."

"We might," said Tommy, still sounding doubtful.
"I still think—"

"Well, what do you still think?" said Tuppence.

"I don't know what to think," said Tommy. "Let's
go to bed and sleep. Don't you think we'd better give
this business up altogether? Why should we want to
know who killed Mary Jordan?"

"Don't you *want* to?"

"No, I don't," said Tommy. "At least—oh, I give in.
You've got me involved now, I admit."

"Haven't *you* found out anything?" asked Tuppence.

"I hadn't time today. But I've got a few more

sources of information. I put that woman I told you about—you know, the one who's quite clever about research—I put *her* onto a few things."

"Oh well," said Tuppence, "we'll still hope for the best. It's all nonsense, but perhaps it *is* rather fun."

"Only I'm not so sure it's going to be as much fun as you think," said Tommy.

"Oh well. No matter," said Tuppence. "We'll have done our best."

"Well, don't go on doing your best all by yourself," said Tommy. "That's exactly what worries me so much—when I'm away from you."

14

Mr. Robinson

"I wonder what Tuppence is doing now?" said Tommy, sighing.

"Excuse me, I didn't quite hear what you said."

Tommy turned his head to look at Miss Collodon more closely. Miss Collodon was thin, emaciated, had gray hair which was slowly passing through the stage of recovering from a peroxide rinse designated to make her look younger (which it had not done). She was now trying various shades of artistic gray, cloudy smoke, steel blue and other interesting shades suitable for a lady between sixty and sixty-five, devoted to the pursuit of research. Her face represented a kind of ascetic superiority and a supreme confidence in her own achievements.

"Oh, it was nothing really, Miss Collodon," said Tommy. "Just—just something I was considering, you know. Just thinking of."

And what is it, I wonder, thought Thomas, being careful this time not to utter the words aloud, that she can be doing today? Something silly, I bet. Half killing herself in that extraordinary, obsolete child's toy that'll come to pieces carrying her down the hill, and she'll probably end up with a broken something or other. Hips, it seems to be nowadays, though I don't see why hips are more vulnerable than anything else. Tuppence, he thought, would at this moment be doing something silly or foolish or, if not that, she would be doing something which might not be silly or foolish but *would* be highly dangerous. Yes, dangerous. It was always difficult keeping Tuppence out of danger. His mind roved vaguely over various incidents in the past. Words of a quotation came into his mind, and he spoke them aloud:

> "Postern of Fate . . .
> Pass not beneath, O Caravan,
> Or pass not singing. Have you heard
> That silence where the birds are dead,
> Yet something pipeth like a bird?"

Miss Collodon responded immediately, giving Tommy quite a shock of surprise.

"Flecker," she said. "Flecker. It goes on:

> "Death's Caravan . . . Disaster's Cavern, Fort of Fear."

Tommy stared at her, then realized that Miss Collodon had thought he was bringing her a poetic problem to be researched, full information on where a certain quotation came from and who the poet had been who had uttered it. The trouble with Miss Collodon was that her research covered such a broad field.

"I was just wondering about my wife," said Tommy apologetically.

"Oh," said Miss Collodon.

She lookd at Tommy with a rather new expression in her eye. Marital trouble in the home, she was deducing. She would presently probably offer him the address of a marriage advice bureau wherein he might seek adjustment in his matrimonial affairs and troubles.

Tommy said hurriedly, "Have you had any success with that inquiry I spoke to you about the day before yesterday?"

"Oh yes. Not very much trouble in *that*. Somerset House is very useful, you know, in all those things. I don't think, you know, that there is likely to be anything particular that you want there, but I've got the names and addresses of certain births, marriages and deaths."

"What, are they all Mary Jordan's?"

"Jordan, yes. A Mary. A Maria and a Polly Jordan. Also a Mollie Jordan. I don't know if any of them are likely to be what you want. Can I pass this to you?"

She handed him a small typewritten sheet.

"Oh, thank you. Thank you very much."

"There are several addresses, too. The ones you asked me for. I have not been able to find out the address of Major Dalrymple. People change their addresses constantly nowadays. However, I think another two days ought to get that information all right. This is Dr. Heseltine's address. He is at present living at Surbiton."

"Thanks very much," said Tommy. "I might start on him, anyway."

"Any more queries?"

"Yes. I've got a list here of about six. Some of them may not be in your line."

"Oh well," said Miss Collodon with complete assurance, "I have to make things my line, you know. You can easily find out first just where you can find out, if that isn't a rather foolish way of speech. But it does explain things, you know. I remember—oh, quite a long time ago, when I was first doing this work, I found how useful Selfridge's advice bureau was. You could ask them the most extraordinary questions about the most extraordinary things and they always seemed to be able to tell you something about it or where you could get the information quickly. But of course they don't do that sort of thing nowadays. Nowadays, you know, most inquiries that are made are—well, you know, if you want to commit suicide, things like that. Samaritans. And legal questions about wills and a lot of extraordinary things for authors, of course. And jobs abroad and immigration problems. Oh yes, I cover a very wide field."

"I'm sure you do," said Tommy.

"And helping alcoholics. A lot of societies there are who specialize in that. Some of them are much better than others. I have quite a list—comprehensive—and some most reliable—"

"I'll remember it," Tommy said, "if I find myself shaping that way any time. It depends how far I get today."

"Oh, I'm sure, Mr. Beresford, I don't see any signs of alcoholic difficulties in you."

"No red nose?" said Tommy.

"It's worse with women," said Miss Collodon. "More difficult, you know, to get them off it, as you might say. Men do relapse, but not so notably. But really, some women, they seem quite all right, quite happy drinking lemonade in large quantities and all that, and then some evening, in the middle of a party—well, it's all there again."

In turn, she looked at her watch.

"Oh dear, I must go on to my next appointment. I have to get to Upper Grosvenor Street."

"Thank you very much," said Tommy, "for all you've done."

He opened the door politely, helped Miss Collodon on with her coat, went back into the room and said:

"I must remember to tell Tuppence this evening that our researches so far have led me to impress a research agent with the idea that my wife drinks and our marriage is breaking up because of it. Oh dear, what next!"

What next was an appointment at an inexpensive restaurant in the neighborhood of Tottenham Court Road.

"Well, I never!" said an elderly man, leaping up from his seat where he was waiting. "Carroty Tom, on my life. Shouldn't have known you."

"Possibly not," said Tommy. "Not much carrots left about me. It's gray-haired Tom."

"Ah well, we're all that. How's your health?"

"Much the same as I always was. Cracking. You know. Decomposing by degrees."

"How long is it since I've seen you? Two years? Eight years? Eleven years?"

"Now you're going too far," said Tommy. "We met at the Maltese Cats dinner last autumn, don't you remember?"

"Ah, so we did. Pity that broke up, you know. I always thought it would. Nice premises, but the food was rotten. Well, what are you doing these days, old boy? Still in the espionage-up-to-date do?"

"No," said Tommy, "I've nothing to do with espionage."

"Dear me. What a waste of your activities."

"And what about you, Mutton-Chop?"

"Oh, I'm much too old to serve my country in that way."

"No espionage going on nowadays?"

"Lots of it, I expect. But probably they put the bright boys onto it. The ones who come bursting out of universities needing a job badly. Where are you now? I sent you a Christmas card this year. Well, I didn't actually post it until January, but anyway it came back to me with 'Not known at this address.'"

"No. We've gone to the country to live now. Down near the sea. Hollowquay."

"Hollowquay. Hollowquay? I seem to remember something. Something in your line going on there once, wasn't there?"

"Not in my time," said Tommy. "I've only just got to hear of it since going to live there. Legends of the past. At least sixty years ago."

"Something to do with a submarine, wasn't it? Plans of a submarine sold to someone or other. I forget who we were selling to at that time. Might have been the Japanese, might have been the Russians—oh, and lots of others. People always seemed to meet enemy agents in Regent's Park or somewhere like that. You know, they'd meet someone like a third secretary

from an Embassy. Not so many beautiful lady spies
around as there used to be once in fiction."

"I wanted to ask you a few things, Mutton-Chop."

"Oh? Ask away. I've had a very uneventful life.
Margery—you remember Margery?"

"Yes, of course I remember Margery. I nearly got
to your wedding."

"I know. But you couldn't make it or something, or
took the wrong train, as far as I remember. A train
that was going to Scotland instead of Southall. Anyway, just as well you didn't. Nothing much came of
it."

"Didn't you get married?"

"Oh yes, I got married. But somehow or other it
didn't take very well. No. A year and a half and it
was done with. She's married again. I haven't, but I'm
doing very nicely. I live at Little Pollon. Quite a de-
cent golf course there. My sister lives with me. She's
a widow with a nice bit of money and we get on
quite well together. She's a bit deaf, so she doesn't
hear what I say, but it only means shouting a bit."

"You said you'd heard of Hollowquay. Was it really
something to do with spying of some kind?"

"Well, to tell you the truth, old boy, it's so long ago
that I can't remember much about it. It made a big
stir at the time. You know, splendid young naval officer absolutely above suspicion in every way, ninety
per cent British, rated about a hundred and five in re-
liability, but nothing of the kind really. In the pay
of—well, I can't remember now who he was in the
pay of. Germany, I suppose. Before the nineteen fourteen war. Yes, I think that was it."

"And there was a woman too, I believe, associated
with it all," said Tommy.

"I seem to remember hearing something about a
Mary Jordan, I think it was. Mind you, I am not clear
about all this. Got into the papers and I think it was
a wife of his—I mean of the above-suspicion naval officer. It was his wife who got in touch with the Rus-

sians and—no, no, that's something that happened
since then. One mixes things up so—they all sound
alike. Wife thought he wasn't getting enough money,
which meant, I suppose, that *she* wasn't getting
enough money. And so—well, why d'you want to dig
up all this old history? What's it got to do with you
after all this time? I know you had something to do
once with someone who was on the *Lusitania* or went
down with the *Lusitania* or something like that,
didn't you? If we go back as far as that, I mean.
That's what you were mixed up in once, or your wife
was mixed up in."

"We were both mixed up in it," said Tommy, "and
it's such a very long time ago that I really can't
remember anything about it now."

"There was some woman associated with that, wasn't
there? Name like Jane Fish, or something like that, or
was it Jane Whale?"

"Jane Finn," said Tommy.

"Where is she now?"

"She's married to an American."

"Oh, I see. Well, all very nice. One always seems to
get talking about one's old pals and what's happened
to them all. When you talk about old friends, either
they are dead, which surprises you enormously because you didn't think they would be, or else they're
not dead and that surprises you even more. It's a very
difficult world."

Tommy said yes it was a very difficult world and
here was the waiter coming. What would they have
to eat . . . The conversation thereafter was gastronomic.

In the afternoon Tommy had another interview arranged. This time with a sad, grizzled man sitting in
an office and obviously grudging the time he was giving to Tommy.

"Well, I really couldn't say. Of course I know
roughly what you're talking about—lot of talk about

it at the time—caused a big political blow-up—but I really have no information about that sort of thing, you know. No. You see, these things, they don't last, do they? They soon pass out of one's mind once the press gets hold of some other juicy scandal."

He opened up slightly on a few of his own interesting moments in life when something he'd never suspected came suddenly to light or his suspicions had suddenly been aroused by some very peculiar event. He said:

"Well, I've just got one thing might help. Here's an address for you and I've made an appointment, too. Nice chap. Knows everything. He's the tops, you know; absolutely the tops. One of my daughters was a godchild of his. That's why he's awfully nice to me and will always do me a good turn if possible. So I asked him if he would see you. I said there were some things you wanted the top news about, I said what a good chap you were and various things, and he said yes, he'd heard of you already. Knew something about you, and he said, Of course, come along. Three forty-five, I think. Here's the address. It's an office in the City, I think. Ever met him?"

"I don't think so," said Tommy, looking at the card and the address. "No."

"Well, you wouldn't think he knew anything, to look at him, I mean. Big, you know, and yellow."

"Oh," said Tommy, "big and yellow."

It didn't really convey much information to his mind.

"He's the tops," said Tommy's grizzled friend, "absolute tops. You go along there. He'll be able to tell you *something* anyway. Good luck, old chap."

Tommy, having successfully got himself to the City office in question, was received by a man of thirty-five to forty years of age who looked at him with the eye of one determined to do the worst without delay. Tommy felt that he was suspected of many things, possibly carrying a bomb in some deceptive container, or prepared to hi-jack or kidnap anyone or to hold up with a revolver the entire staff. It made Tommy extremely nervous.

"You have an appointment with Mr. Robinson? At what time, did you say? Ah, three forty-five." He consulted a ledger. "Mr. Thomas Beresford, is that right?"

"Yes," said Tommy.

"Ah. Just sign your name here, please."

Tommy signed his name where he was told.

"Johnson."

A nervous-looking young man of about twenty-three seemed like an apparition rising out of a glass partitioned desk. "Yes, sir?"

"Take Mr. Beresford up to the fourth floor to Mr. Robinson's office."

"Yes, sir."

He led Tommy to a lift, the kind of lift that always seemed to have its own idea of how it should deal with those who came into it. The doors rolled open. Tommy passed in, the doors very nearly pinched him in doing so and just managed to slam themselves shut about an inch from his spine.

"Cold afternoon," said Johnson, showing a friendly attitude to someone who was clearly being allowed to approach the high one in the highest.

"Yes," said Tommy, "it always seems to be cold in the afternoons."

"Some say it's pollution, some say it's all natural gas they're taking out of the North Sea," said Johnson.

"Oh, I haven't heard that," said Tommy.

"Doesn't seem likely to me," said Johnson.

They passed the second floor and the third floor and finally arrived at the fourth floor. Johnson led Tommy, again escaping the closing doors by a mere inch, along a passage to a door. He knocked, was told to enter, held the door open, insinuated Tommy across the threshold, and said,

"Mr. Beresford, sir. By appointment."

He went out and shut the door behind him. Tommy advanced. The room seemed to be mainly filled by an enormous desk. Behind the desk sat a rather enormous man, a man of great weight and many inches. He had, as Tommy had been prepared for by his friend, a very large and yellow face. What nationality he was Tommy had no idea. He might have been anything. Tommy had a feeling he was probably foreign. A German, perhaps? Or an Austrian? Possibly a Japanese. Or else he might be very decidedly English.

"Ah. Mr. Beresford."

Mr. Robinson got up, shook hands.

"I'm sorry if I come taking a lot of your time," said Tommy.

He had a feeling he had once seen Mr. Robinson before or had had Mr. Robinson pointed out to him. Anyway, on the occasion, whatever it had been, he had been rather shy about it because obviously Mr. Robinson was someone very important, and, he now gathered (or rather felt at once), he was still very important.

"There's something you want to know about, I gather. Your friend, What's-his-name, just gave me a brief résumé."

"I don't suppose—I mean it's something perhaps I oughtn't to bother you about. I don't suppose it's anything of any importance. It was just—just—"

"Just an idea?"

"Partly my wife's idea."

"I've heard about your wife. I've heard about you, too. Let me see, the last time was M or N, wasn't it? Or N or M. Mm. I remember. Remember all the facts and things. You got that commander chap, didn't you? The one who was in the English Navy supposedly but was actually a very important Hun. I still call them Huns occasionally, you know. Of course I know we're all different now we're in the Common

Market. All in the nursery school together, as you
might say. I know. You did a good bit of work there.
Very good bit indeed. And so did your missis. My
word. All those children's books. I remember. Goosey,
goosey, gander, wasn't it—the one that gave the show
away? Where do you wander? Upstairs and downstairs and in my lady's chamber."

"Fancy you remembering that," said Tommy with
great respect.

"Yes, I know. One's always surprised when one
remembers something. It just came back to me at that
minute. So silly, you know, that really you'd never
have suspected it of being anything else, would you?"

"Yes, it was a good show."

"Now, what's the matter now? What are you up
against?"

"Well, it's nothing really," said Tommy. "It's just—"

"Come on, put it in your own words. You needn't
make a thing of it. Just tell me the story. Sit down.
Take the weight off your feet. Don't you know—or
you will know, when you're some years older—resting
your feet is important."

"I'm old enough already, I should think," said
Tommy. "There can't be much ahead of me now except a coffin, in due course."

"Oh, I wouldn't say that. I tell you, once you get
above a certain age, you can go on living practically
forever. Now then, what's all this about?"

"Well," said Tommy, "briefly, my wife and I went
into a new house and there was all the fuss of getting
into a new house—"

"I know," said Mr. Robinson, "yes, I know the sort
of thing. Electricians all over the floor. They pick
holes and you fall into them and—"

"There were some books there the people moving
out wanted to sell. Books that had been in the family
and they didn't care for them. A lot of children's
books, all sorts of things. You know, Henty and things
like that."

"I remember. I remember Henty from my own youth."

"And in one book my wife was reading we found a passage underlined. The letters were underlined and it made a sentence when you put it together. And—this sounds awfully silly, what I'm going to say next—"

"Well, that's hopeful," said Mr. Robinson. "If a things sounds silly, I always want to hear about it."

"It said, *Mary Jordan did not die naturally. It was one of us.*"

"Very, very interesting," said Mr. Robinson. "I've never come across anything like that before. It said that, did it? Mary Jordan did not die a natural death. And who was it who wrote it? Any clue to that?"

"Apparently a boy of school age. Parkinson was the family's name. They all lived in this house and he was one of the Parkinsons, we gathered. Alexander Parkinson. At least, anyway, he's buried there in the churchyard."

"Parkinson," said Mr. Robinson. "Wait a bit. Let me think. Parkinson—yes, you know there was a name like that connected with things, but you don't always remember who or what and where."

"And we've been very keen to learn who Mary Jordan was."

"Because she didn't die a natural death. Yes, I suppose that would be rather your line of country. But it seems very odd. What did you find out about her?"

"Absolutely nothing," said Tommy. "Nobody seems to remember her there much, or say anything about her. At least somebody did say she was what we'd call an *au pair* girl nowadays or a governess or something like that. They couldn't remember. A Mamselle or a Frowline, they said. It's all very difficult, you see."

"And she died—what did she die of?"

"Somebody brought a few foxglove leaves in with some spinach from the garden, by accident, and then they ate it. Mind you, that probably wouldn't kill you."

"No," said Mr. Robinson. "Not enough of it. But if you then put a strong dose of digitalin alkaloid in the coffee and just made sure that Mary Jordan got it in her coffee, or in a cocktail earlier, then—then, as you say, the foxglove leaves would be blamed and it would all be taken to be an accident. But Alexander Parker, or whatever the schoolboy's name was, was too sharp for that. He had other ideas, did he? Anything else, Beresford? When was this? First World War, Second World War, or before that?"

"Before. Rumors passed down through elderly ancestors say she was a German spy."

"I remember that case—made a big sensation. Any German working in England before nineteen fourteen was always said to be a spy. The English officer involved was one always said to be 'above suspicion.' I always look very hard at anyone who is above suspicion. It's all a long time ago, I don't think it's ever been written up in recent years. I mean, not in the way that things are occasionally for public enjoyment when they release a bit of stuff from the records."

"Yes, but it's all rather sketchy."

"Yes, it would be by now. It's always been associated, of course, with the submarine secrets that were stolen around then. There was some aviation news as well. A lot of that side of it, and that's what caught the public interest, as you might say. But there are a lot of other things, you know. There was the political side to it, too. A lot of our prominent politicians. You know, the sort of chaps people say, 'Well, *he* has *real* integrity.' Real integrity is just as dangerous as being above suspicion in the services. Real integrity my foot," said Mr. Robinson. "I remember it with this last war. Some people haven't got the integrity they are credited with. One chap lived down near here, you know. He had a cottage on the beach, I think. Made a lot of disciples, you know, praising Hitler. Saying our only chance was to get in with him. Really, the fellow seemed such a noble man. Had some wonderful ideas. Was so terribly keen to abolish all poverty and difficulties and injustice—things of that kind. Oh yes. Blew the fascist trumpet without calling it fascism. And Spain too, you know. Was in with Franco and all that lot to begin with. And dear old Mussolini, naturally, spouting away. Yes, there are always a lot of sidelines to it just before wars. Things that never came out and nobody ever really knew about."

"You seem to know everything," said Tommy. "I beg your pardon. Perhaps that's rather rude of me. But it really is very exciting to come across someone who does seem to know about everything."

"Well, I've often had a finger in the pie, as you might say. You know, come into things on the sidelines, or in the background. One hears a good deal. One hears a good deal from one's old cronies too, who were in it up to the neck and who knew the lot. I expect you begin to find that, don't you?"

"Yes," said Tommy, "it's quite true. I meet old friends, you know, and they've seen other old friends and there're quite a lot of things that, well, one's friends knew and you knew. You didn't get together just then, but now you *do* hear about them and they're very interesting sometimes."

"Yes," said Mr. Robinson. "I see where you're going—where you're tending, you might say. It's interesting that you should come across this."

"The trouble is," said Tommy, "that I don't really know—I mean, perhaps we're being rather silly. I mean, we bought this house to live in, the sort of house we wanted. We've done it up the way we want and we're trying to get the garden in some kind of shape. But I mean, I don't want to get tied up in this sort of stuff again. It's just pure curiosity on our part. Something that happened long ago and you can't help thinking about it or wanting to know why. But there's no point in it. It's not going to do anybody any good."

"I know. You just want to *know*. Well, that's the way the human being is made. That's what leads us to explore things, to go and fly to the moon, to bother about underwater discoveries, to find natural gas in the North Sea, to find oxygen supplied to us by the sea and not by the trees and forests. Quite a lot of things they're always finding out about. Just through curiosity. I suppose without curiosity a man would be a tortoise. Very comfortable life, a tortoise has. Goes to sleep all the winter and doesn't eat anything more than grass as far as I know, to live all the summer. Not an interesting life perhaps, but a very peaceful one. On the other hand—"

"On the other hand one might say man is more like a mongoose."

"Good. You're a reader of Kipling. I'm so glad. Kipling's not appreciated as much as he should be nowadays. He was a wonderful chap. A wonderful person to read nowadays. His short stories, amazingly good, they are. I don't think it's ever been realized enough."

"I don't want to make a fool of myself," said Tommy. "I don't want to mix myself up with a lot of things which have nothing to do with me. Not anything to do with anybody nowadays, I should say."

"That you never know," said Mr. Robinson.

"I mean, really," said Tommy, who was now completely swamped in a cloud of guilt for having disturbed a very important man, "I mean, I'm not just trying to find out things."

"Got to try and find out things just to satisfy your wife, I suppose. Yes, I've heard of her. I've never had the pleasure of meeting her, I don't think. Rather wonderful person, isn't she?"

"I think so," said Tommy.

"That's good hearing. I like people who stick together and enjoy their marriage and go on enjoying it."

"Really, I'm like the tortoise, I suppose. I mean,

there we are. We're old and we're tired, and although we've got very good health for our age, we don't want to be mixed up in anything nowadays. We're not trying to butt into anything. We just—"

"I know. I know," said Mr. Robinson, "don't keep apologizing for it. You want to know. Like the mongoose, you want to know. And Mrs. Beresford, she wants to know. Moreover, I should say from all I've heard of her and been told of her, I should say she will get to know somehow."

"You think she's more likely to do it than I am?"

"Well, I don't think perhaps you're quite as keen on finding out things as she is, but I think you're just as likely to get onto it because I think you're rather good at finding sources. It's not easy to find sources for something as long ago as that."

"That's why I feel awful about having come and disturbed you. But I wouldn't have done it on my own. It was only Mutton-Chop. I mean—"

"I know who you mean. Had mutton-chop whiskers and was rather pleased with them at one time. That's why he was called that. A nice chap. Done good work in his time. Yes. He sent you to me because he knew that I am interested in anything like that. I started quite early, you know. Poking about, I mean, and finding out things."

"And now," said Tommy, "now you're the tops."

"Now who told you that?" said Mr. Robinson. "All nonsense."

"I don't think it is," said Tommy.

"Well," said Mr. Robinson, "some get to the tops and some have the tops forced upon them. I would say the latter applies to me, more or less. I've had a few things of surpassing interest forced upon me."

"That business connected with—Frankfurt, wasn't it?"

"Ah, *you've* heard rumors, have you? Ah well, don't think about them any more. They're not supposed to be known much. Don't think I'm going to rebuff you for coming here asking me questions. I probably can answer some of the things you want to know. If I said there was something that happened years ago that might result in something being known that would be—possibly—interesting nowadays, something that would give one a bit of information about things that might be going on nowadays, that might be true enough. I wouldn't put it past anyone or anything. I don't know what I can suggest to you, though. It's a question of worry about, listen to people, find out what you can about bygone years. If anything comes along that you think might be interesting to me, just give me a ring or something. We'll find some code words, you know. Just to make ourselves feel excited again, feel as though we really mattered. Crab-apple jelly. How would that be? You know, you say your wife's made some jars of crab-apple jelly and would I like a pot. I'll know what you mean."

"You mean that—that I would have found out something about Mary Jordan. I don't see there's any point in going on with that. After all, she's dead."

"Yes. She's dead. But—well, you see, sometimes one has the wrong ideas about people because of what you've been told. Or because of what's been written."

"You mean we have wrong ideas about Mary Jordan? You mean, she wasn't important at all?"

"Oh yes, she could have been very important." Mr. Robinson looked at his watch. "I have to push you off now. There's a chap coming in, in ten minutes. An awful bore, but he's high up in government circles, and you know what life is nowadays. Government, government, you've got to stand it everywhere. In the office, in the home, in the supermarkets, on the television. Private life. That's what we want more of nowadays. Now this little fun and games that you and your wife are having, you're in private life and you can look at it from the background of private life. Who knows, you might find out something. Something that would be interesting. Yes. You may and you may not.

"I can't tell you anything more about it. I know some of the facts that probably nobody else can tell you and in due course I might be able to tell them to you. But as they're all dead and done with, that's not really practical.

"I'll tell you one thing that will help you perhaps in your investigations. You read about this case, the trial of Commander Whatever-he-was—I've forgotten his name now—and he was tried for espionage, did a sentence for it and richly deserved it. He was a traitor to his country and that's that. But Mary Jordan—"

"Yes?"

"You want to know something about Mary Jordan. Well, I'll tell you one thing that might, as I say, help your point of view. Mary Jordan was—well, you can call it a spy, but she wasn't a German spy. She wasn't an enemy spy. Listen to this, my boy. I can't help calling you 'my boy.'"

Mr. Robinson dropped his voice and leaned forward over his desk.

"*She was one of our lot.*"

Book Three

15

Mary Jordan

"But that alters everything," said Tuppence.

"Yes," said Tommy. "Yes. It was—it was quite a shock."

"Why did he tell you?"

"I don't know," said Tommy. "I thought—well, two or three different things."

"Did he—what's he like, Tommy? You haven't really told me."

"Well, he's yellow," said Tommy. "Yellow and big and fat and very, very ordinary, but at the same time, if you know what I mean, he isn't ordinary at all. He's—well, he's what my friend said he was. He's one of the tops."

"You sound like someone talking about pop singers."

"Well, one gets used to using these terms."

"Yes, but why? Surely that was revealing something that he wouldn't have wanted to reveal, you'd think."

"It was a long time ago," said Tommy. "It's all over, you see. I suppose none of it matters nowadays. I mean, look at all the things they're releasing now. Off the record. You know, not hushing up things any more. Letting it all come out, what really happened. What one person wrote and what another person said and what one row was about and how something else was all hushed up because of something you never heard about."

"You make me feel horribly confused," said Tuppence, "when you say things like that. It makes everything wrong, too, doesn't it?"

"How do you mean, makes everything wrong?"

"Well, I mean, the way we've been looking at it. I mean—what do I mean?"

"Go on," said Tommy. "You must know what you mean."

"Well, what I said. It's all wrong. I mean, we found this thing in *The Black Arrow*, and it was all clear enough. Somebody had written it in there, probably this little boy Alexander, and it meant that somebody—one of them, he said, at least, one of us—I mean he put it that way, but that's what he meant—one of the family or somebody in the house or something, had arranged to bring about the death of Mary Jordan, and we didn't know who Mary Jordan was, which was very baffling."

"Goodness knows it's been baffling," said Tommy.

"Well, it hasn't baffled you as much as me. It's baffled me a great deal. I haven't really found out anything about her. At least—"

"What you found out about her was that she had been apparently a German spy, isn't that what you mean? You found out that?"

"Yes, that is what was believed about her, and I supposed it was true. Only now—"

"Yes," said Tommy, "only now we know that it wasn't true. She was the opposite to a German spy."

"She was a sort of English spy."

"Well, she must have been in the English espionage or security or whatever it was called. And she came here in some capacity to find out something. To find out something about—about—what's his name now? I wish I could remember names better. I mean the naval officer or the army officer, or whatever he was. The one who sold the secret of the submarine or something like that. Yes, I suppose there was a little cluster of German agents here, rather like in N or M all over again, all busy preparing things. You know, like the things that we found out being prepared for."

"It would seem so, yes."

"And she was sent here in that case, presumably, to find out all about it."

"I see."

"So 'one of us' didn't mean what we think it meant. 'One of us' meant—well, it had to be someone who was in this neighborhood. And somebody who had something to do with this house, or was in this house for a special occasion. And so, when she died, her death wasn't a natural one because somebody got wise to what she was doing. And Alexander found out about it."

"She was pretending to spy, perhaps," said Tuppence, "for Germany. Making friends with Commander—whoever it was."

"Call him Commander X," said Tommy, "if you can't remember."

"All right, all right. Commander X. She was getting friendly with him."

"There was also," said Tommy, "an enemy agent living down here. The head of a big organization. He lived in a cottage somewhere, down near the quay, I think it was, and he wrote a lot of propaganda, and used to talk of things and say that really our best plan would be to join with Germany and get together with them—and things like that."

"It is all so confusing," said Tuppence. "All these things—plans, and secret papers and plots and espionage—have been so confusing. Well, anyway, we've probably been looking in all the wrong places."

"Not really," said Tommy. "I don't think so."

"Why don't you think so?"

"Well, because if she, Mary Jordan, was here to find out something, and if she did find out something, then perhaps when *they*—I mean Commander X or other people—there must have been other people too in it—when *they* found out that she'd found out something—"

"Now don't get me muddled again," said Tuppence.

"If you say things like that, it's very muddling. Yes. Go on."

"All right. Well, when they found out that she'd found out a lot of things, well, then they had to—"

"To silence her," said Tuppence.

"You make it sound like Phillips Oppenheim now," said Tommy. "And he was before nineteen fourteen, surely."

"Well, anyway, they had to silence Mary before she could report what she'd found out."

"There must be a little more to it than that," said Tommy. "Perhaps she'd got hold of something important. Some kind of papers or written document. Letters that might have been sent or passed to someone."

"Yes. I see what you mean. We've got to look among a different lot of people. But if she was one of the ones to die because of a mistake that had been made about the vegetables, then I don't see quite how it could be what Alexander called 'one of us.' It presumably wasn't one of *his* family."

"It could have been like this," said Tommy. "It needn't have been actually someone in the house. It's very easy to pick wrong leaves looking alike, bunch 'em all up together and take them into the kitchen, you wouldn't, I think, make them really—I mean, not *really*—too lethal. Just the people at one particular meal would get rather ill after it and they'd send for a doctor and the doctor would get the food analyzed and he'd realize somebody'd made a mistake over vegetables. He wouldn't think anyone had done it on purpose."

"But then everybody at that meal would have died," said Tuppence. "Or everybody would have been ill but *not* died."

"Not necessarily," said Tommy. "Suppose they wanted a certain person—Mary J.—to die, and they were going to give a dose of poison to her, oh, in a cocktail before the lunch or dinner or whatever it was or in coffee or something after the meal—actual digitalin, or aconite or whatever it is in foxgloves—"

"Aconite's in monkshood, I think," said Tuppence.

"Don't be so knowledgeable," said Tommy. "The point is everyone gets a mild dose by what is clearly a mistake, so everyone gets mildly ill—but one person dies. Don't you see, if most people were taken ill after whatever it was—dinner or lunch one day and it was looked into, and they found out about the mistake, well, things *do* happen like that. You know, people eat fungus instead of mushrooms and deadly night-shade berries children eat by mistake because the berries look like fruit. Just a mistake and people are ill, but they don't usually all die. Just one of them does, and the one that did die would be assumed to have been particularly allergic to whatever it was and so *she* had died but the others *hadn't*. You see, it would pass off as really due to the mistake and they wouldn't have looked to see or even suspected there was some other way in which it happened—"

"She might have got a little ill like the others and then the real dose might have been put in her early tea the next morning," said Tuppence.

"I'm sure, Tuppence, that you've lots of ideas."

"About that part of it, yes," said Tuppence. "But what about the other things? I mean who and what and why? Who was the 'one of us'—'one of them' as we'd better say now—who had the opportunity? Someone staying down here, friends of other people perhaps? People who brought a letter, forged perhaps, from a friend saying, 'Do be kind to my friend, Mr. or Mrs. Murray Wilson, or some name, who is down here. She is so anxious to see your pretty garden,' or something. All that would be easy enough."

"Yes, I think it would."

"In that case," said Tuppence, "there's perhaps something still here in the house that would explain what happened to me today and yesterday, too."

"What happened to you yesterday, Tuppence?"

"The wheels came off that beastly little cart and horse I was going down the hill in the other day, and so I came a terrible cropper right down behind the monkey puzzle and into it. And I very nearly—well, I might have had a serious accident. That silly old man Isaac ought to have seen that the thing was safe. He said he *did* look at it. He told me it was quite all right before I started."

"And it wasn't?"

"No. He said afterwards that he thought someone had been playing about with it, tampering with the wheels or something, so that they came off."

"Tuppence," said Tommy, "do you think that's the second or third thing that's happened here to us? You know that other thing that nearly came down on the top of me in the book-room?"

"You mean somebody wants to get rid of *us*? But that would mean—"

"That would mean," said Tommy, "that there must be *something*. Something that's *here*—in the house."

Tommy looked at Tuppence and Tuppence looked at Tommy. It was the moment for consideration. Tuppence opened her mouth three times but checked herself each time, frowning, as she considered. It was Tommy who spoke at last.

"What did he think? What did he say about Truelove? Old Isaac, I mean."

"That it was only to be expected, that the thing was pretty rotten anyway."

"But he said somebody had been monkeying about with it?"

"Yes," said Tuppence, "very definitely. 'Ah,' he said, 'these youngsters have been in tryin' it out, you know. Enjoy pulling wheels off things, they do, young monkeys. Not that I've seen anyone about. But then I suppose they'd be sure that I didn't catch them at it. They'd wait till I'm away from home, I expect.'

"I asked him if he thought it was just—just something mischievous," said Tuppence.

"What did he say to that?" said Tommy.

"He didn't really know what to say."

"It could have been mischief, I suppose," said Tommy. "People do do those things."

"Are you trying to say you think that it was meant in some way so that I should go on playing the fool with the cart and that the wheel would come off and the thing would fall to pieces— Oh, but that is nonsense, Tommy."

"Well, it sounds like nonsense," said Tommy, "but things aren't nonsense sometimes. It depends where and how they happen and why."

"I don't see what 'why' there could be."

"One might make a guess—about the most likely thing," said Tommy.

"Now what do you mean by the most likely?"

"I mean perhaps people want us to go away from here."

"Why should they? If somebody wants the house for themselves, they could make us an offer for it."

"Yes, they could."

"Well, I wondered— Nobody else has wanted this house as far as we know. I mean, there was nobody else looking at it when we were. It seemed to be generally regarded as if it had come into the market rather cheap but not for any other reason, except that it was out of date and needed a lot doing to it."

"I can't believe they wanted to do away with us, maybe it's because you've been nosing about, asking too many questions, copying things out of books."

"You mean that I'm stirring up things that somebody doesn't want to be stirred up?"

"That sort of thing," said Tommy. "I mean, if we suddenly were meant to feel that we didn't like living here, and put the house up for sale and went away, that would be quite all right. They'd be satisfied with that. I don't think that they—"

"Who do you mean by 'they'?"

"I've no idea," said Tommy. "We must get to 'they'

later. Just *they*. There's *we* and there's *they*. We must keep them apart in our minds."

"What about Isaac?"

"What do you mean, what about Isaac?"

"I don't know. I just wondered if he was mixed up in this?"

"He's a very old man, he's been here a long time and he knows a few things. If somebody slipped him a five-pound note or something, do you think he'd tamper with Truelove's wheels?"

"No, I don't," said Tuppence. "He hasn't got the brains to."

"He wouldn't need brains for it," said Tommy. "He'd only need the brains to take the five-pound note and to take out a few screws or break off a bit of wood here or there and just make it so that—well, it would come to grief next time you went down the hill in it."

"I think what you are imagining is nonsense," said Tuppence.

"Well, you've been imagining a few things that are nonsense already."

"Yes, but they fitted in," said Tuppence. "They fitted in with the things we've heard."

"Well," said Tommy, "as a result of my investigations or researches, whatever you like to call them, it seems that we haven't learnt quite the right things."

"You mean what I said just now, that this turns things upside-down. I mean now we know that Mary Jordan wasn't an enemy agent, instead she was a *British* agent. She was here for a purpose. Perhaps she had accomplished her purpose."

"In that case," said Tommy, "now let's get it all clear, with this new bit of knowledge added. Her purpose here was to find out something."

"Presumably to find out something about Commander X," said Tuppence. "You must find out his name, it seems so extraordinarily barren only to be able to say Commander X all the time."

"All right, all right, but you know how difficult these things are."

"And she did find them out, and she reported what she had found out. And perhaps someone opened the letter," said Tuppence.

"What letter?" said Tommy.

"The letter she wrote to whoever was her 'contact.'"

"Yes."

"Do you think he was her father or her grandfather or something like that?"

"I shouldn't think so," said Tommy. "I don't think that's the sort of way things would be done. She might just have chosen to take the name of Jordan, or they thought it was quite a good name because it was not associated in any way, which it wouldn't be if she was partly German, and had perhaps come from some other work that she had been doing for us but not for them.

"For us and not for them," repeated Tommy, "abroad. And so she came here as what?"

"Oh, I don't know," said Tuppence, "we shall have to start all over again finding out *as what*, I suppose ... Anyway, she came here and she found out something and she either passed it on to someone or didn't. I mean, she might not have written a letter. She might have gone to London and reported something. Met someone in Regent's Park, say."

"That's rather the other way about usually, isn't it?" said Tommy. "I mean you meet somebody from whatever embassy it is you're in collusion with and you meet in Regent's Park and—"

"Hide things in a hollow tree sometimes. Do you think they really do that? It sounds so unlikely. It's so much more like people who are having a love affair and putting love letters in."

"I dare say whatever they put in there were written as though they were love letters and really had a code."

"That's a splendid idea," said Tuppence, "only I suppose they— Oh dear, it's such years ago. How difficult it is to get anywhere. The more you know, I mean, the less use it is to you. But we're not going to stop, Tommy, are we?"

"I don't suppose we are for a moment," said Tommy. He sighed.

"You wish we were?" said Tuppence.

"Almost. Yes. Far as I can see—"

"Well," cut in Tuppence, "I can't see you taking yourself off the trail. No, and it would be very difficult to get *me* off the trail. I mean, I'd go on thinking about it and it would worry me. I dare say I should go off my food and everything."

"The point is," said Tommy, "do you think—we know in a way perhaps what this starts from. Espionage. Espionage by the enemy with certain objects in view, some of which were accomplished. Perhaps some which weren't quite accomplished. But we don't know —well—we don't know who was mixed up in it. From the enemy point of view. I mean, there were people here, I should think, people perhaps among security forces. People who were traitors but whose job it was to appear to be loyal servants of the state."

"Yes," said Tuppence, "I'll go for that one. That seems to be very likely."

"And Mary Jordan's job was to get in touch with them."

"To get in touch with Commander X?"

"I should think so, yes. Or with friends of Commander X and to find out about things. But apparently it was necessary for her to come here to get it."

"Do you mean that the Parkinsons—I suppose we're back at the Parkinsons again before we know where we are—were in it? That the Parkinsons were part of the enemy?"

"It seems very unlikely," said Tommy.

"Well then, I can't see what it all means."

"I think the house might have something to do with it," said Tommy.

"The house? Well, other people came and lived here afterwards, didn't they?"

"Yes, they did. But I don't suppose they were people quite like—well, quite like you, Tuppence."

"What do you mean by quite like me?"

"Well, wanting old books and looking through them and finding out things. Being a regular mongoose, in fact. They just came and lived here and I expect the upstairs rooms and the books were probably servants' rooms and nobody went into them. There may be something that was hidden in this house. Hidden perhaps by Mary Jordan. Hidden in a place ready to deliver to someone who would come for them, or deliver them by going herself to London or somewhere on some excuse. Visit to a dentist. Seeing an old friend. Quite easy to do. She had something she had acquired, or got to know, hidden in this house."

"You're not saying it's still hidden in this house?"

"No," said Tommy, "I shouldn't have thought so. But one doesn't know. Somebody is afraid we may find it or have found it and they want to get us out of the house, or they want to get hold of whatever it is they think we've found but that they've never found, though perhaps they've looked for it in past years and then thought it had been hidden somewhere else outside."

"Oh, Tommy," said Tuppence, "that makes it all much more exciting really, doesn't it?"

"It's only what we *think*," said Tommy.

"Now don't be such a wet blanket," said Tuppence. "I'm going to look outside as well as inside—"

"What are you going to do, dig up the kitchen garden?"

"No," said Tuppence. "Cupboards, the cellar, things like that. Who knows? Oh, Tommy!"

"Oh, Tuppence!" said Tommy. "Just when we were looking forward to a delightful, peaceful old age."

"No peace for the pensioners," said Tuppence gaily. "That's an idea, too."

"What?"

"I must go and talk to some old-age pensioners. I hadn't thought of them up to now."

"For goodness' sake, look after yourself," said Tommy. "I think I'd better stay at home and keep an eye on you. But I've got to do more research in London tomorrow."

"I'm going to do some research here," said Tuppence.

16

Research by Tuppence

"I hope," said Tuppence, "that I'm not interrupting you, coming along like this? I thought I'd better ring up first in case you were out, you know, or busy. But, I mean, it's nothing particular so I could go away again at once if you liked. I mean, my feelings wouldn't be hurt or anything like that."

"Oh, I'm delighted to see you, Mrs. Beresford," said Mrs. Griffin.

She moved herself three inches along her chair so as to settle her back more comfortably and looked with what seemed to be distinct pleasure into Tuppence's somewhat anxious face.

"It's a great pleasure, you know, when somebody new comes and lives in this place. We're so used to all our neighbors that a new face, or if I may say so a couple of new faces, is a treat. An absolute *treat!* I hope indeed that you'll both come to dinner one day. I don't know what time your husband gets back. He goes to London, does he not, most days?"

"Yes," said Tuppence. "That's very nice of you. I hope you'll come and see our house when it's more or less finished. I'm always thinking it's going to be finished but it never is."

"Houses are rather like that," said Mrs. Griffin.

Mrs. Griffin, as Tuppence knew very well from her various sources of information which consisted of daily women, old Isaac, Gladys in the post office and sundry others, was ninety-four. The upright position which she enjoyed arranging because it took the rheu-

matic pains out of her back, together with her erect
carriage, gave her the air of someone much younger.
In spite of the wrinkled face, the head of uprising
white hair surmounted by a lace scarf tied round her
head reminded Tuppence of a couple of her great-
aunts in past days. She wore bifocal spectacles and
had a hearing aid which she sometimes, but very seldom as far as Tuppence could see, had to use. And
she looked thoroughly alert and perfectly capable of
reaching the age of a hundred or even a hundred and
ten.

"What have you been doing with yourself lately?"
inquired Mrs. Griffin. "I gather you've got the electricians out of the house now. So Dorothy told me. Mrs.
Rogers, you know. She used to be my housemaid
once and she comes now and cleans twice a week."

"Yes, thank goodness," said Tuppence. "I was always falling into the holes they made. I really came,"
said Tuppence, "and it may sound rather silly but it's
something I just wondered about—I expect you'll
think it's rather silly, too. I've been turning out
things, you know, a lot of old bookshelves and things
like that. We bought some books with the house,
mostly children's books years and years old, but I
found some old favorites among them."

"Ah yes," said Mrs. Griffin, "I quite understand that
you must very much have enjoyed the prospect of
being able to read certain old favorites again. *The
Prisoner of Zenda*, perhaps. My grandmother used to
read *The Prisoner of Zenda*, I believe. I read it once
myself. Really very enjoyable. Romantic, you know.
The first romantic book, I imagine, one is allowed to
read. You know, novel reading was not encouraged.
My mother and my grandmother never approved of
reading anything like a novel in the mornings. A story
book as it was called. You know, you could read history or something serious, but novels were only plea-
surable and so to be read in the afternoon."

"I know," said Tuppence. "Well, I found a good

many books that I liked reading again. Mrs. Molesworth."

"*The Tapestry Room?*" said Mrs. Griffin with imme-
diate comprehension.

"Yes. *The Tapestry Room* was one of my favorites."

"Well, I always liked *Four Winds Farm* best," said
Mrs. Griffin.

"Yes, that was there, too. And several others. Many
different kinds of authors. Anyway, I got down to the
last shelf and I think there must have been an accident there. You know, someone had banged it about a
good deal. When they were moving the furniture, I
expect. There was a sort of hole and I scooped up a
lot of old things out of that. Mostly torn books and
among it there was this."

She produced her parcel wrapped loosely in brown
paper.

"It's a birthday book," she said. "An old-fashioned
birthday book. And it had your name in it. Your
name—I remember you told me—was Winifred Morrison, wasn't it?"

"Yes, my dear. Quite right."

"And it was written in the birthday book. And so I
wondered whether it would amuse you if I brought it
along for you to see. It might have a lot of other old
friends of yours in it and different things or names
which would amuse you."

"Well, that was very nice of you, my dear, and I
should like to see it very much. You know, these
things from the past, one does find very amusing to
read in one's old age. A very kind thought of yours."

"It's rather faded and torn and knocked about,"
said Tuppence, producing her offering.

"Well, well," said Mrs. Griffin, "yes. You know, everyone had a birthday book. Not so much after my
time as a girl. I expect this may be one of the last
ones. All the girls at the school I went to had a birthday book. You know, you wrote your name in your

friend's birthday book and they wrote their names in yours, and so on."

She took the book from Tuppence, opened it and began reading down the pages.

"Oh dear, oh dear," she murmured, "how it takes me back. Yes. Yes indeed. Helen Gilbert—yes, yes of course. And Daisy Sherfield. Sherfield, yes. Oh yes, I remember her. She had to have one of those tooth things in her mouth. A brace, I think they called it. And she was always taking it out. She said she couldn't stand it. And Edie Crone, Margaret Dickson. Ah yes. Good handwriting most of them had. Better than girls have nowadays. As for my nephews' letters; I really can't read them. Their handwriting is like hieroglyphics of some kind. One has to guess what most of the words are. Mollie Short. Ah yes, she had a stammer—it does bring things back."

"I don't suppose there are many of them, I mean—" Tuppence paused, feeling that she might be about to say something tactless.

"You're thinking most of them are dead, I suppose, dear. Well, you're quite right. Most of them are. But not all of them. No. I've still got quite a lot of people living, with whom I was, as they say, girls together. Not living here, because most girls that one knew married and went somewhere else. Either they had husbands who were in the services and they went abroad, or they went to some other different town altogether. Two of my oldest friends live up in Northumberland. Yes, yes, it's very interesting."

"There weren't, I suppose, any Parkinsons left then?" said Tuppence. "I don't see the name anywhere."

"Oh no. It was after the Parkinsons' time. There's something you want to find out about the Parkinsons, isn't there?"

"Oh yes, there is," said Tuppence. "It's pure curiosity, you know, nothing else. But—well, somehow in looking at things I got interested in the boy, Alexander Parkinson, and then, as I was walking through the churchyard the other day, I noticed that he'd died fairly young and his grave was there and that made me think about him more."

"He died young," said Mrs. Griffin. "Yes. Everyone seems to think it was sad that he should have done so. He was a very intelligent boy and they hoped for—well, quite a brilliant future for him. It wasn't really any illness, some food he had in a picnic, I believe. So Mrs. Henderson told me. She remembers a lot about the Parkinsons."

"Mrs. Henderson?" Tuppence looked up.

"Oh, you wouldn't know about her. She's in one of these old people's homes, you know. It's called Meadowside. It's about—oh, about twelve to fifteen miles from here. You ought to go and see her. She'd tell you a lot of things, I expect, about that house you're living in. Swallow's Nest, it was called then, it's called something else, isn't it now?"

"The Laurels."

"Mrs. Henderson is older than I am, although she was the youngest of quite a large family. She was a governess at one time. And then I think she was a kind of nurse-companion with Mrs. Beddingfield who had the Swallow's Nest, I mean The Laurels, then. And she likes talking about old times very much. You ought to go and see her, I think."

"Oh, she wouldn't like—"

"Oh, my dear, I'm sure she *would* like. Go and see her. Just tell her that I suggested it. She remembers me and my sister Rosemary and I do go and see her occasionally, but not of late years because I haven't been able to get about. And you might go and see Mrs. Henley, who lives in—what is it now?—Apple Tree Lodge, I think it is. That's mainly old-age pensioners. Not quite the same class, you know, but it's very well run and there's a lot of gossip going there! I'm sure they'd all be quite pleased with visits. You know, anything to break the monotony."

17

Tommy and Tuppence
Compare Notes

"You look tired, Tuppence," said Tommy as at the close of dinner they went into the sitting room and Tuppence dropped into a chair, uttering several large sighs followed by a yawn.

"Tired? I'm dead beat," said Tuppence.

"What have you been doing? Not things in the garden, I hope."

"I have not been overworking myself physically," said Tuppence coldly. "I've been doing like you. Mental research."

"Also very exhausting, I agree," said Tommy. "Where, particularly? You didn't get an awful lot out of Mrs. Griffin the day before yesterday, did you?"

"Well, I did get a good deal, I think. I didn't get much out of the first recommendation. At least, I suppose I did in a way."

Opening her handbag, she tugged at a notebook of rather tiresome size, and finally got it out.

"I made various notes each time about things. I took some of the china menus along, for one thing."

"Oh. And what did that produce?"

"Well, it set up a large amount of gastronomic remarks. This is the first one. Somebody or other whose name I've now forgotten."

"You must try and remember names better."

"Well, it's not names that I write down so much as the things they say to me and tell me. And they were

144

very thrilled at that china menu because it seemed it was one particular dinner that everyone had enjoyed very much and they had had a wonderful meal—they hadn't had anything like it before, and apparently they had lobster salad for the first time. They'd heard of it being served after the joint in the richest and most fasionable houses, but it hadn't come their way."

"Oh," said Tommy, "that wasn't very helpful."

"Well, yes it was, in a way, because they said they'd always remember that evening. So I said why would they always remember that evening and they said it was because of the census."

"What—a census?"

"Yes. You know what a census is, surely, Tommy? Why, we had one only last year, or was it the year before last? You know—having to say, or making everyone sign or enter particulars. Everyone who slept under your roof on a certain night. You know the sort of thing. On the night of November fifteenth, who did you have sleeping under your roof? And you have to put it down, or they have to sign their names. I forget which. Anyway, they were having a census that day and so everyone had to say who was under their roof, and of course a lot of people were at the party and they talked about it. They said it was very unfair and a very stupid thing to have and that anyway they thought it was really a most disgraceful thing to go on having nowadays, because you had to say if you had children and if you were married, or if you were not married but did have children, and things like that. You had to put down a lot of very difficult particulars and you didn't think it was nice. Not nowadays. So they were very upset about it. I mean, they were upset, not about the old census because nobody minded then. It was just a thing that happened."

"The census might come in useful if you've got the exact date of it," said Tommy.

"Do you mean you could check up about the census?"

"Oh yes. If one knows the right people, I think one could check up fairly easily."

"And they remembered Mary Jordan being talked about. Everyone said what a nice girl she had *seemed* and how fond everyone was of her. And they would never have believed—you know how people say things. Then they said, Well, she was half German so perhaps people ought to have been more careful in engaging her."

Tuppence put down her empty coffee cup and settled back in her chair.

"Anything hopeful?" said Tommy.

"No, not really," said Tuppence, "but it might be. Anyway, the old people talked about it and knew about it. Most of them had heard it from their elderly relations or something. Stories of where they had put things or found things. There was some story about a will that was hidden in a Chinese vase. Something about Oxford and Cambridge, though I don't see how anyone would know about things being hidden in Oxford or Cambridge. It seems very unlikely."

"Perhaps someone had a nephew undergraduate," said Tommy, "who took something back with him to Oxford or Cambridge."

"Possible, I suppose, but not likely."

"Did anyone actually talk about Mary Jordan?"

"Only in the way of hearsay—not of actually knowing definitely about her being a German spy, only from their grandmothers or great-aunts or sisters or mothers' cousins or Uncle John's naval friend who knew all about it."

"Did they talk about how Mary died?"

"They connected her death with the foxglove and spinach episode. Everyone recovered, they said, except her."

"Interesting," said Tommy. "Same story, different setting."

"Too many ideas perhaps," said Tuppence. "Someone called Bessie said, 'Well. It was only my grandmother who talked about that and of course it had all been years before her time and I expect she got some of the details wrong. She usually did, I believe.' You know, Tommy, with everyone talking at once it's all muddled up. There was all the talk about spies and poison on picnics and everything. I couldn't get any exact dates because of course nobody ever knows the exact date of anything your grandmother tells you. If she says, 'I was only sixteen at the time and I was terribly thrilled,' you probably don't know *now* how old your grandmother really was. She'd probably say she was ninety now because people like to say they're older than their age when they get to eighty, or if, of course, she's only about seventy, she says she's only fifty-two."

"*Mary Jordan*," said Tommy thoughtfully, as he quoted the words, "*did not die naturally. He* had his suspicions. Wonder if he ever talked to a policeman about them."

"You mean Alexander?"

"Yes— And perhaps because of that he talked too much. He *had* to die."

"A lot depends on Alexander, doesn't it?" said Tuppence.

"We do know when Alexander died, because of his grave here. But Mary Jordan—we still don't know when or why."

"We'll find out in the end," said Tommy. "You made a few lists of names you've got and dates and things. You'll be surprised. Surprised what one can check up through an odd word or two here and there."

"You seem to have a lot of useful friends," said Tuppence enviously.

"So do you," said Tommy.

"Well, I don't really," said Tuppence.

"Yes, you do, you set people in motion," said Tommy. "You go and see one old lady with a birthday book. The next thing I know you've been all through masses of people in an old pensioners' home or something, and you know all about things that happened at the time of their great-aunts, great-grandmothers, and Uncle Johns and godfathers, and perhaps an old admiral at sea who told tales about espionage and all that. Once we can figure a few dates down and get on with a few inquiries, we might—who knows?—get *something*."

"I wonder who the undergraduates were who were mentioned—Oxford and Cambridge, the ones who were said to have hidden something."

"They don't sound very like espionage," said Tommy.

"No, they don't really," said Tuppence.

"And doctors and old clergymen," said Tommy. "One could, I expect, check up on them, but I don't see it would lead one anywhere. It's all too far away. We're not near enough. We don't know— Has anybody tried anything more funny on you, Tuppence?"

"Do you mean has anyone made an attempt on my life in the last two days? No, they haven't. Nobody's invited me to go on a picnic, the brakes of the car are all right, there's a jar of weed killer in the potting shed, but it doesn't seem to be even opened yet."

"Isaac keeps it there to be handy in case you come out with some sandwiches one day."

"Oh, poor Isaac," said Tuppence. "You are *not* to say things against Isaac. He is becoming one of my best friends. Now I wonder—that reminds me—"

"What does that remind you of?"

"I can't remember," said Tuppence, blinking her eyes. "It reminded me of something when you said that about Isaac."

"Oh dear," said Tommy, and sighed.

"One old lady," said Tuppence, "was said to have always put her things in her mittens every night. Earrings, I think it was. That's the one who thought everyone was poisoning her. And somebody else remembered someone who put things in a missionary box or something. You know, the china thing for the waifs and strays, there was a label stuck onto it. But it wasn't for the waifs and strays at all, apparently. She used to put five-pound notes in it so that she'd always have a nest egg, and when it got too full, she used to take it away and buy another box and break the first one."

"And spend the five pounds, I suppose," said Tommy.

"I suppose that was the idea. My cousin Emlyn used to say," said Tuppence, obviously quoting, "nobody'd rob the waifs and strays or missionaries, would they? If anyone smashed a box like that, somebody'd notice, wouldn't they?"

"You haven't found any books of rather dull-looking sermons, have you, in your book search in those rooms upstairs?"

"No. Why?" asked Tuppence.

"Well, I just thought that'd be a very good place to hide things in. You know, something really boring written about theology. An old crabbed book with the inside scooped out."

"Hasn't been anything like that," said Tuppence. "I should have noticed it if there was."

"Would you have read it?"

"Oh, of course I wouldn't," said Tuppence.

"There you are then," said Tommy. "You wouldn't have read it, you'd have just thrown it away, I expect."

"*The Crown of Success*. That's one book I remember," said Tuppence. "There were two copies of that. Well, let's hope that success will crown our efforts."

"It seems to me very unlikely. Who killed Mary Jordan? That's the book *we'll* have to write one day, I suppose?"

"If we ever find out," said Tuppence gloomily.

18

Possibility of Surgery
on Mathilde

"What are you going to do this afternoon, Tuppence? Go on helping me with these lists of names and dates and things?"

"I don't think so," said Tuppence. "I've had all that. It really is most exhausting writing everything down. Every now and then I do get things a bit wrong, don't I?"

"Well, I wouldn't put it past you. You have made a few mistakes."

"I wish you weren't more accurate than I am, Tommy. I find it so annoying sometimes."

"What are you going to do instead?"

"I wouldn't mind having a good nap. Oh no, I'm not going to actually relax," said Tuppence. "I think I'm going to disembowel Mathilde."

"I beg your pardon, Tuppence."

"I said I was going to disembowel Mathilde."

"What's the matter with you? You seem very set on violence."

"Mathilde—she's in KK."

"What do you mean, she's in KK?"

"Oh, the place where all the dumps are. You know, she's the rocking-horse, the one that's got a hole in her stomach."

"Oh. And—you're going to examine her stomach, is that it?"

"That's the idea," said Tuppence. "Would you like to come and help me?"

"Not really," said Tommy.

"Would you be *kind* enough to come and help me?" suggested Tuppence.

"Put like that," said Tommy, with a deep sigh, "I will force myself to consent. Anyway, it won't be as bad as making lists. Is Isaac anywhere about?"

"No. I think it's his afternoon off. Anyway, we don't want Isaac about. I think I've got all the information I can out of him."

"He knows a good deal," said Tommy thoughtfully. "I found that out the other day. He was telling me a lot of things about the past. Things he can't remember himself."

"Well, he must be nearly eighty," said Tuppence, "I'm quite sure of that."

"Yes, I know, but remembered things really far back."

"People have always *heard* so many things," said Tuppence. "You never know if they're right or not in what they've heard. Anyway, let's go and disembowel Mathilde. I'd better change my clothes first because it's excessively dusty and cobwebby in KK and we have to burrow right inside her."

"You might get Isaac if he's about to turn her up-side-down, then we could get at her stomach more easily."

"You really sound as though in your last reincarnation you must have been a surgeon," said Tommy.

"Well, I suppose it is a little like that. We are now going to remove foreign matter which might be dangerous to the preservation of Mathilde's life, such as is left of it. We might have her painted up and Deborah's twins perhaps would like to ride on her when they next came to stay."

"Oh, our grandchildren have so many toys and presents already."

"That won't matter," said Tuppence. "Children

don't particularly like expensive presents. They'll play
with an old bit of string or a rag doll or something
they call a pet bear which is only a bit of a hearth
rug just made up into a bundle with a couple of black
boot-button eyes put on it. Children have their own
ideas about toys."

"Well, come on," said Tommy. "Forward to Mathilde. To the operating theater."

The reversal of Mathilde to a position suitable for
the necessary operation to take place was not an easy
job. Mathilde was a very fair weight. In addition to
that, she was very well studded with various nails
which would on occasions remove their position, and
which had points sticking out. Tuppence wiped blood
from her hand and Tommy swore as he caught his
pullover which immediately tore itself in a somewhat
disastrous fashion.

"Blow this damned rocking-horse," said Tommy.

"Ought to have been put on a bonfire years ago,"
said Tuppence.

It was at that moment that the aged Isaac suddenly
appeared and joined them.

"Whatever now!" he said with some surprise.
"Whatever be you two doing here now? What do you
want with this old bit of horse-flesh here? Can I help
you at all? What do you want to do with it? Do you
want it taken out of here?"

"Not necessarily," said Tuppence. "We want to turn
it upside-down so that we can get at the hole there
and pull things out."

"You mean pull things out from inside her, as you
might say? Who's been putting that idea into your
head?"

"Yes," said Tuppence, "that's what we do mean to
do."

"What do you think you'll find there?"

"Nothing but rubbish, I expect," said Tommy. "But
it would be nice," he said in a rather doubtful voice,
"if things were cleared up a bit, you know. We might

want to keep other things in here. You know—games, perhaps, a croquet set. Something like that."

"There used to be a crookey lawn once. Long time ago. That was in Mrs. Faulkner's time. Yes. Down where the rose garden is now. Mind you, it wasn't a full-size one."

"When was that?" asked Tommy.

"What, you mean the crookey lawn? Oh, well before my time, it was. There's always people as want to tell you things about what used to happen—things as used to be hidden and why and who wanted to hide them. Lot of tall stories, some of them lies. Some maybe as was true."

"You're very clever, Isaac," said Tuppence. "You always seem to know about everything. How do you know about the croquet lawn?"

"Oh, used to be a box of crookey things in here. Been there for years. Shouldn't think there's much of it left now."

Tuppence relinquished Mathilde and went over to a corner where there was a long wooden box. After releasing the lid with some difficulty, as it had stuck under the ravages of time, it yielded a faded red ball, a blue ball and one mallet bent and warped. The rest of it was mainly cobwebs.

"Might have been in Mrs. Faulkner's time, that might. They do say, you know, as she played in the tournaments in her time," said Isaac.

"At Wimbledon?" said Tuppence, incredulous.

"Well, not exactly at Wimbledon, I don't think it was. No. The locals, you know. They used to have them down here. Pictures I've seen down at the photographer's—"

"The photographer's?"

"Ah. In the village. Durrance. You know Durrance, don't you?"

"Durrance?" said Tuppence vaguely. "Oh yes, he sells films and things like that, doesn't he?"

"That's right. Mind you, he's not the old Durrance,

as manages it now. It's his grandson, or his great-grandson, I shouldn't wonder. He sells mostly post cards, you know, and Christmas cards and birthday cards and things like that. He used to take photographs of people. Got a whole lot tucked away. Somebody come in the other day, you know. Wanted a picture of her great-grandmother, she said. She said she'd had one but she'd broken it or burnt it or lost it or something, and she wondered if there was the negative left. But I don't think she found it. But there's a lot of old albums in there stuck away somewhere."

"Albums," said Tuppence thoughtfully.

"Anything more I can do?" said Isaac.

"Well, just give us a bit of a hand with Jane, or whatever her name is."

"Not Jane, it's Mathilde, and it's not Matilda either, which it ought by rights to be, I should say. I believe it was always called Mathilde, for some reason. French, I expect."

"French or American," said Tommy thoughtfully. "Mathilde. Louise. That sort of thing."

"Quite a good place to have hidden things, don't you think?" said Tuppence, placing her arm into the cavity in Mathilde's stomach. She drew out a dilapidated India rubber ball, which had once been red and yellow but which now had gaping holes in it.

"I suppose that's children," said Tuppence. "They always put things in like this."

"Whenever they see a hole," said Isaac. "But there was a young gentleman once as used to leave his letters in it, so I've heard. Same as though it was a post-box."

"Letters? Who were they for?"

"Some young lady, I'd think. But it was before my time," said Isaac, as usual.

"The things that always happened long before Isaac's time," said Tuppence, as Isaac, having adjusted Mathilde into a good position, left them on the pretext of having to shut up the frames.

Tommy removed his jacket.

"It's incredible," said Tuppence, panting a little as she removed a scratched and dirty arm from the gaping wound in Mathilde's stomach, "that anyone could put so many things or want to put them in this thing, and that nobody should ever have cleaned it out."

"Well, why should anyone clean it out? Why would anyone want to clean it out?"

"That's true," said Tuppence. "We do, though, don't we?"

"Only because we can't think of anything better to do. I don't think anything will come of it, though. Ow!"

"What's the matter?" said Tuppence.

"Oh, I scratched myself on something."

He drew his arm out slightly, readjusted it, and felt inside once more. A knitted scarf rewarded him. It had clearly been the sustenance of moths at one time and possibly after that had descended to an even lower level of social life.

"Disgusting," said Tommy.

Tuppence pushed him aside slightly and fished in with her own arm, leaning over Mathilde while she felt about inside.

"Mind the nails," said Tommy.

"What's this?" said Tuppence.

She brought her find out into the open air. It appeared to be the wheel off a bus or cart of some child's toy.

"I think," she said, "we're wasting our time."

"I'm sure we are," said Tommy.

"All the same, we might as well do it properly," said Tuppence. "Oh dear, I've got three spiders walking up my arm. It'll be a worm in a minute, and I hate worms."

"I don't think there'll be any worms inside Mathilde. I mean, worms like going underground in the

earth. I don't think they'd care for Mathilde as a
boarding house, do you?"

"Oh well, it's getting empty at any rate, I think,"
said Tuppence. "Hullo, what's this? Dear me, it seems
to be a needlebook. What a funny thing to find.
There's still some needles in it, but they're all rusted."

"Some child who didn't like to do her sewing, I expect," said Tommy.

"Yes, that's a good idea."

"I touched something that felt like a book just
now," said Tommy.

"Oh. Well, that might be helpful. What part of Mathilde?"

"I should think the appendix or the liver," said
Tommy in a professional tone. "On her right-hand
side. I'm regarding this as an operation!" he added.

"All right, surgeon. Better pull it out, whatever it
is."

The so-called book, barely recognizable as such,
was of very ancient lineage. Its pages were loose and
stained, and its binding was coming to pieces.

"It seems to be a manual of French," said Tommy.
"Pour les enfants. Le Petit Précepteur."

"I see," said Tuppence. "I've got the same idea as
you had. The child didn't want to learn her French
lesson, so she came in here and deliberately lost it by
putting it into Mathilde. Good old Mathilde."

"If Mathilde was right-side-up, it must have been
very difficult putting things through this hole in her
stomach."

"Not for a child," said Tuppence. "She'd be quite
the right height and everything. I mean, she'd just
kneel and crawl underneath it. Hullo, here's something which feels slippery. Feels rather like an ani-
mal's skin."

"How very unpleasant," said Tommy. "Do you
think it's a dead rabbit or something?"

"Well, it's not furry or anything. I don't think it's
very nice. Oh dear, there's a nail again. Well, it seems

to be hung on a nail. There's a sort of bit of string or cord. Funny it hasn't rotted away, isn't it?"

She drew out her find cautiously.

"It's a sort of pocketbook," she said. "Yes. Yes, it's been quite good leather once, I think. Quite good leather."

"Let's see what's inside it, if there is anything inside it," said Tommy.

"There's something inside it," said Tuppence. "Perhaps it's a lot of five-pound notes, she added hopefully.

"Well, I don't suppose they'd be usable still. Paper would rot, wouldn't it?"

"I don't know," said Tuppence. "A lot of queer things do survive, you know. I think five-pound notes used to be made of wonderfully good paper once, you know. Sort of thin but very durable."

"Oh well, perhaps it's a twenty-pound note. It will help with the housekeeping."

"What? The money'll be before Isaac's time too, I expect, or else he'd have found it. Ah well. Think! It might be a hundred-pound note. I wish it were golden sovereigns. Sovereigns were always in purses. My Great-Aunt Maria had a great purse full of sovereigns. She used to show it to us children. It was her nest egg, she said, in case the French came. I think it was the French. Anyway, it was for extremities or danger. Lovely fat golden sovereigns. I used to think it was wonderful and I'd think how lovely it would be, you know, once one was grown up and you'd have a purse full of sovereigns."

"Who was going to give you a purse full of sovereigns?"

"I didn't think of anyone giving it to me," said Tuppence. "I thought of it as the sort of thing that belonged to you as a right, once you were a grown-up person. You know, a real grownup wearing a mantle—that's what they called the things. A mantle with a sort of fur boa round it and a bonnet. You had this great fat purse jammed full of sovereigns, and if you had a favorite grandson who was going back to school, you always gave him a sovereign as a tip."

"What about the girls, the granddaughters?"

"I don't think they got any sovereigns," said Tuppence. "But sometimes she used to send me half a five-pound note."

"*Half* a five-pound note? That wouldn't be much good."

"Oh yes, it was. She used to tear the five-pound note in half, send me one half first and then the other half in another letter later. You see, it was supposed in that way that nobody'd want to steal it."

"Oh dear, what a lot of precautions everyone did take."

"They did rather," said Tuppence. "Hullo, what's this?"

She was fumbling now in the leather case.

"Let's get out of KK for a minute," said Tommy, "and get some air."

They got outside KK. In the air they saw better what their trophy was like. It was a thick leather wallet of good quality. It was stiff with age, but not in any way destroyed.

"I expect it was kept from damp inside Mathilde," said Tuppence. "Oh, Tommy, do you know what I think this is?"

"No. What? It isn't money anyway. And certainly not sovereigns."

"Oh no, it isn't money," said Tuppence, "but I think it's letters. I don't know whether we'll be able to read them now. They're very old and faded."

Very carefully Tommy arranged the crinkled yellow paper of the letters, pushing them apart when he could. The writing was quite large and had once been written in a very deep blue-black ink.

"Meeting place changed," said Tommy. "Ken Gardens near Peter Pan. Wednesday 25th, 3.30 P.M. Joanna."

"I really believe," said Tuppence, "we might have something at last."

"You mean that someone who'd be going to London was told to go on a certain day and meet someone in Kensington Gardens bringing perhaps the papers or the plans or whatever it was. Who do you think got these things out of Mathilde or put them into Mathilde?"

"It couldn't have been a child," said Tuppence. "It must have been someone who lived in the house and so could move about without being noticed. Got things from the naval spy, I suppose, and took them to London."

Tuppence wrapped up the old leather wallet in the scarf she'd been wearing round her neck and she and Tommy returned to the house.

"There may be other papers in there," said Tuppence, "but most of them I think are perished and will more or less fall to pieces if you touch them. Hallo, what's this?"

On the hall table a rather bulky package was lying. Albert came out from the dining room.

"It was left by hand, madam," he said. "Left by hand this morning for you."

"Ah, I wonder what it is," said Tuppence. She took it.

Tommy and she went into the sitting room together. Tuppence undid the knot of the string and took off the brown paper wrapping.

"It's a kind of album," she said, "I think. Oh, there's a note with it. Ah, it's from Mrs. Griffin.

"Dear Mrs. Beresford, It was so kind of you to bring me the birthday book the other day. I have had great pleasure looking over it and remembering various people from past days. One does forget so soon. Very often one only remembers somebody's Christian name and not their surname, sometimes it's the other way about. I came across, a little time ago, this old album.

It doesn't really belong to me. I think it belonged to
my grandmother, but it has a good many pictures in it
and among them, I think, there are one or two of the
Parkinsons, because my grandmother knew the Parkinsons. I thought perhaps you would like to see it as you
seemed to be so interested in the history of your house
and who has lived in it in the past. Please don't bother
to send it back to me because it means nothing to me
personally really, I can assure you. One has so many
things in the house always belonging to aunts and
grandmothers and the other day when I was looking
in an old chest of drawers in the attic I came across six
needlebooks. Years and years old. I should think almost possibly a hundred years old. And I believe that
was not my grandmother but her grandmother again
who used at one time always to give a needlebook
each to the maids for Christmas and I think these
were some she had bought at a sale and would do for
another year. Of course quite useless now. Sometimes
it seems sad to think of how much waste there has always been.

A photo album," said Tuppence. "Well, that might be
fun. Come along, let's have a look."

They sat down on the sofa. The album was very
typical of bygone days. Most of the prints were faded
by now, but every now and then Tuppence managed
to recognize surroundings that fitted the gardens of
their own house.

"Look, there's the monkey puzzle. Yes—and look,
there's Truelove behind it. That must be a very old
photograph, and a funny little boy hanging on to
Truelove. Yes, and there's the wisteria and there's the
pampas grass. I suppose it must have been a tea
party or something. Yes, there are a lot of people sitting round a table in the garden. They've got names
underneath them too. Mabel. Mabel's no beauty. And
who's that?"

"Charles," said Tommy. "Charles and Edmund.

Charles and Edmund seem to have been playing tennis. They've got rather queer tennis racquets. And there's William, whoever he was, and Major Coates."

"And there's—oh, Tommy, there's Mary."

"Yes. Mary Jordan. Both names there, written under the photograph."

"She was pretty. Very pretty, I think. It is very faded and old, but—oh, Tommy, it really seems wonderful to see Mary Jordan."

"I wonder who took the photograph?"

"Perhaps the photographer that Isaac mentioned. The one in the village here. Perhaps he'd have old photographs, too. I think perhaps one day we'll go and ask."

Tommy had pushed aside the album by now and was opening a letter which had come in the midday post.

"Anything interesting?" asked Tuppence. "There are three letters here. Two are bills, I can see. This one—yes, this one is rather different. I asked you if it was interesting," said Tuppence.

"It may be," said Tommy. "I'll have to go to London tomorrow again."

"To deal with your usual committees?"

"Not exactly," said Tommy. "I'm going to call on someone. Actually it isn't London, it's out of London. Somewhere Harrow way, I gather."

"What is?" said Tuppence. "You haven't told me yet."

"I'm going to call on someone called Colonel Pikeaway."

"What a name," said Tuppence.

"Yes, it is rather, isn't it?"

"Have I ever heard it before?" said Tuppence.

"I may have mentioned it to you once. He lives in a kind of permanent atmosphere of smoke. Have you got any cough lozenges, Tuppence?"

"Cough lozenges! Well, I don't know. Yes, I think I have. I've got an old box of them from last winter.

But you haven't got a cough—not that I've noticed, at
any rate."

"No, but I shall have if I'm going to see Pikeaway.
As far as I can remember, you take two choking
breaths and then you go on choking. You look hopefully at all the windows which are tightly shut, but
Pikeaway would never take a hint of that kind."

"Why do you think he wants to see you?"

"Can't imagine," said Tommy. "He mentions Robinson."

"What—the yellow one? The one who's got a fat
yellow face and is something very hush-hush?"

"That's the one," said Tommy.

"Oh well," said Tuppence, "perhaps what we're
mixed up in here is hush-hush."

"Hardly could be considering it all took place—
whatever it was, if there is anything—years and years
ago, before even Isaac can remember."

"New sins have old shadows," said Tuppence, "if
that's the saying I mean. I haven't got it quite right.
New sins have old shadows. Or is it Old sins make
long shadows?"

"I should forget it," said Tommy. "None of them
sounds right."

"I shall go and see that photographer man this afternoon, I think. Want to come?"

"No," said Tommy. "I think I shall go down and
bathe."

"Bathe? It'll be awfully cold."

"Never mind. I feel I need something cold, bracing
and refreshing to remove all the taste of cobwebs, the
various remains of which seem to be clinging round
my ears and round my neck and some even seem to
have got between my toes."

"This does seem a very dirty job," said Tuppence.
"Well, I'll go and see Mr. Durrell or Durrance, if
that's his name. There was another letter, Tommy,
which you haven't opened."

"Oh, I didn't see it. Ah well, that might be something."

"Who is it from?"

"My researcher," said Tommy in a rather grand voice. "The one who has been running about England, in and out of Somerset House looking up deaths, marriages and births, consulting newspaper files and census returns. She's very good."

"Good and beautiful?"

"Not beautiful so that you'd notice it," said Tommy.

"I'm glad of that," said Tuppence. "You know, Tommy, now that you're getting on in years you might—you might get some rather dangerous ideas about a beautiful helper."

"You don't appreciate a faithful husband when you've got one," said Tommy.

"All my friends tell me you never know with husbands," said Tuppence.

"You have the wrong kind of friends," said Tommy.

19

Interview with Colonel Pikeaway

Tommy drove through Regent's Park, then he passed
through various roads he'd not been through for
years. Once when he and Tuppence had had a flat
near Belsize Park, he remembered walks on Hampstead Heath and a dog they had had who'd enjoyed
the walks. A dog with a particularly self-willed
nature. When coming out of the flat, he had always
wished to turn to the left on the road that would lead
to Hampstead Heath. The efforts of Tuppence or
Tommy to make him turn to the right and go into
shopping quarters were usually defeated. James, a
Sealyham of obstinate nature, had allowed his heavy
sausage-like body to rest flat on the pavement, he
would produce a tongue from his mouth and give every semblance of being a dog tired out by being
given the wrong kind of exercise by those who owned
him. People passing by usually could not refrain from
comment.

"Oh, look at that dear little dog there. You know,
the one with the white hair—looks rather like a sausage, doesn't he? And panting, poor fellow. Those people of his, they won't let him go the way he wants to,
he looks tired out, just tired out."

Tommy had taken the lead from Tuppence and
had pulled James firmly in the opposite direction
from the one he wanted to go.

"Oh dear," said Tuppence, "can't you pick him up, Tommy?"

"What, pick up James? He's too much of a weight."

James, with a clever maneuver, turned his sausage body so that he was facing once more in the direction of his expectation.

"Look, poor little doggie, I expect he wants to go home, don't you?"

James tugged firmly on his lead.

"Oh, all right," said Tuppence, "we'll shop later. Come on, we'll have to let James go where he wants to go. He's such a heavy dog, you can't make him do anything else."

James looked up and wagged his tail. "I quite agree with you," the wag seemed to say. "You've got the point at last. Come on. Hampstead Heath it is." And it usually had been.

Tommy wondered. He'd got the address of the place where he was going. The last time he had been to see Colonel Pikeaway it had been in Bloomsbury. A small poky room full of smoke. Here, when he reached the address, it was a small, nondescript house fronting on the heath not far from the birthplace of Keats. It did not look particularly artistic or interesting.

Tommy rang the bell. An old woman with a close resemblance to what Tommy imagined a witch might look like, with a sharp nose and a sharp chin which almost met each other, stood there, looking hostile.

"Can I see Colonel Pikeaway?"

"Don't know, I'm sure," said the witch. "Who would you be now?"

"My name is Beresford."

"Oh, I see. Yes. He did say something about that."

"Can I leave the car outside?"

"Yes, it'll be all right for a bit. Don't get many of the wardens poking around this street. No yellow lines just along here. Better lock it up, sir. You never know."

Tommy attended to these rules as laid down, and followed the old woman into the house.

"One flight up," she said, "not more."

Already on the stairs there was the strong smell of tobacco. The witch-woman tapped at a door, poked her head in, said, "This must be the gentleman you wanted to see. Says you're expecting him." She stood aside and Tommy passed into what he remembered before, an aroma of smoke which forced him almost immediately to choke and gulp. He doubted he would have remembered Colonel Pikeaway apart from the smoke and the cloud and smell of nicotine. A very old man lay back in an armchair—a somewhat ragged armchair with holes on the arms of it. He looked up thoughtfully as Tommy entered.

"Shut the door, Mrs. Copes," he said, "don't want to let the cold air in, do we?"

Tommy rather thought that they did, but obviously it was his not to reason why, his but to inhale and in due course die, he presumed.

"Thomas Beresford," said Colonel Pikeaway thoughtfully. "Well, well, how many years is it since I saw you?"

Tommy had not made a proper computation.

"Long time ago," said Colonel Pikeaway, "came here with what's-his-name, didn't you? Ah well, never mind, one name's as good as another. A rose by any other name would smell as sweet. Juliet said that, didn't she? Silly things sometimes Shakespeare made them say. Of course, he couldn't help it, he was a poet. Never cared much for Romeo and Juliet myself. All those suicides for love's sake. Plenty of 'em about, mind you. Always happening, even nowadays. Sit down, my boy, sit down."

Tommy was slightly startled at being called "my boy" again, but he availed himself of the invitation.

"You don't mind, sir," he said, dispossessing the only possible seeming chair of a large pile of books.

"No, no, shove 'em all on the floor. Just trying to

look something up, I was. Well, well, I'm pleased to see you. You look a bit older than you did, but you look quite healthy. Ever had a coronary?"

"No," said Tommy.

"Ah! Good. Too many people suffering from hearts, blood pressure—all those things. Doing too much. That's what it is. Running about all over the place, telling everyone how busy they are and the world can't get on without them, and how important they are and everything else. Do you feel the same? I expect you do."

"No," said Tommy, "I don't feel very important. I feel—well, I feel that I really would enjoy relaxing nowadays."

"Well, it's a splendid thought," said Colonel Pike-away. "The trouble is there are so many people about who won't let you relax. What took you to this place of yours where you're living now? I've forgotten the name of it. Just tell me again, will you?"

Tommy obliged with his address.

"Ah yes, ah yes, I put the right thing on the envelope then."

"Yes, I got your letter."

"I understand you've been to see Robinson. He's still going. Just as fat as ever, just as yellow as ever, and just as rich or richer than ever, I expect. Knows all about it, too. Knows about money, I mean. What took you there, boy?"

"Well, we had bought a new house, and a friend of mine advised me that Mr. Robinson might be able to clear up a mystery that my wife and I found connected with it, relating to a long time back."

"I remember now. I don't believe I ever met her, but you've got a clever wife, haven't you? Did some sterling work in the—what is the thing? Sounded like the catechism. N or M, that was it, wasn't it?"

"Yes," said Tommy.

"And now you're onto the same line again, are you? Looking into things. Had suspicions, had you?"

"No," said Tommy, "that's entirely wrong. We only went there because we were tired of the flat we were living in and they kept putting up the rent."

"Nasty trick," said Colonel Pikeaway. "They do that to you nowadays, the landlords. Never satisfied. Talk about Daughters of the Horse Leech—sons of the horse leech are just as bad. All right, you went there to live. *Il faut cultiver son jardin*," said Colonel Pikeaway, with a rather sudden onslaught on the French language. "Trying to rub up my French again," he explained. "Got to keep in with the Common Market nowadays, haven't we? Funny stuff going on there, by the way. You know, behind things. Not what you see on the surface. So you went to live at Swallow's Nest. What took you to Swallow's Nest, I'd like to know?"

"The house we bought—well, it's called The Laurels now," said Tommy.

"Silly name," said Colonel Pikeaway. "Very popular at one time, though. I remember when I was a boy, all the neighbors, you know, they had those great Victorian drives up to the house. Always getting in loads of gravel for putting down on it and laurels on each side. Sometimes they were glossy green ones and sometimes the speckled ones. Supposed to be very showy. I suppose some of the people who've lived there called it that and the name stuck. Is that right?"

"Yes, I think so," said Tommy. "Not the last people. I believe the last people called it Katmandu, or some name abroad because they lived in a certain place they liked."

"Yes, yes. Swallow's Nest goes back a long time. Yes, but one's got to go back sometimes. In fact, that's what I was going to talk to you about. Going back."

"Did you ever know it, sir?"

"What—Swallow's Nest, alias The Laurels? No, I never went there. But it figured in certain things. It's tied up with certain periods in the past. People over a certain period. A period of great anxiety to this country."

"I gather you've come in contact with some information pertaining to someone called Mary Jordan. Or known by that name. Anyway, that's what Mr. Robinson told us," said Tommy.

"Want to see what she looked like? Go over to the mantelpiece. There's a photograph on the left side."

Tommy got up, went across to the mantelpiece and picked up the photograph. It represented an old-world type of photograph. A girl wearing a picture hat and holding up a bunch of roses towards her head.

"Looks damn silly now, doesn't it?" said Colonel Pikeaway. "But she was a good-looking girl, I believe. Unlucky, though. She died young. Rather a tragedy, that was."

"I don't know anything about her," said Tommy.

"No, I don't suppose so," said Colonel Pikeaway. "Nobody does nowadays."

"There was some idea locally that she was a German spy," said Tommy. "Mr. Robinson told me that wasn't the case."

"No, it wasn't the case. She belonged to us. And she did good work for us, too. But somebody got wise to her."

"That was when there were some people called Parkinson living there," said Tommy.

"Maybe. Maybe. I don't know all the details. Nobody does much nowadays. I wasn't personally involved, you know. All this has been raked up since. Because, you see, there's always trouble. There's trouble in every country. There's trouble all over the world now and not for the first time. No. You can go back a hundred years, you'll find trouble, and you can go back another hundred years and you'll find trouble. Go back to the Crusades and you'll find everyone dashing out of the country going to deliver Jerusalem, or you'll find risings all over the country. Wat Tyler and all the rest of them. This, that and the other, there's always trouble."

"Do you mean there's some special trouble now?"

"Of course there is. I tell you, there's always trouble."

"What sort of trouble?"

"Oh, we don't know," said Colonel Pikeaway. "They even come round to an old man like me and ask me what I can tell them, or what I can remember about certain people in the past. Well, I can't remember very much, but I know about one or two people. You've got to look into the past sometimes. You've got to know what was happening then. What secrets people had, what knowledge they had that they kept to themselves, what they hid away, what they pretended was happening and what was really happening. You've done good jobs, you and your missus at different times. Do you want to go on with it now?"

"I don't know," said Tommy. "If—well, do you think there is anything I could do? I'm rather an old man now."

"Well, you look to me as though you've got better health than many people of your age. Look to me as though you've got better health than some of the younger ones, too. And as for your wife, well, she was always good at nosing out things, wasn't she? Yes, good as a well-trained dog."

Tommy could not repress a smile.

"But what is this all about?" said Tommy. "I—of course I'm quite willing to do anything if—if you thought I could, but I don't know. Nobody's *told* me anything."

"I don't suppose they will," said Colonel Pikeaway. "I don't think they want me to tell you anything. I don't suppose that Robinson told you much. He keeps his mouth shut, that large fat man. But I'll tell you, well, the bare facts. You know what the world's like—well, the same things always. Violence, swindles, materialism, rebellion by the young, love of violence and a good deal of sadism, almost as bad as the days of the Hitler Youth. All those things. Well, when you want to find out what's wrong not only with this country but world trouble as well, it's not easy. It's a good thing, the Common Market. It's what we always needed, always wanted. But it's got to be a real Common Market. That's got to be understood very clearly. It's got to be a united Europe. There's got to be a union of civilized countries with civilized ideas and with civilized beliefs and principles. The first thing is, when there's something wrong you've got to know where that something is and that's where that yellow whale of a fellow still knows his oats."

"You mean Mr. Robinson?"

"Yes, I mean Mr. Robinson. They wanted to give him a peerage, you know, but he wouldn't have it. And you know what *he* means."

"I suppose," said Tommy, "you mean he stands for—*money.*"

"That's right. Not materialism, but he *knows* about money. He knows where it comes from, he knows where it goes, he knows why it goes, he knows who's behind things. Behind banks, behind big industrial undertakings, and he has to know who is responsible for certain things, big fortunes made out of drugs, drug pushers, drugs being sent all over the world, being marketed, a worship of money. Money not just for buying yourself a big house and two Rolls-Royces, but money for making more money and doing away with the old beliefs. Beliefs in honesty, in fair trading. You don't want equality in the world, you want the strong to help the weak. You want the rich to finance the poor. You want the honest and the good to be looked up to and admired. Finance! Things are coming back now to finance all the time. What finance is doing, where it's going, what it's supporting, how far hidden it is. There are people you knew, people in the past who had power and brains and their power and brains brought the money and means, and some of their activities were secret, but we've got to find out about them. Find out who their secrets passed to, who they've been handed down to, who may be running things now. Swallow's Nest was a type of headquarters. A headquarters of what I should call evil. Later in Hollowquay there was something else. D'you remember Jonathan Kane at all?"

"It's a name," said Tommy. "I don't remember anything personally."

"Well, he was said to be what was admired at one time—what came to be known later as a fascist. That was the time before we knew what Hitler was going to be like and all the rest of them. The time when we thought that something like fascism might be a splendid idea to reform the world with. This chap Jonathan Kane had followers. A lot of followers. Young followers, middle-aged followers, a lot of them. He had plans, he had sources of power, he knew the secrets of a lot of people. He had the kind of knowledge that gave him power. Plenty of blackmail about as always. We want to know what he knew, we want to know what he did, and I think it's possible that he left both plans and followers behind him. Young people who were enmeshed and perhaps still are in favor of his ideas.

"There have been secrets, you know; there are always secrets that are worth money. I'm not telling you anything exact because I don't know anything exact. The trouble with me is that nobody really knows. We think we know everything because of what we've been through. Wars, turmoil, peace, new forms of government. We think we know it all, but do we? Do we know anything about germ warfare? Do we know everything about gases, about means of inducing pollution? The chemists have their secrets, medical science has its secrets, the services have their secrets, the navy, the air force—all sorts of things. And they're not all in the present; some of them were in the past. Some of them were on the point of being developed, but the development didn't take place. There wasn't time for it. But it was written down, it was committed to paper or committed to certain people, and those people had children and their children had children and maybe some of the things came down. Left in wills, left in documents, left with solicitors to be delivered at a certain time.

"Some people don't know what it is they've got hold of, some of them have just destroyed it as rubbish. But we've got to find out a little more than we do because things are happening all the time. In different countries, in different places, in wars, in Vietnam, in guerrilla wars, in Jordan, in Israel, even in the uninvolved countries. In Sweden and Switzerland—anywhere. There are these things and we want clues to them. And there's some idea that some of the clues could be found in the past. Well, you can't go back into the past, you can't go to a doctor and say, 'Hypnotize me and let me see what happened in nineteen fourteen,' or in nineteen eighteen or earlier still, perhaps. In eighteen ninety, perhaps. Something was being planned, something was never completely developed. Ideas. Just look far back. They were thinking of flying, you know, in the Middle Ages. They had some ideas about it. The ancient Egyptians, I believe, had certain ideas. They were never developed. But once the ideas passed on, once you come to the time when they get into the hands of someone who has the means and the kind of brain that can develop them, anything may happen—bad or good. We have a feeling lately that some of the things that have been invented—germ warfare, for example—are difficult to explain except through the process of some secret development, thought to be unimportant, but it hasn't been unimportant. Somebody in whose hands it's got has made some adaptation of it which can produce very, very frightening results. Things that can change a character, can perhaps turn a good man into a fiend, and usually for the same reason. For money.

Money and what money can buy, what money can get. The power that money can develop. Well, young Beresford, what do you say to all that?"

"I think it's a very frightening prospect," said Tommy.

"That, yes. But do you think I'm talking nonsense? Do you think this is just an old man's fantasies?"

"No, sir," said Tommy. "I think you're a man who knows things. You always have been a man who knew things."

"H'm. That's why they wanted me, wasn't it? They came here, complained about all the smoke, said it stifled them, but—well, you know there's a time—a time when there was that Frankfurt ring business—well, we managed to stop that. We managed to stop it by getting at who was behind it. There's a some-body, not just one somebody—several somebodies who are probably behind this. Perhaps we can know who they are, but even if not, we can know perhaps what the things are."

"I see," said Tommy, "I can almost understand."

"Can you? Don't you think this is all rather non-sense? Rather fantastic?"

"I don't think anything's too fantastic to be true," said Tommy. "I've learnt that, at least, through a pretty long life. The most amazing things are true, things you couldn't believe could be true. But what I have to make you understand is that I have no quali-fications. I have no scientific knowledge. I have been concerned always with security."

"But," said Colonel Pikeaway, "you're a man who has always been able to find out things. You. You—and the other one. Your wife. I tell you, she's got a nose for things. She likes to find out things and you go about and take her about. These women are like that. They can get at secrets. If you're young and beautiful, you do it like Delilah. When you're old—I can tell you, I had an old great-aunt once and there was no secret that she didn't nose into and find out the truth about. There's the money side. Robinson's onto that. He knows about money. He knows where the money goes, why it goes, where it goes to, and where it comes *from* and what it's *doing*. All the rest of it. He knows about money. It's like a doctor feeling your pulse. He can feel a financier's pulse. Where the headquarters of money are. Who's using it, what for and why. I'm putting you onto this because you're in the right place. You're in the right place by accident and you're not there for the reason anyone might suppose you were. For there you are, an ordinary couple, elderly, retired, seeking for a nice house to end your days in, poking about into the corners of it, interested in talking. Some sentence one day will tell you something. That's all I want you to do. Look about. Find out what legends or stories are told about the good old days or the bad old days."

"A naval scandal, plans of a submarine or something, that's talked about still," said Tommy. "Several people keep mentioning it. But nobody seems to know anything really about it."

"Yes, well, that's a good starting point. It was round about then Jonathan Kane lived in that part, you know. He had a cottage down near the sea and he ran his propaganda campaign round there. He had disciples who thought he was wonderful. Jonathan Kane. K-a-n-e. But I would rather spell it a different way. I'd spell it C-a-i-n. That would describe him better. He was set on destruction and methods of destruction. He left England. He went through Italy to countries rather far away, so it's said. How much is rumor, I don't know. He went to Russia. He went to Iceland, he went to the American continent. Where he went and what he did and who went with him and listened to him, we don't know. But we think that he knew things, simple things; he was popular with his neighbors, he lunched with them and they with him. Now, one thing I've got to tell you. Look about you. Ferret out things, but for goodness' sake take care of yourselves, both of you. Take care of that—what's-her-name? Prudence?"

"Nobody ever called her Prudence. Tuppence," said Tommy.

"That's right. Take care of Tuppence and tell Tuppence to take care of you. Take care of what you eat and what you drink and where you go and who is making up to you and being friendly and why should they? A little information comes along. Something odd or queer. Some story in the past that might mean something. Someone perhaps who's a descendant or a relative or someone who knew people in the past."

"I'll do what I can," said Tommy. "We both will. But I don't feel that we'll be able to do it. We're too old. We don't know enough."

"You can have ideas."

"Yes. Tuppence has ideas. She thinks that something might be hidden in our house."

"So it might. Others have had the same idea. Nobody's ever found anything so far, but then they haven't really looked with any assurance at all. Various houses and various families, they change. They get sold and somebody else comes and then somebody else and so they go on. Lestranges and Mortimers and Parkinsons. Nothing much in the Parkinsons except for one of the boys."

"Alexander Parkinson?"

"So you know about him. How did you manage that?"

"He left a message for someone to find in one of Robert Louis Stevenson's books. *Mary Jordan did not die naturally.* We found it."

"The fate of every man we have bound about his neck—some saying like that, isn't there? Carry on, you two. Pass through the Postern of Fate."

20

Postern of Fate

Mr. Durrance's shop was halfway up the village. It was on a corner site, had a few photographs displayed in a window, a couple of marriage groups, a kicking baby in a nudist condition on a rug, one or two bearded young men taken with their girls. None of the photographs were very good; some of them already displayed signs of age. There were also post cards in large numbers; birthday cards and a few special shelves arranged in orders of relationships. To my Husband. To my Wife. One or two bathing groups. There were a few pocketbooks and wallets of rather poor quality and a certain amount of stationery and envelopes bearing floral designs. Boxes of small notepaper decorated with flowers and labeled For Notes.

Tuppence wandered about a little, picking up various specimens of the merchandise and waiting while a discussion about the results obtained from a certain camera were criticized, and advice was asked.

An elderly woman with gray hair and rather lackluster eyes attended to a good deal of the more ordinary requests. A rather tall young man with long flaxen hair and a budding beard seemed to be the principal attendant. He came along the counter towards Tuppence, looking at her questioningly.

"Can I help you in any way?"

"Really," said Tuppence, "I wanted to ask about albums. You know, photograph albums."

"Ah, things to stick your photos in, you mean? Well, we've got one or two of those but you don't get

177

so much of them nowadays, I mean, people go very
largely for transparencies, of course."

"Yes, I understand," said Tuppence, "but I collect
them, you know. I collect old albums. Ones like this."

She produced, with the air of a conjurer, the album
she'd been sent.

"Ah, that goes back a long time, doesn't it?" said
Mr. Durrance. "Ah, well now, over fifty years old, I
should say. Of course, they did do a lot of those
things around then, didn't they? Everyone had an album."

"They had birthday books, too," said Tuppence.

"Birthday books—yes, I remember something about
them. My grandmother had a birthday book, I
remember. Lots of people had to write their name in
it. We've got birthday cards here still, but people
don't buy them much nowadays. It's more valentines,
you know, and Happy Christmases, of course."

"I didn't know whether you had any old albums.
You know, the sort of things people don't want any
more, but they interest me as a collector. I like having different specimens."

"Well, everyone collects something nowadays,
that's true enough," said Durrance. "You'd hardly believe it, the things people collect. I don't think I've
got anything as old as this one of yours, though.
However, I could look around."

He went behind the counter and pulled open a
drawer against the wall.

"Lot of stuff in here," he said. "I meant to turn it
out sometime, but I didn't know as there'd really be
any market for it. A lot of weddings here, of course.
But then, I mean, weddings date. People want them
just at the time of the wedding but nobody comes
back to look for weddings in the past."

"You mean, nobody comes in and says, 'My grandmother was married here. I wonder if you've got any
photographs of her wedding?' "

"Don't think anyone's ever asked me that," said

Durrance. "Still, you never know. They do ask you for queer things sometimes. Sometimes, you know, someone comes in and wants to see whether you've kept a negative of a baby. You know what mothers are. They want pictures of their babies when they were young. Awful pictures, most of them are, anyway. Now and then we've even had the police round. You know, they want to identify someone. Someone who was here as a boy, and they want to see what he looks like—or rather what he looked like then, and whether he's likely to be the same one as one they're looking for now and whom they're after because he's wanted for murder or for swindles. I must say that cheers things up sometimes," said Durrance with a happy smile.

"I see you're quite crime-minded," said Tuppence.

"Oh well, you know, you're reading about things like that every day, why this man is supposed to have killed his wife about six months ago, and all that. Well, I mean, that's interesting, isn't it? Because, I mean, some people say that she's still alive. Other people say that he buried her somewhere and nobody's found her. Things like that. Well, a photograph of him might come in useful."

"Yes," said Tuppence.

She felt that though she was getting on good terms with Mr. Durrance, nothing helpful was coming of it.

"I don't suppose you'd have any photographs of someone called—I think her name was Mary Jordan. Some name like that. But it was a long time ago. About—oh, I suppose sixty years. I think she died here."

"Well, it'd be well before my time," said Mr. Durrance. "Father kept a good many things. You know, he was one of those—hoarders, they call them. Never wanted to throw anything away. Anyone he'd known he'd remember, especially if there was a history about it. Mary Jordan. I seem to remember something about her. Something to do with the Navy, wasn't it, and a submarine? And they said she was a spy, wasn't she? She was half foreign or something. Had a Russian mother or a German mother—might have been a Japanese mother, or something like that."

"Yes. I just wondered if you had any pictures of her."

"Well, I don't think so. I'll have a look around sometime when I've got a little time. I'll let you know if anything turns up. Perhaps you're a writer, are you?" he said hopefully.

"Well," said Tuppence, "I don't make a whole-time job of it, but I am thinking of bringing out a rather small book. You know, recalling the times of about anything from a hundred years ago down till today. You know, curious things that have happened, including crimes and adventures. And, of course, old photographs are very interesting and would illustrate the book beautifully."

"Well, I'll do everything I can to help you, I'm sure. Must be quite interesting, what you're doing. Quite interesting to do, I mean."

"There were some people called Parkinson," said Tuppence. "I think they lived in our house once."

"Ah, you come from the house up on the hill, don't you? The Laruels or Katmandu—I can't remember what it was called last. Swallow's Nest it was called once, wasn't it? Can't think why."

"I suppose there were a lot of swallows nesting in the roof," suggested Tuppence. "There still are."

"Well, may have been, I suppose. But it seems a funny name for a house."

Tuppence, having felt that she'd opened relations satisfactorily, though not hoping very much that any result would come of it, bought a few post cards and some flowered notes in the way of stationery, and wished Mr. Durrance goodbye, got back to the gate, walked up the drive, then checked herself on the way to the house and went up the side path round it to have one more look at KK. She got near the door. She stopped suddenly, then walked on. It looked as though something like a bundle of clothes was lying near the door. Something they'd pulled out of Mathilde and not thought to look at, Tuppence wondered.

She quickened her pace, almost running. When she got near the door, she stopped suddenly. It was not a bundle of old clothes. The clothes were old enough, and so was the body that wore them. Tuppence bent over and then stood up again, steadied herself with a hand on the door.

"Isaac!" she said. "Isaac. Poor old Isaac. I believe—oh, I do believe that he's dead."

Somebody was coming towards her on the path from the house as she called out, taking a step or two.

"Oh, Albert, Albert. Something awful's happened. Isaac, old Isaac. He's lying here and he's dead and I think—I think somebody has killed him."

21

The Inquest

The medical evidence had been given. Two passers-by not far from the gate had given their evidence. The family had spoken, giving evidence as to his state of health; any possible people who had had a reason for enmity towards him (one or two youngish adolescent boys who had before now been warned off by him, had been asked to assist the police and had protested their innocence). One or two of his employers had spoken, including his latest employer, Mrs. Prudence Beresford, and her husband, Mr. Thomas Beresford. All had been said and done and a verdict had been brought in: Wilful murder by a person or persons unknown.

Tuppence came out from the inquest and Tommy put an arm round her as they passed the little group of people waiting outside.

"You did very well, Tuppence," he said, as they returned through the garden gate towards the house. "Very well indeed. Much better than some of those people. You were very clear and you could be heard. The coroner seemed to me to be very pleased with you."

"I don't want anyone to be very pleased with me," said Tuppence. "I don't like old Isaac being coshed on the head and killed like that."

"I suppose someone might have had it in for him," said Tommy.

"Why should they?" said Tuppence.

"I don't know," said Tommy.

"No," said Tuppence, "and I don't know either. But I just wondered if it's anything to do with us."

"Do you mean—what do you mean, Tuppence?"

"You know what I mean really," said Tuppence. "It's this—this place. Our house. Our lovely new house. And garden and everything. It's as though— isn't it just the right place for us? We thought it was."

"Well, I still do," said Tommy.

"Yes," said Tuppence, "I think you've got more hope than I have. I've got an uneasy feeling that there's something—something *wrong* with it all here. Something left over from the past."

"Don't say it again," said Tommy.

"Don't say what again?"

"Oh, just those two words."

Tuppence dropped her voice. She got nearer to Tommy and spoke almost into his ear.

"Mary Jordan?"

"Well, yes. That *was* in my mind."

"And in my mind too, I expect. But I mean, what can anything then have to do with nowadays? What can the past matter?" said Tuppence. "It oughtn't to have anything to do with—now."

"The past oughtn't to have anything to do with the present—is that what you mean? But it does," said Tommy. "It does, in queer ways that one doesn't think of. I mean that one doesn't think would ever happen."

"A lot of things, you mean, happen because of what there was in the past?"

"Yes. It's a sort of long chain. The sort of thing you have, with gaps and then with beads on it from time to time."

"Jane Finn and all that. Like Jane Finn in our adventures when we were young because we wanted adventures."

"And we had them," said Tommy. "Sometimes I look back on it and wonder how we got out of it all alive."

"And then—other things. You know, when we went into partnership, and we pretended to be detective agents."

"Oh, that was fun," said Tommy. "Do you remember—"

"No," said Tuppence, "I'm not going to remember. I'm not anxious to go back to thinking of the past except—well, except as a steppingstone, as you might say. No. Well, anyway, that gave us practice, didn't it? And then we had the next bit."

"Ah," said Tommy. "Mrs. Blenkinsop, eh?"

Tuppence laughed.

"Yes, Mrs. Blenkinsop. I'll never forget when I came into that room and saw you sitting there."

"How you had the nerve, Tuppence, to do what you did, move that wardrobe or whatever it was, and listen in to me and Mr. What's-his-name talking. And then—"

"And then Mrs. Blenkinsop," said Tuppence. She laughed too. "N or M and goosey, goosey, gander."

"But you don't—" Tommy hesitated—"you don't believe that all those were what you called steppingstones to this?"

"Well, they are in a way," said Tuppence. "I mean, I don't suppose that Mr. Robinson would have said what he did to you if he hadn't had a lot of those things in his mind. Me for one of them."

"Very much you for one of them."

"But now," said Tuppence, "this makes it all different. This, I mean. Isaac. Dead. Coshed on the head. Just inside our garden gate."

"You don't think *that's* connected with—"

"One can't help thinking it might be," said Tuppence. "That's what I mean. We're not just investigating a sort of detective mystery any more. Finding out, I mean, about the past and why somebody died in the past and things like that. It's become personal. Quite personal, I think. I mean, poor old Isaac being *dead*."

"He was a very old man and possibly that had something to do with it."

"Not after listening to the medical evidence this morning. Someone wanted to kill him. What for?"

"Why didn't they want to kill us if it was anything to do with us?" said Tommy.

"Well, perhaps they'll try that, too. Perhaps, you know, he could have told us something. Perhaps he *was* going to tell us something. Perhaps he even threatened somebody else that he was going to talk to us, say something he knew about the girl or one of the Parkinsons. Or—or all this spying business in the nineteen fourteen war. The secrets that were sold. And then, you see, he had to be silenced. But if we hadn't come to live here and ask questions and wanted to find out, it wouldn't have happened."

"Don't get so worked up."

"I am worked up. And I'm not doing anything for fun any more. This isn't fun. We're doing something different now, Tommy. We're hunting down a killer. But who? Of course we don't know yet, but we can find out. That's not the past, that's now. That's something that happened—what—only five days ago, six days ago? That's the present. It's here and it's connected with us and it's connected with this house. And we've got to find out and we're going to find out. I don't know how, but we've got to go after all the clues and follow up things. I feel like a dog with my nose to the ground, following a trail. I'll have to follow it *here*, and you've got to be a hunting dog. Go round to different places. The way you're doing now. Finding out about things. Getting your—whatever you call it—research done. There must be people who know things, not of their own knowledge but what people have told them. Stories they've heard. Rumors. Gossip."

"But, Tuppence, you can't really believe there's any chance there of our—"

"Oh yes I do," said Tuppence. "I don't know how or in what way, but I believe that when you've got a real, convincing idea, something that you know is black and bad and evil, and hitting old Isaac on the head *was* black and evil—" She stopped.

"We could change the name of the house again," said Tommy.

"What do you mean? Call it Swallow's Nest and not The Laurels?"

A flight of birds passed over their heads. Tuppence turned her head and looked back towards the garden gate. "Swallow's Nest was once its name. What's the rest of that quotation? The one your researcher quoted. Postern of Death, wasn't it?"

"No, Postern of Fate."

"Fate. That's like a comment on what has happened to Isaac. Postern of Fate—*our* Garden Gate—"

"Don't worry so much, Tuppence."

"I don't know why," said Tuppence. "It's just a sort of idea that came into my mind."

Tommy gave her a puzzled look and shook his head.

"Swallow's Nest is a nice name, really," said Tuppence. "Or it could be. Perhaps it will someday."

"You have the most extraordinary ideas, Tuppence."

"Yet something singeth like a bird. That was how it ended. Perhaps all this will end that way."

Just before they reached the house, Tommy and Tuppence saw a woman standing on the doorstep.

"I wonder who that is," said Tommy.

"Someone I've seen before," said Tuppence. "I don't remember who at the moment. Oh. I think it's one of old Isaac's family. You know they all lived together in one cottage. About three or four boys and this woman and another one, a girl. I may be wrong, of course."

The woman on the doorstep had turned and came towards them.

"Mrs. Beresford, isn't it," she said, looking up at Tuppence.

"Yes," said Tuppence.

"And—I don't expect you know me. I'm Isaac's daughter-in-law, you know. Married to his son, Stephen, I was. Stephen—he got killed in an accident. One of them lorries. The big ones that go along. It was on one of the M roads, the M 1 I think it was. M 1 or the M 5. No, the M 5 was before that. The M 4 it could be. Anyway, there it was. Five or six years ago it was. I wanted to—I wanted just to speak to you. You and—you and your husband—" She looked at Tommy. "You sent flowers, didn't you, to the funeral? Isaac worked in the garden here for you, didn't he?"

"Yes," said Tuppence. "He did work for us here. It was such a terrible thing to have happened."

"I came to thank you. Very lovely flowers they was, too. Good ones. Classy ones. A great bunch of them."

"We thought we'd like to do it," said Tuppence, "because Isaac had been very helpful to us. He'd helped us a lot, you know, with getting into the house. Telling us about things, because we don't know much about the house. Where things were kept, and everything. And he gave me a lot of knowledge about planting things, too."

"Yes, he knew his stuff, as you might say. He wasn't much of a worker because he was old, you know, and he didn't like stooping. Got lumbago a lot, so he couldn't do as much as he'd have liked to do."

"He was very nice and very helpful," said Tuppence firmly. "And he knew a lot about things here, and the people, and told us a lot."

"Ah. He knew a lot, he did. A lot of his family, you know, worked before him. They lived roundabout and they'd known a good deal of what went on in years gone by. Not of their own knowledge, as you might say, but—well, just hearing what went on. Well, ma'am, I won't keep you. I just came up to have a few words and say how much obliged I was."

"That's very nice of you," said Tuppence. "Thank you very much."

"You'll have to get someone else to do a bit of work in the garden, I expect."

"I expect so," said Tuppence. "We're not very good at it ourselves. Do you—perhaps you—" she hesitated, feeling perhaps she was saying the wrong thing at the wrong moment—"perhaps you know of someone who would like to come and work for us."

"Well, I can't say I do offhand, but I'll keep it in mind. You never know. I'll send along Henry—that's my second boy, you know—I'll send him along and let you know if I hear of anyone. Well, good day for now."

"What was Isaac's name? I can't remember," said Tommy, as they went into the house. "I mean, his surname."

"Oh, Isaac Bodlicott, I think."

"So that's a Mrs. Bodlicott, is it?"

"Yes. Though I think she's got several sons, boys and a girl and they all live together. You know, in that cottage halfway up the Marshton Road. Do you think she knows who killed him?" said Tuppence.

"I shouldn't think so," said Tommy. "She didn't look as though she did."

"I don't know how you'd look," said Tuppence. "It's rather difficult to say, isn't it?"

"I think she just came to thank you for the flowers. I don't think she had the look of someone who was— you know—revengeful. I think she'd have mentioned it if so."

"Might. Might not," said Tuppence.

She went into the house looking rather thoughtful.

22

Reminiscences
About an Uncle

The following morning Tuppence was interrupted in her remarks to an electrician who had come to adjust portions of his work which were not considered satisfactory.

"Boy at the door," said Albert. "Wants to speak to you, madam."

"Oh. What's his name?"

"Didn't ask him. He's waiting there outside."

Tuppence seized her garden hat, shoved it on her head and came down the stairs.

Outside the door a boy of about twelve or thirteen was standing. He was rather nervous, shuffling his feet.

"Hope it's all right to come along," he said.

"Let me see," said Tuppence, "you're Henry Bodlicott, aren't you?"

"That's right. That was my—oh, I suppose he was by way of being an uncle, the one I mean whose inquest was on yesterday. Never been to an inquest before, I haven't."

Tuppence stopped herself on the brink of saying, "Did you enjoy it?" Henry had the look of someone who was about to describe a treat.

"It was quite a tragedy, wasn't it?" said Tuppence. "Very sad."

"Oh well, he was an old one," said Henry. "Couldn't have expected to last much longer, I don't think, you know. Used to cough something terrible in

189

the autumn. Kept us all awake in the house. I just
come along to ask if there's anything as you want
done here. I understood—as a matter of fact Mom
told me—as you had some lettuces ought to be thinned
out now and I wonder if you'd like me to do it
for you. I know just where they are because I used to
come up sometimes and talk to Izzy when he was at
work. I could do it now if you liked."

"Oh, that's very nice of you," said Tuppence.
"Come out and show me."

They moved into the garden together and went up
to the spot designated.

"That's it, you see. They've been shoved in a bit
tight and you've got to thin 'em out a bit and put 'em
over there instead, you see, when you've made proper
gaps."

"I don't really know anything about lettuces," Tuppence admitted. "I know a little about flowers. Peas,
Brussels sprouts and lettuces and other vegetables I'm
not very good at. You don't want a job working in the
garden, I suppose, do you?"

"Oh no, I'm still going to school, I am. I takes the
papers round and I do a bit of fruit picking in the
summer, you know."

"I see," said Tuppence. "Well, if you hear of anyone and you let me know, I'll be very glad."

"Yes, I will do that. Well, so long, mum."

"Just show me what you're doing to the lettuces. I'd
like to know."

She stood by, watching the manipulations of Henry
Bodlicott.

"Now that's all right. Yes, nice ones, these, aren't
they? Webb's Wonderful, aren't they? They keep a
long time."

"We finished the Tom Thumbs," said Tuppence.

"That's right. Those are the little early ones, aren't
they? Very crisp and good."

"Well, thank you very much," said Tuppence.

She turned away and started to walk towards the

house. She noted she'd lost her scarf and turned back. Henry Bodlicott, just starting for home, stopped and came across to her.

"Just the scarf," said Tuppence. "Is it—oh, there it is on that bush."

He handed it to her, then stood looking at her, shuffling his feet. He looked so very worried and ill at ease that Tuppence wondered what was the matter with him.

"Is there anything?" she said.

Henry shuffled his feet, looked at her, shuffled his feet again, picked his nose and rubbed his left ear and then moved his feet in a kind of tattoo.

"Just something I—I wondered if you—I mean—if you wouldn't mind me asking you—"

"Well?" said Tuppence. She stopped and looked at him inquiringly.

Henry got very red in the face and continued to shuffle his feet.

"Well, I didn't like to—I don't like to ask, but I just wondered—I mean, people have been saying—they said things . . . I mean, I hear them say . . ."

"Yes?" said Tuppence, wondering what had upset Henry, what he could have heard concerning the lives of Mr. and Mrs. Beresford, the new tenants of The Laurels. "Yes, you've heard what?"

"Oh, just as—as how it's you is the lady what caught spies or something in the last war. You did it, and the gentleman too. You were in it and you found someone who was a German spy pretending to be something else. And you found him out and you had a lot of adventures and in the end it was all cleared up. I mean, you were—I don't know what to call it— I suppose you were one of our secret service people and you did that and they said as you'd been wonderful. Of course, some time ago now, but you was all mixed up with something—something about nursery rhymes too."

"That's right," said Tuppence. "Goosey, goosey, gander was the one in question."

"Goosey, goosey, gander! I remember that. Gosh, years ago, it was. Whither will you wander!"

"That's right," said Tuppence. "Upstairs, downstairs, in my lady's chamber. There he found an old man who wouldn't say his prayers and he took him by the left leg and threw him down the stairs. At least, I think that's right, but it may be a different nursery rhyme I've tacked onto it."

"Well, I never," said Henry. "Well, I mean, it's rather wonderful to have you living here just like anyone else, isn't it? But I don't know why the nursery rhymes were in it."

"Oh, there was a kind of code, a cipher," said Tuppence.

"You mean it had to be sort of read and all that?" said Henry.

"Something of the kind," said Tuppence. "Anyway, it was all found out."

"Well now, isn't that wonderful," said Henry. "You don't mind if I tell my friend, do you? My chum. Clarence, his name is. Silly name, I know. We all laugh at him for it. But he's a good chap, he is, and he'll be ever so thrilled to know as we've got you really living amongst us."

He looked at Tuppence with the admiration of an affectionate spaniel.

"Wonderful!" he said again.

"Oh, it was a long time ago," said Tuppence. "In the nineteen-forties."

"Was it fun, or were you ever so frightened?"

"Bits of both," said Tuppence. "Mostly, I think, I was frightened."

"Oh well, I expect as you would be, too. Yes, but it's odd as you should come here and get mixed up in the same sort of thing. It was a naval gentleman, wasn't it? I mean as called himself an English com-

mander in the Navy, but he wasn't really. He was a
German. At least, that's what Clarence said."

"Something like that," said Tuppence.

"So perhaps that's why you come here. Because,
you know, we had something here once—well, it was
a very, very long time ago—but it was the same thing,
as you might say. He was a submarine officer. He
sold plans of submarines. Mind you, it's only stories
as I've heard people say."

"I see," said Tuppence. "Yes. No, it's not the reason
we came here. We just came here because it's a nice
house to live in. I've heard these same rumors going
about, only I don't know exactly what happened."

"Well, I'll try and tell you sometime. Of course, one
doesn't always know what's right or not, but things
aren't always known properly."

"How did your friend Clarence manage to know so
much about it?"

"Well, he heard from Mick, you know. He used to
live a short time up by where the blacksmith used to
be. He's been gone a long time, but he heard a lot
from different people. And our old Isaac, he knew a
good deal about it. He used to tell us things sometimes."

"So he did know a good deal about it all?" said
Tuppence.

"Oh yes. That's why I wondered, you know, when
he was coshed the other day if that could be the reason. That he might have known a bit too much and—
he told it all to you. So they did him in. That's what
they do nowadays. They do people in, you know, if
they know too much of anything that's going to in-
volve them with the police or anything."

"You think your Uncle Isaac—you think he knew a
good deal about it?"

"Well, I think things got told him, you know. He
heard a lot here and there. Didn't often talk of it, but
sometimes he would. Of an evening, you know, after
smoking a pipe or hearing me and Clarrie talk and

my other friend, Tom Gillingham. He used to want to
know, too, and Uncle Izzy would tell us this, that and
the other. Of course we didn't know if he was making
it up or not. But I think he'd found things and knew
where some things were. And he said if some people
knew where they were there might be something interesting."

"Did he?" said Tuppence. "Well, I think that's very
interesting to us also. You must try and remember
some of the things he said or suggested sometime because, well, it might lead to finding out who killed
him. Because he was killed. It wasn't an accident, was
it?"

"We thought at first it must have been an accident.
You know, he had a bit of a heart or something and
he used to fall down now and again or get giddy or
have turns. But it seems—I went to the inquest, you
know—as though he'd been done in deliberate."

"Yes," said Tuppence, "I think he was done in deliberate."

"And you don't know why?" said Henry.

Tuppence looked at Henry. It seemed to her as
though she and Henry were for the moment two police dogs on the same scent.

"I think it was deliberate, and I think that you, because he was your relation, and I too, would like to
know who it was who did such a cruel and wicked
thing. But perhaps you do know or have some idea
already, Henry."

"I don't have a proper idea, I don't," said Henry.
"One just hears things and I know people that Uncle
Izzy says—said—now and then had got it in for him
for some reason and he said that was because he
knew a bit too much about them and about what
they knew and about something that happened. But
it's always someone who's been dead so many years
ago that one can't really remember it or get at it
properly."

"Well," said Tuppence, "I think you'll have to help us, Henry."

"You mean you'll let me sort of be in it with you? I mean, doing a bit of finding out any time?"

"Yes," said Tuppence, "if you can hold your tongue about what you find out. I mean, tell me, but don't go talking to all your friends about it because that way things would get around."

"I see. And then they might tell the coshers and go for you and Mr. Beresford, mightn't they?"

"They might," said Tuppence, "and I'd rather they didn't."

"Well, that's natural," said Henry. "Well, see here, if I come across anything or hear anything I'll come up and offer to do a bit of work here. How's that? Then I can tell you what I know and nobody'd hear us and—but I don't know anything right at the moment. But I've got friends." He drew himself up suddenly and put on an air clearly adopted from something he'd seen on television. "I know things. People don't know as I know things. They don't think I've listened and they don't think I'd remember, but I know sometimes—you know, they'll say something and then they'll say who else knows about it and then they'll—well, you know, if you keep quiet you get to hear a lot. And I expect it's all very important, isn't it?"

"Yes," said Tuppence, "I think it's important. But we have to be very careful, Henry. You understand that?"

"Oh, I do. Of course I'll be careful. Careful as you know how. He knew a lot about this place, you know," went on Henry. "My Uncle Isaac did."

"About this house, you mean, or this garden?"

"That's right. He knew some of the stories about it, you know. Where people were seen going and what they did with things maybe, and where they met people. Where there were hiding-places and things. He used to talk sometimes, he did. Of course Mom, she

didn't listen much. She'd just think it was all silly.
Johnny—that's my older brother—he thinks it's all
nonsense and he didn't listen. But I listened and
Clarence is interested in that sort of thing. You know,
he likes those kind of films and all that. He said to me,
'Chuck, it's just like a film.' So we talked about it together."

"Did you ever hear anyone talked about whose
name was Mary Jordan?"

"Ah yes, of course. She was the German girl who
was a spy, wasn't she? Got naval secrets out of naval
officers, didn't she?"

"Something of that kind, I believe," said Tuppence,
feeling it safer to stick to that version, though in her
mind apologizing to the ghost of Mary Jordan.

"I expect she was very lovely, wasn't she? Very
beautiful?"

"Well, I don't know," said Tuppence, "because I
mean, she probably died when I was about three
years old."

"Yes, of course, it would be so, wouldn't it? Oh, one
hears her talked about sometimes."

"You seem very excited and out of breath, Tuppence," said Tommy as his wife, dressed in her garden clothes, came in through the door, panting a little
as she came.

"Well," said Tuppence, "I am in a way."

"Not been overdoing it in the garden?"

"No. Actually I haven't been doing anything at all.
I've just been standing by the lettuces talking, or
being talked to—whichever way you put it—"

"Who's been talking to you?"

"A boy," said Tuppence. "A boy."

"Offering to help in the garden?"

"Not exactly," said Tuppence. "That would be very
nice too, of course. No. Actually, he was expressing
admiration."

"Of the garden?"

"No," said Tuppence, "of me."

"Of you?"

"Don't look surprised," said Tuppence, "and oh, don't sound surprised either. Still, I admit these *bonnes bouches* come in sometimes when you least expect them."

"Oh. What is the admiration of—your beauty or your garden overall?"

"My past," said Tuppence.

"Your past!"

"Yes. He was fairly thrilled to think I had been the lady, as he politely put it, who had unmasked a German spy in the last war. A false naval commander, retired, who was nothing of the kind."

"Good gracious," said Tommy. "N or M again. Dear me, shan't we ever be able to live that down?"

"Well, I'm not very sure I want to live it down," said Tuppence. "I mean, why should we? If we'd been a celebrated actress or actor, we'd quite like to be reminded of it."

"I see the point," said Tommy.

"And I think it might be very useful with what we're trying to do here."

"If he's a boy, how old did you say he was?"

"Oh, I should think about ten or twelve. Looks ten, but he's twelve, I think. And he has a friend called Clarence."

"What's that got to do with it?"

"Well, nothing at the moment," said Tuppence, "but he and Clarence are allies and would like, I think, to attach themselves to our service. To find out things or to tell us things."

"If they're ten or twelve, how can they tell us things or remember things we want to know?" said Tommy. "What sort of things did he say?"

"Most of his sentences were short," said Tuppence, "and consisted of mainly 'well, you know,' or 'you see, it was like this' or 'yes, and then you know.' Anyway,

'you know' was always a component part of everything he said."

"And they were all things you didn't know."

"Well, they were attempts at explaining things he'd
heard about."

"Heard about from whom?"

"Well, not first-hand knowledge, as you'd say, and I
wouldn't say second-hand knowledge. I think it might
go up to third-hand, fourth-hand, fifth-hand, sixth-
hand knowledge. It consisted also of what Clarence
had heard and what Clarence's friend, Algernon, had
heard. What Algernon said Jimmy had heard—"

"Stop," said Tommy, "that's enough. And what had
they heard?"

"That's more difficult," said Tuppence, "but I think
one can get round to it. They'd heard certain places
mentioned or stories told and they were very, very
anxious to partake of the joys of what we had clearly
come to do here."

"Which is?"

"To discover something important. Something that's
well known to be hidden here."

"Ah," said Tommy. "Hidden. Hidden how, where
and when?"

"Different stories about all those three," said Tuppence, "but it's exciting, you must admit, Tommy."

Tommy said thoughtfully that perhaps it was.

"It ties in with old Isaac," said Tuppence. "I think
Isaac must have known quite a lot of things which he
could have told us."

"And you think that Clarence and—what's this one's
name again?"

"I'll remember it in a minute," said Tuppence. "I
got so confused with all the other people he'd heard
things from. The ones with the grand names like Algernon and the ones with the ordinary names like
Jimmy and Johnny and Mike.

"Chuck," said Tuppence suddenly.

"Chuck what?" said Tommy.

"No. I didn't mean it that way. I think that's his name. The boy, I mean. Chuck."

"It seems a very odd name."

"His real name is Henry, but I expect his friends call him Chuck. Like Chuck goes the weasel."

"Pop goes the weasel, you mean."

"Well, I know that's correct. But Chuck goes the weasel sounds much the same. Oh, Tommy, what I really want to say to you is that we've got to go on with this, specially now. Do you feel the same?"

"Yes," said Tommy.

"Well, I thought perhaps you did. Not that you've said anything. But we've got to go on with it and I'll tell you why. Mainly because of Isaac. Isaac. Somebody killed him. They killed him because he knew something. He knew something that might have been dangerous to somebody. And we've got to find out who the person was it would be dangerous to."

"You don't think," said Tommy, "that it's just—oh, one of those things. You know, hooliganism or whatever they call it. You know, people go out and want to do people in and don't care who the people are, but they prefer them to be elderly and not be able to put up any kind of a resistance."

"Yes," said Tuppence, "in a way I do mean that. But—I don't think it was that. I think there *is* something, I don't know if hidden is the right word, there's something here. Something that throws light on something that happened in the past, something that someone left here or put here or gave to someone to keep here who has since died or put it somewhere. But something that someone doesn't want discovered. Isaac knew it and they must have been afraid he'd tell us because word's evidently going round now about us. You know, that we're famous anti-espionage people or whatever you call it. We've got a reputation for that sort of thing. And it's tied up in a way, you see, with Mary Jordan and all the rest of it."

"Mary Jordan," said Tommy, "did not die a natural death."

"Yes," said Tuppence, "and old Isaac was killed. We've got to find out who killed him and why. Otherwise—"

"You've got to be careful," said Tommy; "you've got to be careful of yourself, Tuppence. If anyone killed Isaac because he thought he was going to talk about things in the past that he'd heard about, someone may be only too pleased to wait in a dark corner for you one night and do the same thing. They wouldn't think there'd be any worry about it, they'd just think people would say 'Oh, another of those things.'"

"When old ladies are hit on the head and done in," said Tuppence. "Yes, quite so. That's the unfortunate result of having gray hair and walking with a slight arthritic limp. Of course I must be fair game for anyone. I shall look after myself. Do you think I ought to carry a small pistol about with me?"

"No," said Tommy, "certainly not."

"Why? Do you think I'd make some mistake with it?"

"Well, I think you might trip over the root of a tree. You know you're always falling down. And then you might shoot yourself instead of just using the pistol for protection."

"Oh, you don't really think I'd do anything stupid like that, do you?" said Tuppence.

"Yes, I do," said Tommy, "I'm sure you're quite capable of it."

"I could carry a flick knife," said Tuppence.

"I shouldn't carry anything at all," said Tommy. "I should just go about looking innocent and talking about gardening. Say, perhaps, we're not sure we like the house and we have plans for going to live elsewhere. That's what I suggest."

"Who've I got to say that to?"

"Oh, almost anyone," said Tommy. "It'll get round."

"Things always get round," said Tuppence. "Quite a place here for things getting round. Are you going to say the same things, Tommy?"

"Well, roughly. Say, perhaps, that we don't like the house as much as we thought we did."

"But you want to go on, too, don't you?" said Tuppence.

"Yes," said Tommy. "I'm embroiled all right."

"Have you thought how to set about it?"

"Go on doing what I'm doing at present. What about you, Tuppence? Have you got any plans?"

"Not quite yet," said Tuppence. "I've got a few ideas. I can get a bit more out of—what did I say his name was?"

"First Henry—then Clarence."

23

Junior Brigade

Having seen Tommy depart for London, Tuppence was wandering vaguely round the house trying to single out some particular activity which might yield successful results. However, her brain did not seem to be full of bright ideas this morning.

With the general feeling of one returning to the beginning, she climbed up to the book-room and walked round it vaguely, looking at the titles of various volumes. Children's books, lots of children's books, but really one couldn't go any farther than that, could one? She had gone as far as anyone could already. By now she was almost certain that she had looked at every single book in this particular room; Alexander Parkinson had not revealed any more of his secrets.

She was standing there running her fingers through her hair, frowning and kicking at a bottom shelf of theological works whose bindings were nearly all of them scaling away from the books, when Albert came up.

"Someone as wants to see you downstairs, madam."

"What do you mean by someone?" said Tuppence. "Anyone I know?"

"I dunno. Shouldn't think so. Boys they are, mainly. Boys and a girl or two all in a hump. Spect they want a subscription for something or other."

"Oh. They didn't give any names or say anything?"

"Oh, one of them did. Said he was Clarence and you'd know all about him."

202

"Oh," said Tuppence. "Clarence." She considered for a moment.

Was this the fruit from yesterday? Anyway, it could do no harm to follow it up.

"Is the other boy here too? The one I was talking to yesterday in the garden?"

"Don't know. They all look much alike. Dirty, you know, and all the rest of it."

"Oh well," said Tuppence, "I'll come down."

When she had reached the ground floor, she turned inquiringly to her guide.

Albert said, "Oh, I didn't let them come into the house. Wouldn't be safe, I think. Never know what you might lose, these days. They're out in the garden. They said to tell you they was by the gold mine."

"They was by the what?" asked Tuppence.

"The gold mine."

"Oh," said Tuppence.

"What way would that be?"

Tuppence pointed.

"Past the rose garden, and then right by the dahlia walk. I think I know. There's a sort of water thing there. I don't know if it's a brook or a canal or has once been a pond that had had goldfish in it. Anyway, give me my gumboots and I'd better take my mackintosh as well in case someone pushes me into it."

"I should put it on if I was you, ma'am, it's going to rain presently."

"Oh dear," said Tuppence. "Rain, rain. Always rain."

She went out and came fairly quickly to what seemed to be a considerable deputation waiting for her. There were, she thought, about ten or twelve of assorted ages, mainly boys flanked by two long-haired girls, all looking rather excited. One of them said in a shrill voice as Tuppence approached,

"Here she comes! Here she is. Now then, who's

going to speak? Go on, George, you'd better talk. You're the one who always talks."

"Well, you're not going to now. I'm going to talk," said Clarence.

"You shut up, Clarrie. You know your voice is weak. It makes you cough if you talk."

"Now look here, this is my show. I—"

"Good morning, all," said Tuppence, breaking in. "You've come to see me about something, have you? What is it?"

"Got something for you, we have," said Clarence. "Information. That's what you're after, isn't it?"

"It depends," said Tuppence. "What kind of information?"

"Oh, not information about nowadays. All long ago."

"Historical information," said one of the girls, who appeared to be the intellectual chief of the group. "Most interesting if you're doing research into the past."

"I see," said Tuppence, concealing the fact that she did not see. "What's this place here?"

"It's a gold mine."

"Oh," said Tuppence. "Any gold in it?"

She looked about her.

"Well, really, it's a goldfish pool," explained one of the boys. "Used to be a goldfish in it once, you know. Special ones with lots of tails, from Japan or somewhere. Oh, wonderful it used to be. That was in old Mrs. Forrester's time. That's—oh, that's ten years ago."

"Twenty-four years ago," said one of the girls.

"Sixty years ago," said a very small voice, "every bit of sixty years ago. Lots of goldfish there were. Ever so many. Said to be valuable, they was. They used to die sometimes. Sometimes they ate each other, sometimes they were just lying on top, floating about, you know."

"Well," said Tuppence, "what do you want to tell

me about them? There are no goldfish to see here now."

"No. It's information," said the intellectual girl.

A large outbreak of voices occurred. Tuppence waved her hand.

"Not all at once," she said. "One or two speak at a time. What's all this about?"

"Something perhaps you ought to know about where things was hidden once. Hidden once and said to be very important."

"And how do you know about them?" said Tuppence.

This provoked a chorus of replies. It was not very easy to hear everyone at once.

"It was Janie."

"It was Janie's Uncle Ben," said one voice.

"No, it wasn't. It was Harry, it was ... Yes, it was Harry. Harry's Cousin Tom ... Much younger than that. It was his grandmother told him and his grandmother had been told by Josh. Yes. I don't know who Josh was. I think Josh was her husband ... No, he wasn't her husband, he was her uncle."

"Oh dear," said Tuppence.

She looked over the gesticulating crowd and picked out a choice.

"Clarence," she said. "You're Clarence, aren't you? Your friend told me about you. Yes, well, what do you know and what's it all about?"

"Well, if you want to find out, you've got to go to the PPC."

"Go to the what?" said Tuppence.

"The PPC."

"What's the PPC?"

"Don't you know? Hasn't anyone told you? PPC is the Pensioners' Palace Club."

"Oh dear," said Tuppence, "that sounds very grand."

"It isn't grand at all," said one boy of about nine. "It isn't grand a bit. It's only old-age pensioners saying things and getting together. Pack of lies, some people say they tell about things they knew. You know, knew of the last war and knew after it. Oh, all sorts of things they say."

"Where is this PPC?" asked Tuppence.

"Oh, it's along at the end the the village. Halfway to Morton Cross, it is. If you're a pensioner, you get a ticket for it and you go there and you have bingo and you have all sorts of things there. It's quite fun, it is. Oh, some of them are very old. Some of them are deaf and blind and everything else. But they all—well, they like getting together, you know."

"Well, I should like to pay a visit to it," said Tuppence. "Certainly. Is there any particular time one goes there?"

"Well, any time you like, I suppose, but the afternoon would be a good time, you know. Yes. That's when they like visits. In the afternoon. Then if they can say they've got a friend coming—if they've got a friend coming, they get extra things for tea, you know. Biscuits sometimes, with sugar on. And crisps sometimes. Things like that. What did you say, Fred?"

Fred took a step forward. He gave a somewhat pompous bow to Tuppence.

"I shall be very happy," he said, "to escort you. Shall we say about half-past three this afternoon?"

"Ah, be yourself," said Clarence. "Don't go talking like that."

"I shall be very pleased to come," said Tuppence. She looked at the water. "I can't help being rather sorry that there aren't any goldfish any more."

"You ought to have seen the one with five tails. Wonderful, they was. Somebody's dog fell in here once. Mrs. Faggett's, it was."

He was contradicted. "Not it wasn't. It was somebody else, her name was Follyo, not Fagot—"

"It was Foliatt and it was spelt with plain 'f.' Not a capital letter."

"Ah, don't be silly. It was someone quite different.

It was that Miss French, that was. Two small ffs she spelt it with."

"Did the dog drown?" asked Tuppence.

"No, he didn't drown. He was only a puppy, you see, and his mother was upset and she went along and she pulled at Miss French's dress. Miss Isabel was in the orchard picking apples and the mother dog pulled at her dress and Miss Isabel she come along and she saw the puppy drowning and she jumped right into this here and pulled it out. Wet through, she was, and the dress she was wearing was never fit for wearing again."

"Oh dear," said Tuppence, "what a lot of things seem to have gone on here. All right," she said, "I'll be ready this afternoon. Perhaps two of you or three would come for me and take me to this Pensioners' Palace Club."

"What three? Who's going to come?"

Uproar happened immediately.

"I'm coming ... No, I'm not ... No, Betty is ... No, Betty shan't come. Betty went the other day. I mean, she went to the cinema party the other day. She can't go again."

"Well, settle it between you," said Tuppence, "and come here at half-past three."

"I hope you'll find it interesting," said Clarence.

"It will be of historical interest," said the intellectual girl firmly.

"Oh, shut up, Janet," said Clarence. He turned to Tuppence. "She's always like that," he said, "Janet is. She goes to grammar school, that's why. She boasts about it, see? A comprehensive wasn't good enough for her and her parents made a fuss and now she's at grammar school. That's why she goes on like this all the time."

Tuppence wondered, as she finished her lunch, whether the events of the morning would produce any sequel. Would anybody really come to escort her

this afternoon and take her to the PPC? Was there
any such thing really as the PPC, or was it a
nickname of some kind that the children had invented? Anyway, it might be fun, Tuppence thought, to
sit waiting in case someone came.

However, the deputation was punctual to the minute. At half-past three the bell rang, Tuppence rose
from her seat by the fire, clapped a hat upon her
head—an India rubber hat because she thought it
would probably rain—and Albert appeared to escort
her to the front door.

"Not going to let you go with just anyone," he
breathed into her ear.

"Look here, Albert," whispered Tuppence, "is there
really such a place as the PPC here?"

"I thought that had something to do with visiting
cards," said Albert, who was always prone to show
his complete knowledge of social customs. "You
know, what you leave on people when you're going
away or when you're arriving, I'm not sure which."

"I think it's something to do with pensioners."

"Oh yes, they've got a sort of a place. Yes. Built
just two or three years ago, I think it was. You know,
it's just down after you pass the rectory and then you
turn right and then you see it. It's rather an ugly
building, but it's nice for the old folk and any who
like can go meeting there. They have games and
things, and there's a lot of ladies goes and helps with
things. Gets up concerts and—sort of—well, rather
like, you know, Women's Institute. Only it's specially
for the elderly people. They're all very, very old, and
most of them deaf."

"Yes," said Tuppence, "yes. It sounded rather like
that."

The front door was opened. Janet, by reason of her
intellectual superiority, stood there first. Behind her
was Clarence, and behind him was a tall boy with a
squint who appeared to answer to the name of Bert.

"Good afternoon, Mrs. Beresford," said Janet. "Everybody is so pleased that you are coming. I think perhaps you'd better take an umbrella. The weather forecast was not very good today."

"I've got to go that way anyway," said Albert, "so I'll come with you a short part of it."

Certainly, Tuppence thought, Albert was always very protective. Perhaps just as well, but she did not think that either Janet, Bert or Clarence was likely to be a danger to her. The walk took about twenty minutes. When the red building was reached, they went through the gate, up to the door and were received by a stout woman of about seventy.

"Ah, so we've got visitors. I'm so pleased you could come, my dear, so pleased." She patted Tuppence upon the shoulder. "Yes, Janet, thank you very much. Yes. This way. Yes. None of you need wait unless you like, you know."

"Oh, I think the boys will be very disappointed if they didn't wait to hear a little about what all this is about," said Janet.

"Well, I think, you know, there are not so very many of us here. Perhaps it would be better for Mrs. Beresford, not so worrying if there weren't too many of us. I wonder, Janet, if you would just go into the kitchen and tell Mollie that we are quite ready for tea to be brought in now."

Tuppence had not really come for tea, but she could hardly say so. Tea appeared rather rapidly. It was excessively weak, it was served with some biscuits and some sandwiches with a rather nasty type of paste in between them with an extra fishy taste. Then they sat around and seemed slightly at a loss.

An old man with a beard who looked to Tuppence as though he was about a hundred came and sat firmly by her.

"I'd best have a word with you first, I think, my lady," he said, elevating Tuppence to the peerage.

"Seeing as I'm about the oldest here and have heard more of the stories of the old days than anyone else. A lot of history about this place, you know. Oh, a lot of things has happened here, not that we can go into everything at once, can we? But we've all—oh, we've all heard something about the things that went on."

"I gather," said Tuppence, hastily rushing in before she could be introduced to some topic in which she had no interest whatever, "I understand that quite a lot of interesting things went on here, not so much in the last war, but in the war before that, or even earlier. Not that any of your memories would go back as far as that. But one wonders perhaps if you could have heard things, you know, from your elderly relations."

"Ah, that's right," said the old man, "that's right. Heard a lot, I did, from my Uncle Len. Yes, ah, he was a great chap, was Uncle Len. He knew about a lot of things. He knew what went on. It was like what went on down in the house on the quay before the last war. Yes, a bad show, that. What you call one of those fakists—"

"Fascists," said one of the elderly ladies, a rather prim one with gray hair and a lace fichu rather the worse for wear round her neck.

"Well, fascist if you like to say it that way, what does it matter? Ah yes, one of those he was. Yes. Same sort of thing as that chap in Italy. Mussolini or something, wasn't it? Anyway, some sort of fishy name like that. Mussels or cockles. Oh yes, he did a lot of harm here. Had meetings, you know. All sorts of things like that. Someone called Mosley started it all."

"But in the First War there was a girl called Mary Jordan, wasn't there?" said Tuppence, wondering if this was a wise thing to say or not.

"Ah yes. Said to be quite a good-looker, you know. Yes. Got hold of secrets out of the sailors and the soldiers."

A very old lady piped up in a thin voice.

"He's not in the Navy and he's not in the Army,
But he's just the man for me.
Not in the Navy, not in the Army,
        he's in the Royal Ar-till-er-rie!"

The old man took up his personal chant when she
had got thus far:

"It's a long way to Tipperary,
It's a long way to go,
It's a long way to Tipperary
And the rest of it I don't know."

"Now that's enough, Benny, that's quite enough,"
said a firm-looking woman who seemed to be either
his wife or his daughter.

Another old lady sang in a quavering voice,

"All the nice girls love a sailor,
All the nice girls love a tar,
All the nice girls love a sailor,
And you know what sailors are."

"Oh, shut up, Maudie, we're tired of that one. Now
let the lady hear something," said Uncle Ben. "Let the
lady hear something. She's come here to hear something. She wants to hear where that thing there was
all the fuss about was hidden, don't you? And all about
it."

"That sounds very interesting," said Tuppence,
cheering up. "Something *was* hidden?"

"Ah yes, long before my time it was, but I heard all
about it. Yes. Before nineteen fourteen. Word was
handed down, you know, from one to another. Nobody knew exactly what it was and why there was all
this excitement."

"Something to do with the boat race, it had," said
an old lady. "You know, Oxford and Cambridge. I
was taken once. I was taken to see the boat race in

London under the bridges and everything. Oh, it was a wonderful day. Oxford won by a length."

"A lot of nonsense you're all talking," said a grim-looking woman with iron-gray hair. "You don't know anything about it, you don't. I know more than most of you although it happened a long time before I was born. It was my Great-Aunt Matilda who told me and she were told by her Aunty Lou. And that was a good forty years before then. Great talk about it, it was, and people went around looking for it. Some people thought it was a gold mine, you know. Yes, a gold ingot brought back from Australia. Somewhere like that."

"Damn silly," said an old man, who was smoking a pipe with an air of general dislike of his fellow members. "Mixed it up with goldfish, they did. Was as ignorant as that."

"It was worth a lot of money, whatever it was, or it wouldn't have been hidden," said someone else. "Yes, lots of people come down from the government, and yes, police too. They looked around but they couldn't find anything."

"Ah well, they didn't have the right clues. There are clues, you know, if you know where to look for them." Another old lady nodded her head wisely. "There's always clues."

"How interesting," said Tuppence. "Where? Where are these clues, I mean? In the village or somewhere outside it or—"

This was a rather unfortunate remark, as it brought down at least six different replies, all uttered at once.

"On the moor, beyond Tower West," one was saying.

"Oh no, it's past Little Kenny, it was. Yes, quite near Little Kenny."

"No, it was the cave. The cave by the sea front. Over as far as Baldy's Head. You know, where the red rocks age. That's it. There's an old smugglers' tunnel. Wonderful, it must be. Some people say as it's there still."

"I saw a story once of an old Spanish main or something. Right back to the time of the Armada, it was. A Spanish boat as went down there. Full of doubloons."

24

Attack on Tuppence

"Good gracious!" said Tommy, as he returned that evening. "You look terribly tired, Tuppence. What have you been doing? You look worn out."

"I am worn out," said Tuppence. "I don't know that I shall ever recover again. Oh dear."

"What *have* you been doing? Not climbing up and finding more books or anything?"

"No, no," said Tuppence, "I don't want to look at books again. I'm off books."

"Well, what is it? What have you been doing?"

"Do you know what a PPC is?"

"No," said Tommy, "at least, well, yes. It's something—" He paused.

"Yes, Albert knows," said Tuppence, "but it's not that kind of one. Now then, I'll just tell you in a minute, but you'd better have something first. A cocktail or a whisky or something. And I'll have something too."

She more or less put Tommy wise to the events of the afternoon. Tommy said "good gracious" again and added: "The things you get yourself into, Tuppence. Was any of it interesting?"

"I don't know," said Tuppence. "When six people are talking at once, and most of them can't talk properly and they all say different things—you see, you don't really know what they're saying. But yes, I think I've got a few ideas for dealing with things."

"What do you mean?"

"Well, there is a lot of legend, I think, going on

about something that was once hidden here and was a secret connected with the nineteen fourteen war, or even before it."

"Well, we know that already, don't we?" said Tommy. "I mean, we've been briefed to know that."

"Yes. Well, there are a few old tales still going around the village here. And everybody has got ideas about it put into their heads by their Aunt Marias or their Uncle Bens and it's been put into their Aunt Marias by their Uncle Stephens or Aunty Ruth or Grandmother Something-else. It's been handed down for years and years. Well, one of the things might be the right one, of course."

"What, lost among all the others?"

"Yes," said Tuppence, "like a needle in a haystack. Exactly."

"And how are you going to find the needle in the haystack?"

"I'm going to select a few what I call likely possibilities. People who might tell one something that they really *did* hear. I shall have to isolate them from everybody else, at any rate for a short period of time, and get them to tell me exactly what their Aunt Agatha or Aunt Betty or old Uncle James told them. Then I shall have to go on to the next one and possibly one of them might give me a further inkling. There must be something, you know, somewhere."

"Yes," said Tommy, "I think there's something, but we don't know what it is."

"Well, that's what we're trying to do, isn't it?"

"Yes, but I mean you've got to have some idea what a thing actually is before you go looking for it."

"I don't think it's gold ingots on a Spanish Armada ship," said Tuppence, "and I don't think it's anything hidden in the smugglers' cave."

"Might be some super brandy from France," said Tommy hopefully.

"It might," said Tuppence, "but that wouldn't be really what we're looking for, would it?"

"I don't know," said Tommy. "I think it might be what I'm looking for sooner or later. Anyway, it's something I should enjoy finding. Of course it might be a sort of letter or something. A sexy letter that you could blackmail someone about, about sixty years ago. But I don't think it would cut much ice nowadays, do you?"

"No, I don't. But we've got to get some idea sooner or later. Do you think we'll *ever* get anywhere, Tommy?"

"I don't know," said Tommy. "I got a little bit of help today."

"Oh. What about?"

"Oh, about the census."

"The what?"

"The census. There seems to have been a census in one particular year—I've got the year written down—and there were a good many people staying in this house with the Parkinsons."

"How on earth did you find all that out?"

"Oh, by various methods of research by my Miss Collodon."

"I'm getting jealous of Miss Collodon."

"Well, you needn't be. She's very fierce and she ticks me off a good deal, and she is no ravishing beauty."

"Well, that's just as well," said Tuppence. "But what has the census got to do with it?"

"Well, when Alexander said *It was one of us* it could have meant, you see, someone who was in the house at that time and therefore you had to enter up their name on the census register. Anyone who spent the night under the roof, and I think probably there are records of these things in the census files. And if you know the right people—I don't mean I know them now, but I can get to know them through people I do know—then I think I could perhaps get a short list."

"Well, I admit," said Tuppence, "you have ideas all

right. For goodness' sake let's have something to eat and perhaps I shall feel better and not so faint from trying to listen to sixteen very ugly voices all at once."

Albert produced a very passable meal. His cooking was erratic. It had its moments of brilliance which tonight was exemplified by what he called cheese pudding, and Tuppence and Tommy preferred to call cheese soufflé. Albert reproved them slightly for the wrong nomenclature.

"Cheese soufflé is different," he said, "got more beaten-up white of egg in it than this has."

"Never mind," said Tuppence, "it's very good whether it's cheese pudding or cheese soufflé."

Both Tommy and Tuppence were entirely absorbed with the eating of food and did not compare any more notes as to their procedure. When, however, they had both drunk two cups of strong coffee, Tuppence leaned back in her chair, uttered a deep sigh and said:

"Now I feel almost myself again. You didn't do much washing before dinner, did you, Tommy?"

"I couldn't be bothered to wait and wash," said Tommy. "Besides, I never know with you. You might have made me go upstairs to the book-room and stand on a dusty ladder and poke about on the shelves."

"I wouldn't be so unkind," said Tuppence. "Now wait a minute. Let's see where we are."

"Where we are or where you are?"

"Well, where I am, really," said Tuppence. "After all, that's the only thing I know about, isn't it? You know where you are and I know where I am. Perhaps, that is."

"May be a bit of perhaps about it," said Tommy.

"Pass me over my bag, will you, unless I've left it in the dining room?"

"You usually do, but you haven't this time. It's under the foot of your chair. No—the other side."

Tuppence picked up her handbag.

"Very nice present, this was," she said. "Real crocodile, I think. Bit difficult to stuff things in sometimes."

"And apparently to take them out again," said Tommy.

Tuppence was wrestling.

"Expensive bags are always very difficult for getting things out of," she said breathlessly. "Those basketwork ones are the most comfortable. They bulge to any extent and you can stir them up like you stir up a pudding. Ah! I think I've got it."

"What is it? It looks like a washing bill or something."

"Oh, it's a little sort of notebook. Yes, I used to write washing things in it, you know, what I had to complain about—torn pillowcase or something like that. But I thought it would come in useful, you see, because only three or four pages of it had been used. I put down here, you see, things we've heard. A great many of them don't seem to have any point, but there it is. I added census, by the way, when you first mentioned it. I didn't know what it meant at that time or what you meant by it. But anyway I did add it."

"Fine," said Tommy.

"And I put down Mrs. Henderson and someone called Dodo."

"Who was Mrs. Henderson?"

"Well, I don't suppose you'll remember and I needn't go back to it now but those were two of the names I put down that Mrs. What's-her-name, you know, the old one, Mrs. Griffin mentioned. And then there was a message or a notice. Something about Oxford and Cambridge. And I've come across another thing in one of the old books."

"What about Oxford and Cambridge? Do you mean an undergraduate?"

"I'm not sure whether there was an undergraduate or not, I think really it was a bet on the boat race."

"Much more likely," said Tommy. "Not awfully apt to be useful to us."

"Well, one never knows. So there's Mrs. Henderson and there's somebody who lives at something called Apple Tree Lodge and there's something I found on a dirty bit of paper shoved into one of the books upstairs. I don't know if it was *Catriona* or whether it was a book called *Shadow of the Throne*."

"That's about the French Revolution. I read it when I was a boy," said Tommy.

"Well, I don't see how that comes in. At any rate, I put it down."

"Well, what is it?"

"It seems to be three pencil words. Grin, g-r-i-n, then hen, h-e-n, and then Lo, capital l-o."

"Let me guess," said Tommy. "Cheshire cat—that's a grin—Henny-Penny, that's another fairy story, isn't it, for the hen, and Lo—"

"Ah," said Tuppence, "Lo does you in, does it?"

"Lo and behold," said Tommy, "but it doesn't seem to make sense."

Tuppence spoke rapidly. "Mrs. Henley, Apple Tree Lodge—I haven't done her yet, she's in Meadowside." Tuppence recited quickly: "Now, where are we? Mrs. Griffin, Oxford and Cambridge, bet on a boat race, census, Cheshire cat, Henny-Penny, the story where the hen went to the Dovrefell—Hans Andersen or something like that—and Lo. I suppose Lo means when they got there. Got to the Dovrefell, I mean. I don't think there's much else," said Tuppence. "There's the Oxford and Cambridge boat race or the bet."

"I should think the odds are on our being rather silly. But I think if we go on being silly long enough, some gem of great price might come out of it, concealed among the rubbish, as you might say. Just as we found one significant book on the bookshelves upstairs."

"Oxford and Cambridge," said Tuppence thoughtfully. "That makes me think of something. It makes me remember something. Now what could it be?"

"Mathilde?"

"No, it wasn't Mathilde, but—"

"Truelove," suggested Tommy. He grinned from ear to ear. "True love. Where can I my true love find?"

"Stop grinning, you ape," said Tuppence. "You've got that last thing on your brain. Grin-hen-Lo. Doesn't make sense. And yet—I have a kind of feeling—Oh!"

"What's the Oh about?"

"Oh! Tommy, I've got an idea. Of course."

"What's of course?"

"Lo," said Tuppence. "Lo. Grin is what made me think of it. You grinning like a Cheshire cat. Grin. Hen and then Lo. Of course. That must be it somehow."

"What on earth are you talking about?"

"Oxford and Cambridge boat race."

"Why does grin-hen-Lo make you think of Oxford and Cambridge boat race?"

"I'll give you three guesses," said Tuppence.

"Well, I give up at once because I don't think it could possibly make sense."

"It does really."

"What, the boat race?"

"No, nothing to do with the boat race. The color. Colors, I mean."

"What *do* you mean, Tuppence?"

"Grin-hen-Lo. We've been reading it the wrong way round. It's meant to be read the other way round."

"What do you mean? Ol, then n-e-h—it doesn't make sense. You couldn't go on n-i-r-g. Nirg or some word like that."

"No. Just take the three words. A little bit, you know, like what Alexander did in the book—the first book that we looked at. Read those three words the other way round. Lo-hen-grin."

Tommy scowled.

"Still haven't got it?" said Tuppence. "Lohengrin, of course. The swan. The opera. You know. You know, *Lohengrin*, Wagner."

"Well, there's nothing to do with a swan."

"Yes, there is. These two pieces of china we found. Stools for the garden. You remember? One was a dark blue and one was a light blue and old Isaac said to us, at least I think it was Isaac, he said, 'That's Oxford, you see, and that's Cambridge.'"

"Well, we smashed the Oxford one, didn't we?"

"Yes. But the Cambrdige one is still there. The light blue one. Don't you see? Lohengrin. Something was hidden in one of those two swans. Tommy, the next thing we have to do is to go and look at the Cambridge one. The light blue one, it's still in KK. Shall we go now?"

"What—at eleven o'clock at night—no."

"We'll go tomorrow. You haven't got to go to London tomorrow?"

"No."

"Well, we'll go tomorrow and we'll see."

"I don't know what you're doing about the garden," said Albert. "I did a spell once in a garden for a short time, but I'm not up in vegetables very much. There's a boy here that wants to see you, by the way, madam."

"Oh, a boy," said Tuppence, "do you mean the red-haired one?"

"No. I mean the other one, the one with a lot of messy yellow hair half down his back. Got rather a silly name. Like a hotel. You know, the Royal Clarence. That's his name. Clarence."

"Clarence, but not Royal Clarence."

"Not likely," said Albert. "He's waiting in the front

door. He says, madam, as he might be able to assist
you in some way."

"I see. I gather he used to assist old Isaac occasionally."

She found Clarence sitting on a decayed basket
chair on the veranda or loggia, whichever you liked
to call it. He appeared to be making a late breakfast
off potato crisps and held a bar of chocolate in his
left hand.

"Morning, missis," said Clarence. "Come to see if I
could be any help."

"Well," said Tuppence, "of course we do want help
in the garden. I believe you used to help Isaac at one
time."

"Ah well, now and again I did. Not that I know
very much. Don't say that Isaac knew much neither.
Lot of talk with him, lot of talking saying what a
wonderful time he used to have. What a wonderful
time it was for the people who employed him. Yes, he
used to say he was the head gardener to Mr. Bolingo.
You know, as lives further along the river. Great big
house. Yes, it's turned into a school now. Head gardener there, he said he used to be. But my grandmother says there isn't a word of truth in that."

"Well, never mind," said Tuppence. "Actually, I
wanted to turn a few more things out of that little
greenhouse place."

"What, d'you mean the shed, the glass shed? KK,
isn't it?"

"Quite right," said Tuppence. "Fancy your knowing
the proper name for it."

"Oh well, it was always used to be called that. Everybody says so. They say it's Japanese. I don't know
if that's true."

"Come on," said Tuppence. "Let's go there."

A procession formed consisting of Tommy, Tuppence, Hannibal the dog, with Albert abandoning
the washing up of breakfast for something more interesting bringing up the rear. Hannibal displayed a

great deal of pleasure after attending to all the useful smells in the neighborhood. He rejoined them at the door of the KK and sniffed in an interested manner.

"Hullo, Hannibal," said Tuppence, "are you going to help us? You tell us something."

"What kind of a dog is he?" asked Clarence. "Somebody said as he is the kind of dog they used to keep for rats. Is that so?"

"Yes, that's quite true," said Tommy. "He's a Manchester terrier, an old English Black and Tan."

Hannibal, knowing he was being talked about, turned his head, waggled his body, beat his tail with a good deal of exuberance. He then sat down and looked proud of himself.

"He bites, doesn't he?" said Clarence. "Everyone says so."

"He's a very good guard dog," said Tuppence. "He looks after me."

"That's quite right. When I'm away he looks after you," said Tommy.

"The postman said he nearly got bitten four days ago."

"Dogs are rather like that with postmen," said Tuppence. "Do you know where the key of KK is?"

"I do," said Clarence. "Hanging up in the shed. You know, the shed where the flowerpots are."

He went off and returned shortly with the once rusty but now more or less oiled key.

"Been oiling this key, Isaac must have," he said.

"Yes, it wouldn't turn very easily before," said Tuppence.

The door was opened.

The Cambridge china stool with the swan wreathed round it was looking rather handsome. Obviously Isaac had polished it up and washed it, with the idea of transferring it to the veranda when the weather was suitable for sitting out.

"Ought to be a dark blue one too," said Clarence. "Isaac used to say Oxford and Cambridge."

"Is that true?"

"Yes. Dark blue Oxford and pale blue Cambridge. Oh, and Oxford was the one that smashed, was it?"

"Yes. Rather like the boat race, isn't it?"

"By the way, something's happened to that rocking-horse, hasn't it? There's a lot of mess about in KK."

"Yes."

"Funny name like Matilda, hasn't she?"

"Yes. She had to have an operation," said Tuppence.

Clarence seemed to think this very amusing. He laughed heartily.

"My Great-Aunt Edith had to have an operation," he said. "Took out a good part of her inside, but she got well."

He sounded slightly disappointed.

"I suppose there's no real way of getting inside these things," said Tuppence.

"Well, I suppose you can smash them like the dark blue one was smashed."

"Yes. There's no other way, is there? Funny those sort of S-kind of slits around the top. Why, you could post things in there, couldn't you, like a postbox."

"Yes," said Tommy, "one could. It's an interesting idea. Very interesting, Clarence," he said kindly.

Clarence looked pleased.

"You can unscrew 'em, you know," he said.

"Unscrew them, can you?" said Tuppence. "Who told you that?"

"Isaac. I've seen 'im do it often. You turn them upside-down and then you begin to swing the top round. It's stiff sometimes. You pour a little oil round all the cracks and when it's soaked in a bit, you can turn it round."

"Oh."

"The easiest way is to put it upside-down."

"Everything here always seems to have to be turned

upside-down," said Tuppence. "We had to do that to Mathilde before we could operate."

For the moment Cambridge seemed to be entirely obstreperous, then quite suddenly the china began to revolve and very shortly afterwards they managed to unscrew it completely and lift it off.

"Lot of rubbish in here, I should think," said Clarence.

Hannibal came to assist. He was a dog who liked helping in anything that was going on. Nothing, he thought, was complete unless he took a hand or a paw in it. But with him it was usually a nose in the investigation. He stuck his nose down, growled gently, retired an inch or two and sat down.

"Doesn't like it much, does he?" said Tuppence, and looked down into the somewhat unpleasant mass inside.

"Ow!" said Clarence.

"What's the matter?"

"Scratched myself. There's something hanging down from a nail on the side here. I don't know if it's a nail or what it is. It's something. Ow!"

"Wuff, wuff!" said Hannibal, joining in.

"There's something hung on a nail just inside. Yes, I've got it. No. It's slipping. Yes, here I am. I've got it."

Clarence lifted out a dark tarpaulin package.

Hannibal came and sat at Tuppence's feet. He growled.

"What's the matter, Hannibal?" said Tuppence.

Hannibal growled again. Tuppence bent down and smoothed the top of his head and ears.

"What's the matter, Hannibal?" said Tuppence. "Did you want Oxford to win and now Cambridge have won, you see. Do you remember," said Tuppence to Tommy, "how we let him watch the boat race once on television?"

"Yes," said Tommy, "he got very angry towards the

end and started barking so that we couldn't hear anything at all."

"Well, we could still see things," said Tuppence; "that was something. But if you remember, he didn't like Cambridge winning."

"Obviously," said Tommy, "he studied at the Oxford Dogs' University."

Hannibal left Tuppence and came to Tommy and wagged his tail appreciatively.

"He likes your saying that," said Tuppence; "it must be true. I myself," she added, "think he has been educated at the Dogs' Open University."

"What were his principal studies there?" asked Tommy, laughing.

"Bone disposal."

"You know what he's like."

"Yes, I know," said Tuppence. "Very unwisely, you know, Albert gave him the whole bone of a leg of mutton once. First of all I found him in the drawing room putting it under a cushion, then I forced him out through the garden door and shut it. And I looked out of the window and he went into the flower bed where I'd got gladioli, and buried it very carefully there. He's very tidy with his bones, you know. He never tries to eat them. He always puts them away for a rainy day."

"Does he ever dig them up again?" asked Clarence, assisting on this point of dog lore.

"I think so," said Tuppence. "Sometimes when they're very, very old and would have been better if they had been left buried."

"Our dog doesn't like dog biscuits," said Clarence.

"He leaves them on the plate, I suppose," said Tuppence, "and eats the meat first."

"He likes sponge cake, though, our dog does," said Clarence.

Hannibal sniffed at the trophy just disinterred from the inside of Cambridge. He wheeled round suddenly then and barked.

"See if there's anyone outside," said Tuppence. "It might be a gardener. Somebody told me the other day, Mrs. Herring, I think it was, that she knew of an elderly man who'd been a very good gardener in his time and who did jobbing."

Tommy opened the door and went outside. Hannibal accompanied him.

"Nobody here," said Tommy.

Hannibal barked. First he growled again, then he barked and barked more loudly.

"He thinks there's someone or something in that great clump of pampas grass," said Tommy. "Perhaps someone is un-burying one of his bones there. Perhaps there's a rabbit there. Hannibal's very stupid about rabbits. He needs an awful lot of encouragement before he'll chase a rabbit. He seems to have a kindly feeling about them. He goes after pigeons and large birds. Fortunately he never catches them."

Hannibal was now sniffing round the pampas grass, first growling, after which he then began to bark loudly. At intervals he turned his head towards Tommy.

"I expect there's a cat in there," said Tommy. "You know what he's like when he thinks a cat is around. There's that big black cat that comes round here and the little one. The one that we call the Kitty-cat."

"That's the one that's always getting into the house," said Tuppence. "It seems to get through the smallest chinks. Oh, do stop, Hannibal. Come back."

Hannibal heard and turned his head. He was expressing a very high degree of fierceness. He gave Tuppence a look, went back a little way, then turned his attention once more to the clump of pampas grass and began barking furiously.

"There's something worries him," said Tommy. "Come on, Hannibal."

Hannibal shook himself, shook his head, looked at Tommy, looked at Tuppence and made a prancing attack on the pampas grass, barking loudly.

There was a sudden sound. Two sharp explosions.

"Good Lord, somebody must be shooting rabbits," exclaimed Tuppence.

"Get back. Get back inside KK," said Tommy.

Something flew past his ear. Hannibal, now fully alerted, was racing round and round the pampas grass. Tommy ran after him.

"He's chasing someone now," he said. "He's chasing someone down the hill. He's running like mad."

"Who was it—what was it?" said Tuppence.

"You all right, Tuppence?"

"No, I'm not quite all right," said Tuppence. "Something—something, I think, hit me here, just below the shoulder. Was it—what was it?"

"It was someone shooting at us. Someone who was hidden inside that pampas grass."

"Someone who was watching what we were doing," said Tuppence. "Do you think that's it, perhaps?"

"I expect it's them Irish," said Clarence hopefully. "The IRA. You know. They've been trying to blow this place up."

"I don't think it's of any political significance," said Tuppence.

"Come into the house," said Tommy. "Come quickly. Come on, Clarence, you'd better come too."

"You don't think your dog will bite me?" said Clarence uncertainly.

"No," said Tommy, "I think he is busy for the moment."

They had just turned the corner into the garden door when Hannibal reappeared suddenly. He came racing up the hill very out of breath. He spoke to Tommy in the way a dog does speak. He came up to him, shook himself, put a paw on Tommy's knee, caught Tommy by his trouser leg and tried to pull him in the direction from which he had just come.

"He wants me to go with him after whoever the man was," said Tommy.

"Well, you're not to," said Tuppence. "If there's anyone there with a rifle or a pistol or something that shoots, I'm not going to have you shot. Not at your age. Who would look after me if anything happened to you? Come on, let's get indoors."

They went into the house quickly. Tommy went out into the hall and spoke on the telephone.

"What are you doing?" said Tuppence.

"Telephoning the police," said Tommy. "Can't let anything like this pass. They may get onto someone if we're in time."

"I think," said Tuppence, "that I want something put on my shoulder. This blood is ruining my best jumper."

"Never mind your jumper," said Tommy.

Albert appeared at that moment with a complete service of first aid.

"Well, I never," said Albert, "you mean some dirty guy has shot at the missis? Whatever's happening next in this country."

"You don't think you ought to go to the hospital, do you?"

"No, I don't," said Tuppence. "I'm quite all right, but I want an outsize Band-aid or something to stick on here. Put on something like friars' balsam first."

"I've got some iodine."

"I don't want iodine. It stings. Besides, they say now in hospitals that it isn't the right thing to put on."

"I thought friars' balsam was something you breathed in out of an inhaler," said Albert hopefully.

"That's one use," said Tuppence, "but it's very good to put on slight scratches or scars or if children cut themselves or anything like that. Have you got the thing all right?"

"What thing, what do you mean, Tuppence?"

"The thing we just got out of the Cambridge Lohengrin. That's what I mean. The thing that was hanging on a nail. Perhaps it's something important, you know. They saw us. And so if they tried to kill us—and tried to get whatever it was—that really would be something!"

25

Hannibal Takes Action

Tommy sat with the police inspector in his office. The police officer, Inspector Norris, was nodding his head gently.

"I hope with any luck we may get results, Mr. Beresford," he said. "Dr. Crossfield, you say, is attending your wife."

"Yes," said Tommy, "it isn't serious, I gather. It was just grazing by a bullet and it bled a good deal, but she's going to be all right, I think. There's nothing really dangerous, Dr. Crossfield said."

"She's not very young, though, I suppose," said Inspector Norris.

"She's over seventy," said Tommy. "We're both of us getting on, you know."

"Yes, yes. Quite so," said Inspector Norris. "I've heard a good deal about her locally, you know, since you came here to live. People have taken to her in a big way, down here. We've heard about her various activities. And about yours."

"Oh dear," said Tommy.

"Can't live down your record, you know, whatever it is, good or bad," said Inspector Norris in a kindly voice. "You can't live down your record if you're a criminal and you can't live down your record if you've been a hero either. Of one thing I can assure you. We'll do all we can to clear things up. You can't describe whoever it was, I suppose?"

"No," said Tommy. "When I saw him, he was run-

ning with our dog after him. I should say he was not
very old. He ran easily, I mean."

"Difficult age round about fourteen, fifteen on-
wards."

"It was someone older than that," said Tommy.

"Not had any telephone calls or letters, demands
for money or anything like that?" said the inspector.
"Asking you to get out of your house, maybe?"

"No," said Tommy, "nothing like that."

"And you've been here—how long?"

Tommy told him.

"Hmmm. Not very long. You go to London, I
gather, most days of the week."

"Yes," said Tommy. "If you want particulars—"

"No," said Inspector Norris, "no. No, I don't need
any particulars. The only thing I should suggest is
that—well, you don't go away too often. If you can
manage to stay at home and look after Mrs. Beresford
yourself . . ."

"I thought of doing that anyway," said Tommy. "I
think this is a good excuse for my not turning up always at the various appointments I've got in
London."

"Well, we'll do all we can to keep an eye on things,
and if we could get hold of this whoever it is . . ."

"Do you feel—perhaps I oughtn't to ask this—" said
Tommy—"do you feel you know who it is? Do you
know his name or his reasons?"

"Well, we know a good many things about some of
the chaps around here. More than they think we
know very often. Sometimes we don't make it appar-
ent how much we do know because that's the best
way to get at them in the end. You find out then who
they're mixed up with, who's paying them for some of
the things they do, or whether they thought of it
themselves out of their own heads. But I think—well,
I think somehow that this isn't one of our locals, as
you might say."

"Why do you think that?" asked Tommy.

"Ah. Well, one hears things, you know. One gets information from various headquarters elsewhere."

Tommy and the inspector looked at each other. For about five minutes neither of them spoke. They were just looking.

"Well," said Tommy, "I—I see. Yes. Perhaps I see."

"If I may say one thing," said Inspector Norris.

"Yes?" said Tommy, looking rather doubtful.

"This garden of yours. You want a bit of help in it, I understand."

"Our gardener was killed, as you probably know."

"Yes, I know all about that. Old Isaac Bodlicott, wasn't it? Fine old chap. Told tall stories now and then about the wonderful things he'd done in his time. But he was a well-known character and a fellow you could trust, too."

"I can't imagine why he was killed or who killed him," said Tommy. "Nobody seems to have had any idea or to have found out."

"You mean *we* haven't found out. Well, these things take a little time, you know. It doesn't come out at the time the inquest's on, and the coroner sums up and says, 'Murder by some person unknown.' That's only the beginning sometimes. Well, what I was going to say was it's likely someone may come and ask you whether you'd like a chap to come and do a bit of jobbing gardening for you. He'll come along and say that he could come two or three days a week. Perhaps more. He'll tell you, for reference, that he worked for some years for Mr. Solomon. You'll remember that name, will you?"

"Mr. Solomon," said Tommy.

There seemed to be something like a twinkle for a moment in Inspector Norris's eye.

"Yes, he's dead, of course. Mr. Solomon, I mean. But he *did* live here and he *did* employ several different jobbing gardeners. I'm not quite sure what name this chap will give you. We'll say I don't quite remember it. It might be one of several—it's likely to be Crispin, I think. Between thirty and fifty or so, and he worked for Mr. Solomon. If anyone comes along and says he can do some jobbing gardening for you and *doesn't* mention Mr. Solomon, in that case, I wouldn't accept him. That's just a word of warning."

"I see," said Tommy. "Yes. I see. At least, I hope I see the point."

"That's the point," said Inspector Norris. "You're quick on the uptake, Mr. Beresford. Well, I suppose you've had to be quite often in your activities. Nothing more you want to know that we could tell you?"

"I don't think so," said Tommy. "I wouldn't know what to ask."

"We shall be making inquiries, not necessarily round here, you know. I may be in London or other parts looking round. We all help to look round. Well, you'd know that, wouldn't you?"

"I want to try and keep Tuppence—keep my wife from getting herself too mixed up in things because—but it's difficult."

"Women are always difficult," said Inspector Norris.

Tommy repeated that remark later as he sat by Tuppence's bedside and watched her eating grapes.

"Do you really eat all the pips of grapes?"

"Usually," said Tuppence. "It takes so much time getting them out, doesn't it? I don't think they hurt you."

"Well, if they haven't hurt you by now, and you've been doing it all your life, I shouldn't think they would," said Tommy.

"What did the police say?"

"Exactly what we thought they would say."

"Do they know who it's likely to have been?"

"They say they don't think it's a local."

"Who did you see? Inspector Watson his name is, isn't it?"

"No. This was an Inspector Norris."

"Oh, that's one I don't know. What else did he say?"

"He said women were always very difficult to restrain."

"Really!" said Tuppence. "Did he know you were coming back to tell me that?"

"Possibly not," said Tommy. He got up. "I must put in a telephone call or two to London. I'm not going up for a day or two."

"You can go up all right. I'm quite safe here! There's Albert looking after me and all the rest of it. Dr. Crossfield has been terribly kind and rather like a sort of broody hen watching over me."

"I'll have to go out to get things for Albert. Anything you want?"

"Yes," said Tuppence, "you might bring me back a melon. I'm feeling very inclined to fruit. Nothing but fruit."

"All right," said Tommy.

Tommy rang up a London number.

"Colonel Pikeaway?"

"Yes. Hullo. Ah, it's you, Thomas Beresford, is it?"

"Ah, you recognized my voice. I wanted to tell you that—"

"Something about Tuppence. I've heard it all," said Colonel Pikeaway. "No need to talk. Stay where you are for the next day or two or a week. Don't come up to London. Report anything that happens."

"There may be some things which we ought to bring you."

"Well, hang onto them for the moment. Tell Tuppence to invent a place to hide them until then."

"She's good at that sort of thing. Like our dog. He hides bones in the garden."

"I hear he chased the man who shot at you both, and saw him off the place—"

"You seem to know all about it."

"We always know things here," said Colonel Pikeaway.

"Our dog managed to get a snap at him and came
back with a sample of his trousers in his mouth."

26

Oxford, Cambridge
and Lohengrin

"Good man," said Colonel Pikeaway, puffing out smoke. "Sorry to send for you so urgently, but I thought I'd better see you."

"As I expect you know," said Tommy, "we've been having something a little unexpected lately."

"Ah! Why should you think I know?"

"Because you always know everything here."

Colonel Pikeaway laughed.

"Hah! Quoting me to myself, aren't you? Yes, that's what I say. We know everything. That's what we're here for. Did she have a very narrow escape? Your wife, I'm talking about, as you know."

"She didn't have a narrow escape, but there might have been something serious. I expect you know most of the details, or do you want me to tell you?"

"You can run over it quickly if you like. There's a bit I didn't hear," said Colonel Pikeaway, "the bit about Lohengrin. Grin-hen-Lo. She's sharp, you know, your wife is. She saw the point of that. It seems idiotic, but there it was."

"I've brought you the results today," said Tommy. "We hid them in the flour bin until I could get up to see you. I didn't like to send them by post."

"No. Quite right—"

"In a kind of tin—not tin but a better metal than that—box and hanging in Lohengrin. Pale blue Lohengrin. Cambridge. Victorian china outdoor garden stool."

"Remember them myself in the old days. Had an aunt in the country who used to have a pair."

"It was well preserved, sewn up in tarpaulin. Inside it are letters. They are somewhat perished and that, but I expect with expert treatment—"

"Yes, we can manage that sort of thing all right."

"Here they are then," said Tommy, "and I've got a sort of list for you of things that we've noted down, Tuppence and I. Things that have been mentioned or told us."

"Names?"

"Yes. Three or four. The Oxford and Cambridge clue and the mention of Oxford and Cambridge graduates staying there—I don't think there was anything in that, because really it referred simply to the Lohengrin porcelain stools, I suppose."

"Yes—yes—yes, there are one or two other things here that are quite interesting."

"After we were fired at," said Tommy, "I reported it of course to the police."

"Quite right."

"Then I was asked to go down to the police station the next day and I saw Inspector Norris there. I haven't come in contact with him before. I think he must be rather a new officer."

"Yes. Probably on a special assignment," said Colonel Pikeaway. He puffed out more smoke.

Tommy coughed.

"I expect you know all about him."

"I know about him," said Colonel Pikeaway. "We know everything here. He's all right. He's in charge of this inquiry. Local people will perhaps be able to spot who it was who's been following you about, finding out things about you. You don't think, do you, Beresford, that it would be well if you left the place for a while and brought your wife along?"

"I don't think I could do that," said Tommy.

"You mean she wouldn't come?" said Colonel Pikeaway.

"Again," said Tommy, "if I may mention it, you seem to know everything. I don't think you could draw Tuppence away. Mind you, she's not badly hurt, she's not ill and she's got a feeling now that—well, that we're onto something. We don't know what it is and we don't know what we shall find or do."

"Nose around," said Colonel Pikeaway, "that's all you can do in a case of this kind." He tapped a nail on the metal box. "This little box is going to tell us something, though, and it's going to tell us something we've always wanted to know. Who was involved a great many years ago in setting things going and doing a lot of dirty work behind the scenes."

"But surely—"

"I know what you're going to say. You're going to say whoever it was is now dead. That's true. But it tells us nevertheless what was going on, how it was set in motion, who helped, who inspired it and who has inherited or carried on with something of the same business ever since. People who don't seem to amount to much but possibly they amount to more than we've ever thought. And people who've been in touch with the same group, as one calls it—one calls anything a group nowadays—the same group which may have different people in it now but who have the same ideas, the same love of violence and evil and the same people to communicate with elsewhere and other groups. Some groups are all right but some groups are worse because they are groups. It's a kind of technique, you know. We've taught it to ourselves in the last, oh, say fifty to a hundred years. Taught that if people cohere together and make a tight little mob of themselves, it's amazing what they are able to accomplish and what they are able to inspire other people to accomplish for them."

"May I ask you something?"

"Anyone can always ask," said Colonel Pikeaway. "We know everything here but we don't always tell, I have to warn you of that."

"Does the name of Solomon mean anything to you?"

"Ah," said Colonel Pikeaway. "Mr. Solomon. And where did you get that name from?"

"It was mentioned by Inspector Norris."

"I see. Well, if you're going by what Norris said, you're going right. I can tell you that. You won't see Solomon personally, I don't mind telling you. He's dead."

"Oh," said Tommy, "I see."

"At least you don't quite see," said Colonel Pikeaway. "We use his name sometimes. It's useful, you know, to have a name you can use. The name of a real person, a person who isn't there any longer but although dead is still highly regarded in the neighborhood. It's sheer chance you ever came to live in The Laurels at all and we've got hopes that it may lead to a piece of luck for us. But I don't want it to be a cause of disaster to you or to your missis. Suspect everyone and everything. It's the best way."

"I only trust two people there," said Tommy. "One's Albert, who's worked for us for years—"

"Yes, I remember Albert. Red-haired boy, wasn't he?"

"Not a boy any longer—"

"Who's the other one?"

"My dog Hannibal."

"Hm. Yes—you may have something there. Who was it—Dr. Watts who wrote a hymn beginning, 'Dogs delight to bark and bite, It is their nature too.'— What is he, an Alsatian?"

"No, he's a Manchester terrier."

"Ah, an old English Black and Tan, not as big as a Doberman pinscher but the kind of dog that knows his stuff."

27

Visit from Miss Mullins

Tuppence, walking along the garden path, was accosted by Albert coming down at a quick pace from the house.

"Lady waiting to see you," he said.

"Lady? Oh, who is it?"

"Miss Mullins, she says she is. Recommended by one of the ladies in the village to call on you."

"Oh, of course," said Tuppence. "About the garden, isn't it?"

"Yes, she said something about the garden."

"I think you'd better bring her out here," said Tuppence.

"Yes, madam," said Albert, falling into his role of experienced butler.

He went back to the house and returned a few moments later bringing with him a tall masculine-looking woman in tweed trousers and a Fair Isle pullover.

"Chilly wind this morning," she said.

Her voice was deep and slightly hoarse.

"I'm Iris Mullins. Mrs. Griffin suggested I should come along and see you. Wanting some help in the garden. Is that it?"

"Good morning," said Tuppence, shaking hands. "I'm very pleased to see you. Yes, we do want some help in the garden."

"Only just moved in, haven't you?"

"Well, it feels almost like years," said Tuppence, "because we've only just got all the workmen out."

"Ah yes," said Miss Mullins, giving a deep hoarse chuckle. "Know what it is to have workmen in the

241

house. But you're quite right to come in yourself and not leave it to them. Nothing gets finished until the owner's moved in and even then you usually have to get them back again to finish something they've forgotten about. Nice garden you've got here, but it's been let go a bit, hasn't it?"

"Yes, I'm afraid the last people who lived here didn't care much about how the garden looked."

"People called Jones or something like that, weren't they? Don't think I actually know them. Most of my time here, you know, I've lived on the other side, the moor side, of the town. Two houses there I go to regularly. One, two days a week and the other one, one day. Actually, one day isn't enough, not to keep it right. You had old Isaac working here, didn't you? Nice old boy. Sad he had to get himself done in by some of this violent guerrilla material that's always going about bashing someone. The inquest was about a week ago, wasn't it? I hear they haven't found out who did it yet. Go about in little groups they do, and mug people. Nasty lot. Very often the younger they are, the nastier they are. That's a nice magnolia you've got there. Soulangeana, isn't it? Much the best to have. People always want the more exotic kinds, but it's better to stick to old friends when it's magnolias, in my opinion."

"It's really been more the vegetables that we're thinking about."

"Yes, you want to build up a good working kitchen garden, don't you? There doesn't seem to have been much attention paid before. People lose their spirit and think it's better really to buy their vegetables, and not try and grow them."

"I'd always want to grow new potatoes and peas," said Tuppence, "and I think French beans too, because you then can have them all young."

"That's right. You might as well add runner beans. Most gardeners are so proud of their runner beans that they like them a foot and a half in length. They think that's a fine bean. Always takes a prize at a local show. But you're quite right, you know. Young vegetables are the things that you really enjoy eating."

Albert appeared suddenly.

"Mrs. Redcliffe on the telephone, madam," he said. "Wanted to know if you could lunch tomorrow?"

"Tell her I'm very sorry," said Tuppence. "I'm afraid we may have to go to London tomorrow. Oh—wait a minute, Albert. Just wait while I write a word or two."

She pulled out a small pad from her bag, wrote a few words on it and handed it to Albert.

"Tell Mr. Beresford," she said. "Tell him Miss Mullins is here and we're in the garden. I forgot to do what he asked me to do, give him the name and address of the person he is writing to. I've written it here—"

"Certainly, madam," said Albert, and disappeared.

Tuppence returned to the vegetable conversation.

"I expect you're very busy," she said, "as you are working three days already."

"Yes, and as I said it's rather the other side of the town. I live the other side of the town. I've got a small cottage there."

At that moment Tommy arrived from the house. Hannibal was with him, running round in large circles. Hannibal reached Tuppence first. He stopped still for a moment, spread out his paws, and then rushed at Miss Mullins with a fierce array of barking. She took a step or two back in some alarm.

"This is our terrible dog," said Tuppence. "He doesn't really bite, you know. At least very seldom. It's usually only the postman he likes to bite."

"All dogs bite postmen, or try to," said Miss Mullins.

"He's a very good guard dog," said Tuppence. "He's a Manchester terrier, you know, and they are good guard dogs. He protects the house in a wonderful way. He won't let anyone near it or come inside, and he looks after me very carefully. He evidently regards me as his principal charge in life."

"Oh well, of course I suppose it's a good thing nowadays."

"I know. There are so many robberies about," said Tuppence. "Lots of our friends, you know, have had burglars. Some even who come in in broad daylight in the most extraordinary way. They set up ladders and take window sashes out or pretend to be windowcleaners—up to all kinds of tricks. So it's a good thing to let it be known that there's a fierce dog in the house, I think."

"I think perhaps you're quite right."

"Here is my husband," said Tuppence. "This is Miss Mullins, Tommy. Mrs. Griffin very kindly told her that we wanted someone who could possibly do some gardening for us."

"Would this be too heavy work for you perhaps, Miss Mullins?"

"Of course not," said Miss Mullins in her deep voice. "Oh, I can dig with anyone. You've got to dig the right way. It's not only trenching the sweet peas, it's everything needs digging, needs manuring. The ground's got to be prepared. Makes all the difference."

Hannibal continued to bark.

"I think, Tommy," said Tuppence, "you'd really better take Hannibal back to the house. He seems to be in rather a protective mood this morning."

"All right," said Tommy.

"Won't you come back to the house," said Tuppence to Miss Mullins, "and have something to drink? It's rather a hot morning and I think it would be a good thing, don't you? And we can discuss plans together perhaps."

Hannibal was shut into the kitchen and Miss Mullins accepted a glass of sherry. A few suggestions were made, then Miss Mullins looked at her watch and said she must hurry back.

"I have an appointment," she explained. "I mustn't be late." She bade them a somewhat hurried farewell and departed.

"She *seems* all right," said Tuppence.

"I know," said Tommy. "But one can't ever be sure—"

"One could ask questions?" said Tuppence doubtfully.

"You must be tired going all round the garden. We must leave our expedition this afternoon for another day—you have been ordered to rest."

28

Garden Campaign

"You understand, Albert," said Tommy.

He and Albert went together in the pantry where Albert was washing up the tea tray he had just brought down from Tuppence's bedroom.

"Yes, sir," said Albert. "I understand."

"You know, I think you will get a bit of a warning—you know what I mean—from Hannibal."

"He's a good dog in some ways," said Albert. "Doesn't take to everyone, of course."

"No," said Tommy, "that's not his job in life. Not one of those dogs who welcome in the burglars and wag their tails at the wrong person. Hannibal knows a few things. But I have made it quite clear to you, haven't I?"

"Yes. I don't know what I am to do if the missis— well, am I to do what the missis says or tell her what you said or—"

"I think you'll have to use a certain amount of diplomacy," said Tommy. "I'm making her stay in bed today. I'm leaving her in your charge more or less."

Albert had just opened the front door to a youngish man in a tweed suit.

Albert looked up doubtfully at Tommy. The visitor stepped inside and advanced one step, a friendly smile on his face.

"Mr. Beresford? I've heard you want a bit of help in your garden—just moved in here lately, haven't you? I noticed coming up the drive that it was getting rather overgrown. I did some work locally a couple of years ago—for a Mr. Solomon—you may have heard of him."

"Mr. Solomon, yes, someone did mention him."

"My name's Crispin, Angus Crispin. Perhaps we might take a look at what wants doing."

"About time someone did something about the garden," said Mr. Crispin, as Tommy led him on a tour of the flower beds and the vegetable garden.

"That's where they used to grow the spinach along this kitchen garden path here. Behind it were some frames. They used to grow melons too."

"You seem to be very well aware of all this."

"Well, one heard a lot you know of what had been everywhere in the old days. Old ladies tell you about the flower beds and Alexander Parkinson told a lot of his pals about the foxglove leaves."

"He must have been a rather remarkable boy."

"Well, he had ideas and he was very keen on crime," said Tommy. "He made a kind of code message out in one of Stevenson's books: *The Black Arrow.*"

"Rather a good one that, isn't it? I read it myself about five years ago. Before that I'd never got further than *Kidnapped.* When I was working for—" He hesitated.

"Mr. Solomon?" suggested Tommy.

"Yes, yes, that's the name. I heard things. Heard things from old Isaac. I gather, unless I've heard the wrong rumors, I gather that old Isaac must have been, oh, getting on for a hundred and did some work for you here."

"Yes," said Tommy. "For his age he was rather wonderful, really. He knew a lot of things he used to tell us, too. Things he couldn't have remembered himself."

"No, but he liked the gossip of the old days. All things like that. He's got relations here still, you know, who have listened to his tales and checked up on his stories. I expect you've heard a good many things yourself."

"So far," said Tommy, "everything seems to work out in lists of names. Names from the past but names, naturally, that don't mean anything to me. They can't."

"All hearsay?"

"Mostly. My wife has listened to a lot of it and made some lists. I don't know whether any of them mean anything. I've got one list myself. It only came into my hands yesterday, as a matter of fact."

"Oh. What's your list?"

"Census," said Tommy. "You know, there's a census on—I've got the date written down so I'll give it to you—and the people who were entered up that day because they spent the night here. There was a big party. A dinner party."

"So you know on a certain date—and perhaps quite an interesting date—who was here?"

"Yes," said Tommy.

"It might be valuable. It might be quite significant. You've only just moved in here, haven't you?"

"Yes," said Tommy, "but it's possible we might just want to move out of here."

"Don't you like it? It's a nice house, and this garden—well, this garden could be made very beautiful indeed. You've got some fine shrubs—wants a bit of clearing out, superfluous trees and bushes, flowering shrubs that haven't flowered lately and may never flower again by the look of them. Yes, I don't know why you'd want to go and move."

"The associations with the past aren't terribly pleasant here," said Tommy.

"The past," said Mr. Crispin. "How does the past tie up with the present?"

"One thinks it doesn't matter, it's all behind us. But there's always somebody left, you know. I don't mean walking about, but somebody who comes alive when people tell you about her or him or it or them. You really would be prepared to do a bit of—"

"Bit of jobbing gardening for you? Yes, I would. It would interest me. It's rather a—well, it's rather a hobby of mine, gardening."

"There was a Miss Mullins who came yesterday."

"Mullins? Mullins? Is she a gardener?"

"I gather something in that line. It was a Mrs.—a Mrs. Griffin, I think it was—who mentioned her to my wife and who sent her along to see us."

"Did you fix up with her or not?"

"Not definitely," said Tommy. "As a matter of fact we've got a rather enthusiastic guard dog here. A Manchester terrier."

"Yes, they can be very enthusiastic at guarding. I suppose he thinks your wife is his business and he practically never lets her go anywhere alone. He's always there."

"Quite right," said Tommy, "and he's prepared to tear anyone limb from limb who lays a finger on her."

"Nice dogs. Very affectionate, very loyal, very self-willed, very sharp teeth. I'd better look out for him, I suppose."

"He's all right at the moment. He's up in the house."

"Miss Mullins," said Crispin thoughtfully. "Yes. Yes, that's interesting."

"Why is it interesting?"

"Oh, I think it's because—well, I wouldn't know her by that name, of course. Is she between fifty and sixty?"

"Yes. Very tweedy and countrified."

"Yes. Got some county connections, too. Isaac could have told you something about her, I expect. I heard she'd come back to live here. Not so very long ago, either. Things tie up, you know."

"I expect you know things about this place that I don't," said Tommy.

"I shouldn't think so. Isaac could have told you a

lot, though. He knew things. Old stories, as you say, but he had a memory. And they talk it over. Yes, in these clubs for old people, they talk things over. Tall stories—some of them not true, some of them based on fact. Yes, it's all very interesting. And—I suppose he knew too much."

"It's a shame about Isaac," said Tommy. "I'd like to get even with whoever did him in. He was a nice old boy and he was good to us and did as much as he could to help us here. Come on, anyway, let's go on looking round."

29

Hannibal Sees Active Service with Mr. Crispin

Albert tapped on the bedroom door and in answer to Tuppence's "Come in" advanced his head round the side of it.

"The lady as came the other morning," he said. "Miss Mullins. She's here. Wants to speak to you for a minute or two. Suggestions about the garden, I understand. I said as you was in bed and I wasn't sure if you were receiving."

"The words you use, Albert," said Tuppence. "All right. I am receiving."

"I was just going to bring your morning coffee up."

"Well, you can bring that up and another cup. That's all. There'll be enough for two, won't there?"

"Oh yes, madam."

"Very well, then. Bring it up, and put it on the table over there, and then bring Miss Mullins up."

"What about Hannibal?" said Albert. "Shall I take him down and shut him up in the kitchen?"

"He doesn't like being shut up in the kitchen. No. Just push him into the bathroom and shut the door of it when you've done so."

Hannibal, resenting the insult which was being put upon him, allowed with a bad grace Albert's pushing him into the bathroom and adjustment to the door. He gave several loud fierce barks.

"Shut up!" Tuppence shouted to him. "Shut up!"

Hannibal consented to shut up as far as barking

went. He lay down with his paws in front of him and his nose pressed to the crack under the door and uttered long, noncooperative growls.

"Oh, Mrs. Beresford," cried Miss Mullins, "I'm afraid I am intruding, but I really thought you'd like to look at this book I have on gardening. Suggestions for planting at this time of year. Some very rare and interesting shrubs and they do quite well in this particular soil although some people say they won't ... Oh dear—oh no, oh, it's very kind of you. Yes, I would like a cup of coffee. Please let me pour it out for you, it's so difficult when you're in bed. I wonder, perhaps—" Miss Mullins looked at Albert, who obligingly drew up a chair.

"That be all right for you, miss?" he demanded.

"Oh yes, very nice indeed. Dear me, is that another bell downstairs?"

"Milk, I expect," said Albert. "Or might be the grocer. It's his morning. Excuse me, won't you."

He went out of the room, shutting the door behind him. Hannibal gave another growl.

"That's my dog," said Tuppence. "He's very annoyed at not being allowed to join the party, but he makes so much noise."

"Do you take sugar, Mrs. Beresford?"

"One lump," said Tuppence.

Miss Mullins poured out a cup of coffee. Tuppence said, "Otherwise black."

Miss Mullins put down the coffee beside Tuppence and went to pour out a cup for herself.

Suddenly she stumbled, clutched at an occasional table, and went down on her knees with an exclamation of dismay.

"Have you hurt yourself?" demanded Tuppence.

"No, oh no, but I've broken your vase. I caught my foot in something—so clumsy—and your beautiful vase is smashed. Dear Mrs. Beresford, what will you think of me? I assure you it was an accident."

"Of course it was," said Tuppence kindly. "Let me see. Well, it looks as if it could be worse. It's broken in two, which means we shall be able to glue it together. I dare say the join will hardly show."

"I shall still feel awful about it," declared Miss Mullins. "I know you must perhaps be feeling ill and I oughtn't to have come today, but I did so want to tell you—"

Hannibal began to bark again.

"Oh, the poor wee doggie," said Miss Mullins, "shall I let him out?"

"Better not," said Tuppence. "He's not very reliable sometimes."

"Oh dear, is that another bell downstairs?"

"No," said Tuppence, "I think that's the telephone."

"Oh. Does it need to be answered?"

"No," said Tuppence. "Albert'll answer it. He can always bring up a message if necessary."

It was, however, Tommy who answered the telephone.

"Hello," he said, "yes? Oh, I see. Who? I see—yes. Oh. An enemy, definite enemy. Yes, that's all right. We've taken the countermeasures all right. Yes. Thank you very much."

He dropped the receiver back and looked at Mr. Crispin.

"Words of warning?" said Mr. Crispin.

"Yes," said Tommy.

He continued to look at Mr. Crispin.

"Difficult to know, isn't it? I mean, who's your enemy and who's your friend."

"Sometimes when you know, it's too late. Postern of Fate, Disaster's Cavern," said Tommy.

Mr. Crispin looked at him in some surprise.

"Sorry," said Tommy. "For some reason or other we've got in the habit of reciting poetry in this house."

"Flecker, isn't it? Gates of Baghdad or is it the Gates of Damascus?"

"Come up, will you?" said Tommy. "Tuppence is only resting, she's not suffering from any peculiar disease or anything. Not even a sneezing cold in the head."

"I've taken up coffee," said Albert, reappearing suddenly, "and an extra cup for Miss Mullins wot's up there now with a gardening book or something."

"I see," said Tommy. "Yes. Yes, it's all going very well. Where's Hannibal?"

"Shut him in the bathroom."

"Did you latch the door very tight, because he won't like that, you know."

"No, sir, I've done just what you said."

Tommy went upstairs. Mr. Crispin came just behind him. Tommy gave a little tap on the bedroom door and then went in. From the bathroom door Hannibal gave one more outspoken bark of defiance, then he leapt at the door from the inside, the latch gave, he shot out into the room. He gave one quick glance at Mr. Crispin, then came forward and lunged with all his might, growling furiously, at Miss Mullins.

"Oh dear," said Tuppence, "oh dear."

"Good boy, Hannibal," said Tommy, "Good boy. Don't you think so?"

He turned his head to Mr. Crispin.

"Knows his enemies, doesn't he—and your enemies."

"Oh dear," said Tuppence. "Has Hannibal bitten you?"

"A very nasty nip," said Miss Mullins, rising to her feet and scowling at Hannibal.

"His second one, isn't it?" said Tommy. "Chased you out of our pampas grass, didn't he?"

"He knows what's what," said Mr. Crispin. "Doesn't he, Dodo, my dear? Long time since I've seen you, Dodo, isn't it?"

Miss Mullins got up, shot a glance at Tuppence, at Tommy and at Mr. Crispin.

"Mullins," said Mr. Crispin. "Sorry I'm not up to

date. Is that a married name or are you now known
as Miss Mullins?"

"I am Iris Mullins, as I always was."

"Ah, I thought you were Dodo. You used to be
Dodo to me. Well, dear, I think—nice to have seen
you, but I think we'd better get out of here quickly.
Drink your coffee. I expect that's all right. Mrs.
Beresford? I'm very pleased to meet you. If I might
advise you, I shouldn't drink *your* coffee."

"Oh dear, let me take the cup away."

Miss Mullins pressed forward. In a moment Crispin
stood between her and Tuppence.

"No, Dodo dear, I wouldn't do that," he said. "I'd
rather have charge of it myself. The cup belongs to
the house, you know, and of course it would be nice
to have an analysis of exactly what's in it just now.
Possibly you brought a little dose with you, did you?
Quite easy to put a little dose into the cup as you're
handing it to the invalid or the supposed invalid."

"I assure you I did no such thing. Oh, do call your
dog off."

Hannibal showed every desire to pursue her down
the staircase.

"He wants to see you off the premises," said
Tommy; "he's rather particular about that. He likes
biting people who are going out through the front
door. Ah, Albert, there you are. I thought you'd be
just outside the other door. Did you see what happened, by any chance?"

Albert put his head round the dressing-room door
across the room.

"I saw, all right. I watched her through the crack
of the hinge. Yes. Put something in the missis's cup,
she did. Very neat. Good as a conjurer, but she did it,
all right."

"I don't know what you mean," said Miss Mullins.
"I—oh dear, oh dear, I must go. I've got an appointment. It's very important."

She shot out of the room and down the stairs. Hannibal gave one glance and went after her. Mr. Crispin showed no sign of animosity, but he too left hurriedly in pursuit.

"I hope she's a good runner," said Tuppence, "because if she isn't, Hannibal will catch up with her. My word, he's a good guard dog, isn't he?"

"Tuppence, that was Mr. Crispin, sent us by Mr. Solomon. Came at a very good moment, didn't he? I think he's been waiting his time to see what might be going to happen. Don't break that cup and don't pour any of that coffee away until we've got a bottle or something to put it in. It's going to be analyzed and we're going to find out what's in it. Put your best dressing gown on, Tuppence, and come down to the sitting room and we'll have some drinks there before lunch."

"And now, I suppose," said Tuppence, "we shall never know what any of it means or what it is all about."

She shook her head in deep despondency. Rising from her chair, she went towards the fireplace.

"Are you trying to put a log on?" said Tommy. "Let me. You've been told not to move about much."

"My arm's quite all right now," said Tuppence. "Anyone would think I'd broken it or something. It was only a nasty scrape or graze."

"You have more to boast about than that," said Tommy. "It was definitely a bullet wound. You have been wounded in war."

"War it seems to have been all right," said Tuppence. "Really!"

"Never mind," said Tommy, "we dealt with the Mullins very well, I think."

"Hannibal," said Tuppence, "was a very good dog there, wasn't he?"

"Yes," said Tommy, "he told us. Told us very definitely. He just leapt for that pampas grass. His nose told him, I suppose. He's got a wonderful nose."

"I can't say my nose warned me," said Tuppence. "I just thought she was rather an answer to prayer, turning up. And I quite forgot we were only supposed to take someone who had worked for Mr. Solomon. Did Mr. Crispin tell you anything more? I suppose his name isn't really Crispin."

"Possibly not," said Tommy.

"Did he come to do some sleuthing too? Too many of us here, I should say."

"No," said Tommy, "not exactly a sleuth. I think he was sent for security purposes. To look after you."

"To look after me," said Tuppence, "and you, I should say. Where is he now?"

"Dealing with Miss Mullins, I expect."

"Yes, well, it's extraordinary how hungry these excitements make one. Quite peckish, as one might say. Do you know, there's nothing I can imagine I'd like to eat more than a nice hot crab with a sauce made of cream with just a touch of curry powder."

"You're well again," said Tommy. "I'm delighted to hear you feeling like that about food."

"I've never been ill," said Tuppence. "I've been wounded. That's quite different."

"Well," said Tommy, "anyway you must have realized as I did that when Hannibal let go all out and told you an enemy was close at hand in the pampas grass, you must have realized that Miss Mullins was the person who, dressed as a man, hid there and shot at you—"

"But then," said Tuppence, "we thought that she'd have another go. I was immured with my wound in bed and we made our arrangements. Isn't that right, Tommy?"

"Quite right," said Tommy, "quite right. I thought probably she wouldn't leave it too long to come to the conclusion that one of her bullets had taken effect and that you'd be laid up in bed."

"So she came along full of feminine solicitude," said Tuppence.

"And our arrangement was very good, I thought," said Tommy. "There was Albert on permanent guard, watching every step she took, every single thing she did—"

"And also," said Tuppence, "bringing me up on a tray a cup of coffee and adding another cup for the visitor."

"Did you see Mullins—or Dodo, as Crispin called her—put anything in your cup of coffee?"

"No," said Tuppence, "I must admit that I didn't. You see, she seemed to catch her foot in something and she knocked over that little table with our nice vase on it, made a great deal of apology, and my eye of course was on the broken vase and whether it was too bad to mend. So I didn't see her."

"Albert did," said Tommy. "Saw it through the hinge where he'd enlarged it a crack so that he could look through."

"And then it was a very good idea to put Hannibal in confinement in the bathroom but leaving the door only half latched because, as we know, Hannibal is very good at opening doors. Not of course if they're completely latched, but if they only look latched or feel latched he takes one great spring and comes in like a—oh, like a Bengal tiger."

"Yes," said Tommy, "that is quite a good description."

"And now I suppose Mr. Crispin or whatever his name is has finished making his inquiries, although how he thinks Miss Mullins can be connected with Mary Jordan, or with a dangerous figure like Jonathan Kane who only exists in the past—"

"I don't think he only exists in the past. I think there may be a new edition of him, a rebirth, as you might say. There are a lot of young members, lovers of violence, violence at any price, the merry muggers society if there's anything called that, and the super-fascists regretting the splendid days of Hitler and his merry group."

"I've just been reading *Count Hannibal*," said Tuppence. "Stanley Weyman. One of his best. It was among the Alexander books upstairs."

"What about it?"

"Well, I was thinking that nowadays it's really still like that. And probably always has been. All the poor children who went off to the Children's Crusade so full of joy and pleasure and vanity, poor little souls. Thinking they'd been appointed by the Lord to deliver Jerusalem, that the seas would part in front of them so that they could walk across, like in the Bible Moses did. And now all these pretty girls and young men who appear in courts the whole time, because they've smashed down some wretched old-age pensioner or elderly person who had just got a little money or something in the bank. And there was St. Bartholomew's Massacre. You see, all these things *do* happen again. Even the new fascists were mentioned the other day in connection with a perfectly respectable university. Ah well, I suppose nobody will ever really tell us anything. Do you really think that Mr. Crispin will find out something more about a hiding place that nobody's yet discovered? Cisterns. You know, bank robberies. They often hid things in cisterns. Very damp place, I should have thought, to hide something. Do you think when he's finished making his inquiries or whatever it is, he'll come back here and continue looking after me—and you, Tommy?"

"I don't need him to look after me," said Tommy.

"Oh, that's just arrogance," said Tuppence.

"I think he'll come to say goodbye," said Tommy.

"Oh yes, because he's got very nice manners, hasn't he?"

"He'll want to make sure that you're quite all right again."

"I'm only wounded and the doctor's seen to that."

"He's really very keen on gardening," said Tommy.

"I realize that. He really did work for a friend of his who happened to be Mr. Solomon, who has been dead for some years, but I suppose it makes a good cover, that, because he can say he worked for him and people will know he worked for him. So he'll appear to be quite *bona fide*."

"Yes, I suppose one has to think of all those things," said Tuppence.

The front door bell rang and Hannibal dashed from the room, tiger-style, to kill any intruder who might be wishing to enter the sacred precincts which he guarded. Tommy came back with an envelope.

"Addressed to us both," he said. "Shall I open it?"

"Go ahead," said Tuppence.

He opened it.

"Well," he said, "this raises possibilities for the future."

"What is it?"

"It's an invitation from Mr. Robinson. To you and to me. To dine with him on a date the week after next, when he hopes you'll be fully recovered and yourself again. In his country house. Somewhere in Sussex, I think."

"Do you think he'll tell us anything then?" said Tuppence.

"I think he might," said Tommy.

"Shall I take my list with me?" said Tuppence. "I know it by heart now."

She read rapidly.

"*Black Arrow*, Alexander Parkinson, Oxford and Cambridge porcelain Victorian seats, grin-hen-Lo, KK, Mathilde's stomach, Cain and Abel, Truelove . . ."

"Enough," said Tommy, "it sounds mad."

"Well, it is mad, all of it. Think there'll be anyone else at Mr. Robinson's?"

"Possibly Colonel Pikeaway."

"In that case," said Tuppence, "I'd better take a cough lozenge with me, hadn't I? Anyway, I do want to see Mr. Robinson. I can't believe he's as fat and yellow as you say he is— Oh—but, Tommy, isn't it the week after next that Deborah is bringing the children to stay with us?"

"No," said Tommy, "it's this *next* weekend as ever is."

"Thank goodness, so that's all right," said Tuppence.

30

The Birds Fly South

"Was that the car?"

Tuppence came out of the front door peering anxiously along the curve of the drive, eagerly awaiting the arrival of her daughter Deborah and the three children.

Albert emerged from the side door.

"They won't be here yet. No, that was the grocer, madam. You wouldn't believe it—eggs have gone up *again*. Never vote for this government again, I won't. I'll give the Liberals a go."

"Shall I come and see to the rhubarb and strawberry fool for tonight?"

"I've seen to that, madam. I've watched you often and I know just how you do it."

"You'll be a *cordon bleu* chef by the time you've finished, Albert," said Tuppence. "It's Janet's favorite sweet."

"Yes, and I made a treacle tart—Master Andrew loves treacle tart."

"The rooms are all ready?"

"Yes. Mrs. Shacklebury came in good time this morning. I put the Guerlain sandalwood soap in Miss Deborah's bathroom. It's her favorite, I know."

Tuppence breathed a sigh of relief at the knowledge that all was in order for the arrival of her family.

There was the sound of a motor horn and a few minutes later the car came up the drive with Tommy at the wheel and a moment later the guests were decanted on the doorstep—daughter Deborah still a very handsome woman, nearly forty, and Andrew, fifteen, Janet, eleven, and Rosalie, seven.

"Hullo, Grandma," shouted Andrew.

"Where's Hannibal?" called Janet.

"I want my tea," said Rosalie, showing a disposition to burst into tears.

Greetings were exchanged. Albert dealt with the disembarkation of all the family treasures, including a budgerigar, a bowl of goldfish and a hamster in a hutch.

"So this is the new home," said Deborah, embracing her mother. "I like it—I like it very much."

"Can we go round the garden?" asked Janet.

"After tea," said Tommy.

"I want my tea," reiterated Rosalie with an expression on her face of: First things first.

They went into the dining room where tea was set out and met with general satisfaction.

"What's all this I've been hearing about you, Mum?" demanded Deborah, when they had finished tea and repaired to the open air—the children racing around to explore the possible pleasures of the garden in the joint company of Thomas and Hannibal, who had rushed out to take part in the rejoicings.

Deborah, who always took a stern line with her mother, whom she considered in need of careful guardianship, demanded, "What *have* you been doing?"

"Oh. We've settled in quite comfortably by now," said Tuppence.

Deborah looked unconvinced.

"You've been doing things. She has, hasn't she, Dad?"

Tommy was returning with Rosalie riding him piggyback, Janet surveying the new territory and Andrew looking around with an air of taking a full grown-up view.

"You have been *doing* things." Deborah returned to

the attack. "You've been playing at being Mrs. Blenkinsop all over again. The trouble with you is, there's no holding you—N or M—all over again. Derek heard something and wrote and told me." She nodded as she mentioned her brother's name.

"Derek—what could *he* know?" demanded Tuppence.

"Derek always gets to know things."

"You too, Dad." Deborah turned on her father. "*You've* been mixing yourself up in things, too. I thought you'd come here, both of you, to retire, and take life quietly—and enjoy yourselves."

"That *was* the idea," said Tommy, "but Fate thought otherwise."

"Postern of Fate," said Tuppence. "Disaster's Cavern, Fort of Fear—"

"Flecker," said Andrew, with conscious erudition. He was addicted to poetry and hoped one day to be a poet himself. He carried on with a full quotation:

> "Four great gates has the city of Damascus . . .
> Postern of Fate, the Desert Gate . . .
> Pass not beneath, O Caravan,
> Or pass not singing. Have you heard
> That silence where the birds are dead,
> Yet something pipeth like a bird? . . ."

With singularly apposite cooperation birds flew suddenly from the roof of the house over their heads.

"What are all those birds, Grannie?" asked Janet.

"Swallows flying south," said Tuppence.

"Won't they ever come back again?"

"Yes, they'll come back next summer."

"And pass through the Postern of Fate!" said Andrew with intense satisfaction.

"This house was called Swallow's Nest once," said Tuppence.

"But you aren't going on living here, are you?" said

Deborah. "Dad wrote and said you're looking out for another house."

"Why?" asked Janet—the Rosa Dartle of the family. "I like this one."

"I'll give you a few reasons," said Tommy, plucking a sheet of paper from his pocket and reading aloud:

"*Black Arrow*
Oxford and Cambridge
Alexander Parkinson
Oxford and Cambridge
Victorian china garden stools
Grin-hen-Lo
KK
Mathilde's stomach
Cain and Abel
Gallant Truelove."

"Shut up, Tommy—that's *my* list. It's nothing to do with you," said Tuppence.

"But what does it *mean?*" asked Janet, continuing her quiz.

"It sounds like a list of clues from a detective story," said Andrew, who in his less poetical moments was addicted to that form of literature.

"It *is* a list of clues. It's the reason why we are looking for another house," said Tommy.

"But I like it here," said Janet, "it's lovely."

"It's a nice house," said Rosalie. "Chocolate biscuits," she added, with memories of recently eaten tea.

"I like it," said Andrew, speaking as an autocratic Czar of Russia might speak.

"Why don't *you* like it, Grandma?" asked Janet.

"I *do* like it," said Tuppence with a sudden unexpected enthusiasm. "I want to live here—to go on living here."

"Postern of Fate," said Andrew. "It's an exciting name."

"It used to be called Swallow's Nest," said Tuppence. "We could call it that again—"

"All those clues," said Andrew. "You could make a story out of them—even a book—"

"Too many names, too complicated," said Deborah. "Who'd read a book like that?"

"You'd be surprised," said Tommy, "what people *will* read—and enjoy."

Tommy and Tuppence looked at each other.

"Couldn't I get some paint tomorrow?" asked Andrew. "Or Albert could get some and he'd help me. We'd paint the new name on the gate."

"And then the swallows would know they could come back next summer," said Janet.

She looked at her mother.

"Not at all a bad idea," said Deborah.

"*La Reine le Veut,*" said Tommy and bowed to his daughter, who always considered that giving the Royal assent in the family was her perquisite.

31

Last Words:
Dinner with Mr. Robinson

"What a lovely meal," said Tuppence. She looked round at the assembled company.

They had passed from the dining table and were now assembled in the library round the coffee table.

Mr. Robinson, as yellow and even larger than Tuppence had visualized him, was smiling behind a big and beautiful George II coffeepot—next to him was Mr. Crispin, now, it seemed, answering to the name of Horsham. Colonel Pikeaway sat next to Tommy, who had, rather doubtfully, offered him one of his own cigarettes.

Colonel Pikeaway, with an expression of surprise, said: "I *never* smoke after *dinner*."

Miss Collodon, whom Tuppence had found rather alarming, said, "Indeed, Colonel Pikeaway? How *very, very* interesting." She turned her head towards Tuppence. "What a very well-behaved dog you have got, Mrs. Beresford."

Hannibal, who was lying under the table with his head resting on Tuppence's foot, looked out with his misleading best angelic expression and moved his tail gently.

"I understood he was a very *fierce* dog," said Mr. Robinson, casting an amused glance at Tuppence.

"You should see him in action," said Mr. Crispin—alias Horsham.

"He has party manners when he is asked out to

267

dinner," explained Tuppence. "He loves it, feels he's really a prestige dog going into high society." She turned to Mr. Robinson. "It was really very, *very* nice of you to send him an invitation and to have a plateful of liver ready for him. He loves liver."

"All dogs love liver," said Mr. Robinson. "I understand"—he looked at Crispin-Horsham—"that if I were to pay a visit to Mr. and Mrs. Beresford at their *own* home, I might be torn to pieces."

"Hannibal takes his duties very seriously," said Mr. Crispin. "He's a well-bred guard dog and never forgets it."

"You understand his feelings, of course, as a security officer," said Mr. Robinson.

His eyes twinkled.

"You and your husband have done a very remarkable piece of work, Mrs. Beresford," said Mr. Robinson. "We are indebted to you. Colonel Pikeaway tells me that *you* were the initiator in the affair."

"It just happened," said Tuppence, embarrassed. "I got—well—curious. I wanted to find out—about certain things—"

"Yes, I gathered that. And now, perhaps you feel an equally natural curiosity as to what all this has been about?"

Tuppence became even more embarrassed, and her remarks became slightly incoherent.

"Oh—oh, of course—I mean—I do understand that all this is quite secret—I mean all very hush-hush—and that we can't ask questions—because you couldn't tell us things. I do understand that perfectly."

"On the contrary, it is I who want to ask you a question. If you will answer it by giving me the information, I shall be enormously pleased."

Tuppence stared at him with wide-open eyes.

"I can't imagine—" She broke off.

"You have a list—or so your husband tells me. He didn't tell me what that list was. Quite rightly. That list is *your* secret property. But I, too, know what it is to suffer curiosity."

Again his eyes twinkled. Tuppence was suddenly aware that she liked Mr. Robinson very much.

She was silent for a moment or two, then she coughed and fumbled in her evening handbag.

"It's terribly silly," she said. "In fact it's rather more than silly. It's mad."

Mr. Robinson responded unexpectedly: " 'Mad, mad, all the world is mad.' So Hans Sachs said, sitting under his elder tree in *The Meistersingers*—my favorite opera. How right he was!"

He took the sheet of foolscap she handed to him.

"Read it aloud if you like," said Tuppence. "I don't really mind."

Mr. Robinson glanced at it, then handed it to Crispin. "Angus, you have a clearer voice than I have."

Mr. Crispin took the sheet and read in an agreeable tenor with good enunciation:

"*Black Arrow*
Alexander Parkinson
Mary Jordan did not die naturally
Oxford and Cambridge porcelain Victorian seats
Grin-hen-Lo
KK
Mathilde's stomach
Cain and Abel
Truelove"

He stopped, looking at his host, who turned his head towards Tuppence.

"My dear," said Mr. Robinson. "Let me congratulate you—you must have a most unusual mind. To arrive from this list of clues at your final discoveries is really most remarkable."

"Tommy was hard at it too," said Tuppence.

"Nagged into it by you," said Tommy.

"Very good research he did," said Colonel Pikeaway appreciatively.

"The census date gave a very good pointer."

"You are a gifted pair," said Mr. Robinson. He looked at Tuppence again and smiled. "I am still assuming that though you have displayed no indiscreet curiosity, you really want to know what all this has been about?

"Oh," exclaimed Tuppence. "Are you really going to tell us something? How wonderful!"

"Some of it begins, as you surmised, with the Parkinsons," said Mr. Robinson. "That is to say, in the distant past. My own great-grandmother was a Parkinson. Some things I learnt from her—

"The girl known as Mary Jordan was in our service. She had connections in the Navy—her mother was Austrian and so she herself spoke German fluently.

"As you may know, and as your husband certainly knows already, there are certain documents which will shortly be released for publication.

"The present trend of political thinking is that hush-hush, necessary as it is at certain times, should not be preserved indefinitely. There are things in the records that should be made known as a definite part of our country's past history.

"Three or four volumes are due to be published within the next couple of years authenticated by documentary evidence.

"What went on in the neighborhood of Swallow's Nest (that was the name of your present house at that time) will certainly be included.

"There were leakages—as always there are leakages in times of war, or preceding a probable outbreak of war.

"There were politicians who had prestige and who were thought of very highly. There were one or two leading journalists who had enormous influence and used it unwisely. There were men even before the First World War who were intriguing against their own country. After that war there were young men who graduated from universities and who were fervent believers and often active members of the Communist Party without anyone knowing of that fact. And even more dangerous, fascism was coming into favor with a full progressive program of eventual union with Hitler, posing as a lover of peace and thereby bringing about a quick end to the war.

"And so on. A continuous behind the scenes picture. It has happened before in history. Doubtless it will always happen: a fifth column that is both active and dangerous, run by those who believed in it—as well as those who sought financial gain, those who aimed at eventual power being placed in their hands in the future. Some of this will make interesting reading. How often has the same phrase been uttered in all good faith: 'Old B.? A traitor? Nonsense. Last man in the world! Absolutely trustworthy!'

"The complete confidence trick. The old, old story. Always on the same lines.

"In the commercial world, in the services, in political life. Always a man with an honest face—a fellow you can't help liking and trusting. Beyond suspicion. 'The last man in the world.' Et cetera, et cetera, et cetera. Someone who's a natural for the job, like the man who can sell you a gold brick outside the Ritz.

"Your present village, Mrs. Beresford, became the headquarters of a certain group just before the First World War. It was such a nice old world village—nice people had always lived there—all patriotic, doing different kinds of war work. A good naval harbor—a good-looking young naval commander—came of a good family, father had been an admiral. A good doctor practicing there—much loved by all his patients—they enjoyed confiding their troubles to him. Just in general practice—hardly anyone knew that he had had a special training in chemical warfare—in poison gases.

"And later, before the Second World War, Mr. Kane—spelt with a K—lived in a pretty thatched cottage by the harbor and had a particular political creed—not fascist—oh no! Just Peace before Everything to save the world—a creed rapidly gaining a following on the Continent and in numerous other countries abroad.

"None of that is what you really want to know, Mrs. Beresford—but you've got to realize the background first, a very carefully contrived one. That's where Mary Jordan was sent to find out, if she could, just what was going on.

"She was born before my time. I admired the work she had done for us when I heard the story of it—and I would have liked to have known her—she obviously had character and personality.

"Mary was her own Christian name, though she was always known as Molly. She did good work. It was a tragedy she should die young."

Tuppence had been looking up to the wall at a picture which for some reason looked familiar. It was a mere sketch of a boy's head.

"Is that—surely—"

"Yes," said Mr. Robinson. "That's the boy Alexander Parkinson. He was only eleven then. He was a grandson of a great-aunt of mine. That's how Molly went to the Parkinsons' in the role of a nursery governess. It seemed a good safe observation post. One wouldn't ever have thought—" He broke off. "What would come of it."

"It wasn't—one of the Parkinsons?" asked Tuppence.

"Oh no, my dear. I understand that the Parkinsons were not involved in any way. But there were others—guests and friends—staying in the house that night. It was your Thomas who found out that the evening in question was the date of a census return. The names of everyone sleeping under that roof had to be entered as well as the usual occupants. One of those names linked up in a significant manner. The daughter of the local doctor about whom I have just told you came down to visit her father as she often did and asked the Parkinsons to put her up that night as she had brought two friends with her. Those friends were all right—but later her father was found to be heavily involved in all that was going on in that part of the world. She herself, it seemed, had helped the Parkinsons in garden work some weeks earlier and was responsible for foxgloves and spinach being planted in close proximity. It was she who had taken the mixture of leaves to the kitchen on the fatal day. The illness of all the participants of the meal passed off as one of those unfortunate mistakes that happen sometimes. The doctor explained he had known such a thing happen before. His evidence at the inquest resulted in a verdict of Misadventure. The fact that a cocktail glass had been swept off a table and smashed by accident that same night attracted no attention.

"Perhaps, Mrs. Beresford, you would be interested to know that history might have repeated itself. You were shot at from a clump of pampas grass, and later the lady calling herself Miss Mullins tried to add poison to your coffee cup. I understand she is actually a granddaughter or great-niece of the original criminal doctor, and before the Second World War she was a disciple of Jonathan Kane. That's how Crispin knew of her, of course. And your dog definitely disapproved of her and took prompt action. Indeed we now know that it was she who coshed old Isaac.

"We now have to consider an even more sinister character. The genial kindly doctor was idolized by everyone in the place, but it seems most probable on the evidence that it was the doctor who was responsible for Mary Jordan's death, though at the time no one would have believed it. He had wide scientific interests, and expert knowledge of poisons and did pioneering work in bacteriology. It has taken sixty years before the facts have become known. Only Alexander Parkinson, a schoolboy at the time, began having ideas."

"*Mary Jordan did not die naturally,*" quoted Tuppence softly. "*It was one of us.*" She asked: "Was it the doctor who found out what Mary was doing?"

"No. The doctor had not suspected. But somebody had. Up till then she had been completely successful. The naval commander had worked with her as planned. The information she passed to him was genuine and he didn't realize that it was mainly stuff that didn't matter—though it had been made to sound important. So-called naval plans and secrets which he passed to her, she duly delivered on her days off in London, obeying instructions as to when and where. Queen Mary's Garden in Regent's Park was one, I believe—and the Peter Pan statue in Kensington Gardens was another. We learned a good deal from these meetings and the minor officials in certain embassies concerned.

"But all that's in the past, Mrs. Beresford—long, long in the past."

Colonel Pikeaway coughed and suddenly took over. "But history repeats itself, Mrs. Beresford. Everyone learns that sooner or later. A nucleus recently reformed in Hollowquay. People who knew about it set things up again. Perhaps that's why Miss Mullins returned. Certain hiding-places were used again. Secret meetings took place. Once more money became significant—where it came from, where it went to. Mr. Robinson here was called in. And then our old friend Beresford came along and started giving me some very interesting information. It fitted in with what we had already suspected. Background scenery being set up in anticipation. A future being prepared to be controlled and run by one particular political figure in this country. A man with a certain reputation and making more converts and followers every day. The confidence trick in action once again. Man of Great Integrity—Lover of Peace. Not fascism—oh no! Just something that looks like fascism. Peace for all—and financial rewards to those who cooperate."

"Do you mean it's still going on?" Tuppence's eyes opened wide.

"Well, we know more or less all we want and need to know now. And that's partly because of what you two have contributed—the operation of a surgical nature on a rocking-horse was particularly informative—"

"Mathilde!" exclaimed Tuppence. "I *am* glad! I can hardly believe it. Mathilde's stomach!"

"Wonderful things, horses," said Colonel Pikeaway. "Never know what they will do, or won't do. Ever since the wooden horse of Troy."

"Even Truelove helped, I hope," said Tuppence. "But, I mean, if it's all going on still. With children about—"

"It isn't," said Mr. Crispin. "You don't need to worry. That area of England is purified—the wasp's nest cleared up. It's suitable for private living again. We've reason to believe they've shifted operations to the neighborhood of Bury St. Edmunds. And we'll be keeping an eye on you, so you needn't worry at all."

Tuppence gave a sigh of relief. "Thank you for telling me. You see, my daughter Deborah comes to stay from time to time and brings her three children—"

"You needn't worry," said Mr. Robinson. "By the way, after the N or M business, didn't you adopt the child that figured in the case—the one that had the nursery rhyme books, Goosey Gander and all the rest of it?"

"Betty?" said Tuppence. "Yes. She's done very well at university and she's gone off now to Africa to do research on how people live—that sort of thing. A lot of young people are very keen on that. She's a darling—and very happy."

Mr. Robinson cleared his throat and rose to his feet. "I want to propose a toast. To Mr. and Mrs. Thomas Beresford in acknowledgment of the service they have rendered to their country."

It was drunk enthusiastically.

"And if I may, I will propose a further toast," said Mr. Robinson. "To Hannibal."

"There, Hannibal," said Tuppence, stroking his head. "You've had your health drunk. Almost as good as being knighted or having a medal. I was reading Stanley Weyman's *Count Hannibal* only the other day."

"Read it as a boy, I remember," said Mr. Robinson. "'Who touches my brother touches Tavanne,' if I've got it right. Pikeaway, don't you think? Hannibal, may I be permitted to tap you on the shoulder?"

Hannibal took a step towards him, received a tap on the shoulder and gently wagged his tail.

"I hereby create you a Count of this Realm."

"Count Hannibal. Isn't that lovely?" said Tuppence. "What a proud dog you ought to be!"

ABOUT THE AUTHOR

AGATHA CHRISTIE, the great mystery story writer, was born in England. Since the publication of her first mystery in 1922, she has written over sixty books. She is one of the few writers of detective and mystery fiction whose books consistently appear on bestseller lists. In addition to her fiction, she has also written successful plays, including *Witness for the Prosecution,* and many of her books and plays have been made into movies.